A TIME TO BE BORN

Data made his way back through the sundered starship *Seattle* to the gash in her underbelly where he had entered. Braving the debris smacking against the scorched hull, he stuck his head out the gash and looked around. The vortex appeared so close that he could touch it. The battered husk of the *Seattle* arced toward destruction on an erratic, decaying orbit. Other hulks raced beside them, banging into each other like fanciful vehicles in a mad race. In such chaos, the silence was eerie. He reactivated his emotion chip to experience every moment of this spectacular scene. It could possibly be the last thing he ever saw. . . .

Current books in this series:

A Time to Be Born by John Vornholt

Forthcoming books in this series:

STAR TREK®
A Time to Be Born

JOHN VORNHOLT

Based upon
STAR TREK: THE NEXT GENERATION™
created by Gene Roddenberry

POCKET BOOKS
New York   London   Toronto   Sydney

This book is a work of fiction. Names, characters, places and incidents are products of the author's imagination or are used fictitiously. Any resemblance to actual events or locales or persons, living or dead, is entirely coincidental.

An *Original* Publication of POCKET BOOKS

POCKET BOOKS, a division of Simon & Schuster, Inc.
1230 Avenue of the Americas, New York, NY 10020

A VIACOM COMPANY

STAR TREK is a Registered Trademark of Paramount Pictures.

This book is published by Pocket Books, a division of Simon & Schuster, Inc., under exclusive license from Paramount Pictures.

ISBN: 978-1-4516-5557-5

First Pocket Books printing February 2004

10   9   8   7   6   5   4   3   2   1

POCKET and colophon are registered trademarks of Simon & Schuster, Inc.

Manufactured in the United States of America

For information regarding special discounts for bulk purchases, please contact Simon & Schuster Special Sales at 1-800-456-6798 or business@simonandschuster.com

For Penny

Chapter One

THE GAUNT WOMAN, wearing a ragged shift and shoes made of discarded insulation material, knelt in the gully and ran her fingers through the grimy soil. While the sun beat down mercilessly, she searched until she found a shriveled root, which she popped into her mouth and chewed ravenously until it was gone. So intent was she upon her search that she hardly noticed the shuttlecraft that set down in a cloud of blowing sand not fifty meters away. Thrusters clicked off; then a hatch opened. Even when three humanoids in flight suits emerged from the craft and approached the old woman, she continued her desperate search for food.

All of this was observed by a nondescript male of her species who sat on a bench about twenty meters away. He, too, wore rags and makeshift shoes, but he was not hungry, at least not for food. Behind him stood a row of deserted buildings that had once been stores, homes, and places of recreation and worship. Most of these dusty structures were collapsed or falling apart, and their hinges creaked in the constant wind. *A ghost town,* this place would have been called on another planet far, far away, the man on the bench decided.

The three strangers approached the woman. One of them said kindly, "Madam, we are here from the Relocation Bureau. Are you ready to go?"

She looked up at the men with unbridled hostility and spat at them, although she barely had enough spittle to wet her fingertip. "This is my *home!*" she rasped. "Who told you I was going anywhere?" She continued scrounging for roots.

The three strangers looked uneasily at one another, and another one of the men said, "Look around you, madam. This planet is finished—nothing will grow in this irradiated soil. Your leaders have agreed to this relocation, and all of your neighbors have already left." He glanced for a moment at the man on the bench. "You two are the only ones left on this whole continent."

"Damn the Federation! Damn the Dominion! *Damn them all!*" shrieked the woman. She sobbed and pounded the worthless soil. "Why did you have to make war *here?* Why did it have to be *our* world? What did we ever do to anyone? We just wanted to live in peace—to raise our children, to raise our crops. Now they're all gone . . . all gone." She buried her face in the scorched dirt and sobbed pitifully.

The three men tried to help her up. She fought them

off with screams and flailing fists. That was enough for the observer on the bench, who rose slowly and walked toward them with a creaky gait that belied his youthful appearance. None of them could really tell how old he was, and their descriptions of him would later vary.

He motioned the trio back. They obeyed him without question. Then the nondescript man bent down and put his arms around the gaunt woman. "Mother," he said tenderly, "these men are not at fault for what happened here. No one chooses to be in a war, nor do they choose the place to fight it. Yes, our beloved world was once good to us, but now it's spent. Let's leave it as a shrine to the dead and departed. It's best to leave now, Mother, and go with these men. They will be kind to you and give you plenty of food. They have your welfare at heart. Go with them, please."

She gazed fondly at her neighbor, and her gnarled hand patted his. "Do I know you?"

He smiled. "Yes, you do, but you've forgotten. It doesn't matter. Let me help you up."

The neighbor gently lifted the woman to her feet and handed her off to her would-be rescuers. "Thanks for your help," said one of them. "Where are her belongings?"

"Belongings?" asked the local with amusement. "The Dominion War took care of everything she considered dear. Just take her and go."

They led the woman toward the shuttlecraft, expecting the man to follow. When he didn't, one of the officers walked back to him and said, "You have to go too, sir."

"I have my own transportation," he answered.

The man shook his head skeptically. "What transportation? There's nothing here but—" He motioned around at the derelict buildings and arid fields.

"This is your last chance, sir. By the end of the day, there won't be anyone on this planet but you. You're signing your own death warrant."

"I won't be dying here," the local assured him with a smile. "You're doing a good job . . . a necessary job. But your work here is finished. Go on home."

The officer looked unconvinced; then he turned and strode after his companions, who had ushered the woman into the shuttlecraft. In a flurry of dust, the small vessel took off and streaked into the pale sky.

The man on the ground sighed, and he looked his true age of twenty-seven Terran years. "This planet died too young."

"I know," replied a kindly voice beside him. "That's the nature of war—death at an early age. It will take many generations for the Alpha Quadrant to recover from the Dominion War. You did well on this vigil, Wesley, however you came close to interfering in that woman's life."

Wes turned to gaze at his slight, bald, unobtrusive friend, a being he had known for a dozen years without ever knowing his name, only his extraordinary existence as the Traveler.

"When you helped me save my mom's life, weren't you interfering a little?" asked Wesley.

"Just a little," agreed the Traveler. "There's always a price to pay when we interfere. In your case, I had to take on a protégé."

The young man gazed at the stark landscape and

said, "It was painful, watching this planet and these people suffer . . . then wither away and die. They tried so hard to reclaim their world "

"I know," answered the Traveler with sympathy. "We all experienced what you did, remember. Their suffering will not be forgotten. You performed well in this trial."

"This trial?" asked the young man, angrily. "I have sat too many vigils in the last six years—all that training, never seeing my mother, never having the companionship of my own kind. Most of all, never being myself. I don't *feel* what you feel. Watching this suffering and not being able to help . . . it only left me depressed."

"You must submerge yourself," said his guide sternly. "But soon you will feel what every Traveler feels, because this was your last trial, Wesley. I will no longer be able to call you by that name, because your identity will merge with ours. You will be born anew as a Traveler."

The human stared at his mentor in surprise. He had been waiting for this moment—with dread and anticipation—and now it had arrived. "Will I be able to go anywhere?" he asked. "By myself?"

"Yes," answered the Traveler, casting his pale eyes downward. "Any place, any dimension, any time—they are open. Our combined focus will enable you. However the temptation will be great for you to do more than watch and record. Remember, no experience will be yours alone, it will belong to all of us. You can visit the *Enterprise,* but you won't see it as you once did. I believe it was a human who said, 'You can't go home again.' "

"Thomas Wolfe," replied Wes with a nod. "I feel so

old already, after all the training and vigils, but I don't feel that much wiser."

Now the Traveler smiled. "That's because you're aware of everything you *don't* know. To most cultures, what we do is magic, but the more we discover about life and how to focus, the more inadequate we feel. The more we witness, the more we hunger to see."

The young man didn't contradict his friend, but he really hungered for warmth and familiarity—a poker game, a scratch on the back, a birthday card. Seeing the triumphs and suffering of others was not the same as experiencing them, even if he had godlike powers to move through dimensions and blend in with a crowd until he was barely noticeable. Living without being in danger, without having to suffer—that was both exhilarating and weakening. He had always thought his intense studies and lonesome vigils would be rewarded when the Travelers finally took him into their fellowship. If it really happened, he faced the end of his quest, unsure what he had learned except that, at his core, he was still human.

What if I've spent six years in a futile search for perfection and knowledge, when they're just an illusion?

The Traveler laid a hand on his shoulder in a comforting gesture he rarely used. "You are expanding your mind, Wesley. That you have gotten this far is wonderful for one of your species, but it goes to prove that humans are wasting a large degree of their potential. You have always trained to be a pioneer, an explorer, and we've just continued your education. Are you ready to be born?"

Wes nodded warily. It was asking if he no longer wanted to be human. When he embarked on this journey, he knew there would be a destination, a border that he couldn't cross and expect to come back the same.

"Will I change much?" asked Wesley.

"You'll be changed," admitted the guide, "and we'll be changed by you. Perhaps you have less changing to do than you think."

My mind will be transformed, thought Wesley, remembering his lessons. *Regions I didn't use before I will now use, and subconscious areas of my brain will multiprocess in focus with the minds of all the other Travelers. When I use all my potential, I will Travel.*

The Traveler's vigil had lasted more than a year, so he hadn't Traveled any great distance since he arrived here. It was never as easy for the human as for his companion.

"Shall we go?" asked his comrade. "I will ease the way."

"All right," said Wesley with relief. While his mentor kept a hand on his shoulder, the young man cleared his mind and began to focus. This process seemed magical but was based on shared, amplified manipulation of brain waves unknown to or nonexistent in most species. So Traveling was less physical than mental, even if the end result was physical relocation.

If it was familiar to him, Wes could conjure his own image of the place he wanted to go. If it was unknown in his limited knowledge, or he was being assigned to a vigil, the fellowship could focus and send him directly.

When he was sent, the young man felt swept away, as he was on this dusty afternoon in the last ghost town on a dead planet.

To Wesley's surprise, he arrived at the Travelers' homeworld, a place he had visited only once before during his eight years of service. He knew where he was instantly. He saw a youthful individual of their nondescript, gray-skinned species. The child was running across a field, pursuing a soap bubble larger than herself. Not every member of this species became a Traveler; in fact, it was less than one percent, he recalled. Few were capable of getting through the rigorous training, and even fewer were cut out for such a demanding life. Among the Travelers were several members of other races, like himself, but they always had this pool of their own kind from which to recruit.

He had been surprised to find that Travelers lived normal life spans, although Wesley suspected they could improve that condition if they chose. Since their feelings and experiences lived on in every other Traveler, there seemed little point in making themselves immortal.

The human looked around for his mentor, but he was alone in the meadow, except for the little girl. She stopped, shook her fists, and shuffled toward him. "It broke," she complained. "My bubble broke."

"Perhaps you can make a new one," suggested Wesley, leaning down to study the child. She looked about six in Terran years, with subtle head ridges and a lone braid of hair at the back of her skull.

She smiled at him flirtatiously. "You're handsome and very hairy. You're not from the Dell, are you?"

"No," he admitted, gazing at the feathery fields and orange and crimson wildflowers. "But I feel at home here."

"Lendal!" called a voice that seemed to waft on the breeze. Wes wondered if it was more telepathic than real.

"They're calling me," said the girl sadly as she shuffled away from him. She ran off, and at the last moment turned to wave. Her pout became a smile when she shouted, "See you tomorrow!"

"Tomorrow!" called Wesley, and he knew this was no idle prediction, but a fact. He also felt a familiar presence at his side, so he asked, "Who is that?"

"Your mother," answered the Traveler. "Of course, this is her past. She hasn't yet chosen the path that will unite the two of you."

Wes wanted to protest that he already had a mother, but he chose not to since he knew very little about this "borning" process. That had to be contributing to his uneasiness.

The Traveler gazed after the departing child. "We wanted you to see that she's just a normal person, from a normal background. She's unexceptional except for what she becomes later in life. But we don't want to stay here long or interact too much—"

"I know," said Wesley, fully understanding the taboos associated with Travelers going into the past. They tried to avoid affecting the lives of those they observed in the present. Only in dire emergencies did they even dare interfere. To change events in the past was unforgivable, considering the unexpected consequences

9

that might result. Travelers would no more use their focus to change the past than to commit murder. Possessing great power and knowing how to use it sparingly were the ultimate goals of their existence.

"You look confused," said his companion sympathetically. The breeze carried flower petals across the lush grassland, as the Traveler was uncharacteristically searching for words. "If you were of my species, I would know how to prepare you. Seeing this child would be comforting to *us.*"

"That's okay," Wesley assured him, realizing that his mentor was also nervous about doing his best under unfamiliar circumstances.

"I'm a human," said the former Starfleet officer. "What's best for humans is to push them into the swimming hole, throw them out of the plane—plunge them into it and don't let them think too much."

"Of course," said the Traveler with a knowing smile. "But I warn you, after you join the fellowship, there is one more trial before your focus is honed. It may be trivial, it may be terrifying—we have no control over what you see. Once you are a Traveler, you must gaze into the Pool of Prophecy."

"I will," agreed Wesley immediately. He had little direct knowledge of the sacred miratorium, only that it consisted of shared impressions of the future, unexplainable except to one with the right experience.

"So you're ready now?" asked his guide. "Do you need any more time to prepare?"

"I've been preparing my whole life to take the path less traveled," answered the young man. "I never knew what it was until you invited me on the vision quest—I only knew that the path kept eluding me. For all the years I've known you, I've been preparing. It hasn't been easy. I grew so lonely and discouraged. I wanted to quit many times, but quitting is in my past. I'll go through with it; however, don't make me consider it too long—"

"Enough said," replied his mentor, warmly placing his hand on Wes's shoulder. "The fellowship has been summoned."

The human felt himself being swept away, as the combined brain waves of every Traveler in existence bent time and space to whisk him to a familiar chamber. Wes was never sure if this was a genuine location on the physical plane or another dimension, but he knew the Travelers felt safe here. To the human, the natural cavity seemed like the weightless center of a hollow asteroid, but it could be more complicated than that. A hundred or more Travelers floated in the blackness, lit only by the globes of liquid nourishment which circulated among them via telekinesis. He had never seen so many Travelers gathered at one time. In addition, they were all watching him. In the past, those resting in the chamber had paid him little attention. On this occasion, they smiled and nodded at the human as he moved among them, letting him know that he was indeed the guest of honor.

Wesley gravitated slowly toward the center of the vast gathering, releasing his will so that his subconscious mind would conduct his actions. This was one of the stress-reducing techniques he had learned early on.

It allowed him to immerse himself physically and mentally without fear. Under the circumstances, he had a feeling that would be a good idea. In time, he saw his destination—a filmy bubble at the center of the hollow asteroid. Except for its immense size, it was not much different from the soap bubble the little girl had been chasing in the meadow.

The elastic globe shimmered in the darkness, its thin membrane quivering with every movement of air in the cavern. As the human drew closer, he was shocked to see that the immense bubble was attached to the cranium of an old female, who floated beneath it. Her frail body was dressed in a slight shift, revealing her purple veins and desiccated limbs. He tried not to cringe at the thought that the elastic sphere actually *was* the woman's cranium, although that's what it looked like. Wesley feared that she wasn't alive, just some mummified remains kept in a strange suspension.

He dropped closer to the withered crone, and she opened her eyes and stared at him with blazing turquoise pupils. He knew at once that she was the little girl he had met in the meadow . . . at least a century ago.

The elder studied his concerned face and said in a hoarse whisper, "It's like a dampening field—to contain all that we know. I must channel it for you, as you will immerse yourself. In this way, we shall imprint your being with all of our experiences and knowledge. This will unlock the last regions of your brain that you must control to be a real Traveler. When you are full, you will be born."

Wes sighed with relief, realizing that the membrane

bubble was not any part of the woman's head, although it was an extension of her mind. Before anything else was explained to him, the elder shut her eyes. Subtle beams radiated from the sphere to every Traveler floating in the vast reaches of the cavern. He marveled as the darkness was crisscrossed by hundreds of these slender beams, which seemed no more substantial than dust particles floating in a sliver of light.

The young man felt himself moving physically, beyond his will. He passed through the filmy barrier into the very heart of the Travelers' existence, surrounded by an impossible array of images, sensations, glimpses, and thoughts. In a nanosecond, Wes experienced all war, joy, failure, triumph—the humdrum of everyday existence and the extraordinary moments that defined each and every life. The great moments of history, a thousand dark ages, the march of progress, and the deprivations of brutality—all assaulted him without demanding explanation . . . just acceptance.

Wesley thought his eyes had been opened during his six years of apprenticeship; now he knew that he had been spared the true scope of what they had witnessed. *Take the bad with the good* was the only thought he clung to . . . while his mind drowned in a morass of searing images and emotions. An eternity passed—or mere seconds—and the human felt ravaged, overwhelmed, and unable to absorb any more. Still he watched, as if viewing a horrible accident and being unable to look away. He screamed in agony, but there was no relief from the ordeal. It was like a newborn infant being shown everything he would ever see in his life the moment he was expelled from the womb.

In desperation, Wesley found himself clawing to get out. He ripped apart the past and the future, shredding the veneer that any of it made sense. It was madness . . . spiders weaving webs by day and tearing them apart at night . . . death on an incomprehensible scale, followed by the screaming of newborns . . . the protoplasm of a cell looking as wide and deep as an ocean. Panting from the exertion, the young Traveler tore through the filmy membrane and emerged in blinding light—strong white beams that were as warm as sunlight. He had left the collective experience of his fellow Travelers to bask in their collective love. In this way, they welcomed him into their unique fellowship.

The light gradually faded, and Wes felt real hands patting his back, tousling his hair, and touching the tears on his face. He felt full yet drained, wise beyond his years but insufferably stupid. The new Traveler touched his own cheek and was shocked to see that he had grown several days' worth of beard. *How long have I been in there?* he thought to himself as he accepted the wishes of his peers. *How much have I changed?*

"You'll need sleep," said a familiar voice, and he turned to see his mentor, who looked as proud and fulfilled as any father.

The others were gone, including his ageless mother. Wesley and his mentor were standing in a wooded hollow on a golden-hued planet that he knew was in another dimension. A simple hut made of leaves and native materials rested in the shade. He could tell that the pillows and sleeping mat were intended for him. The new Traveler was exhausted yet strangely energized, as one often is after an ordeal. He knew he would be able to find his way back here any time he wished, then stay as long as he liked without wasting a moment in the reality he had once known.

I can also go to Earth in the blink of an eye, thought the Traveler. *The* Enterprise, *my home, my childhood . . . past, present, or future . . , any place I choose.*

He yawned with satisfaction. "I am very tired," he admitted. "Thank you, I'll lie down now."

"Wait," said his mentor, tugging gently on his arm. "Remember, you have one final task before your well-deserved rest. You must gaze into the Pool of Prophecy, which will show you an event from the future. Although we have all shared to create the Pool, we have no control over what you will witness. Rest assured, this vision will mean something to you, and only you."

"Let me see the Pool," answered the young Traveler with confidence. After what he had been through, he figured he could see one more vision, no matter where it came from.

With a comforting arm on his elbow, the young Traveler allowed himself to be guided down a wooded path suffused with golden light. Orange and scarlet blossoms the length of his hand grew in profusion, and the floral scents were almost overpowering. He thought he heard birds chirping in the willowy trees, until he heard familiar languages and realized that the forest hummed with voices from all creatures. In seconds, he grew accustomed to the cacophony of low-pitched conversations, like whispers in the room next door.

The path led them to a pond that was lined with rough stones and looked much too dark for the sunlit glen. Leaves and a bit of green slime floated in one forgotten eddy of the pool, and the murky depths looked as if they couldn't reveal anything but a tadpole. Wesley glanced around for his mentor at the same moment that he realized he was alone.

With a shrug, the young Traveler leaned over the Pool of Prophecy and gazed upon its inky surface. For once, he didn't physically go anywhere; he simply saw an image dance atop the water until it grew as sharp as an image on an *Enterprise* viewscreen. When he saw some Starfleet markings, he realized that it *was* a viewscreen on the *Enterprise*-E, a ship he had never visited. On a portion of the screen a countdown was running, with the bright red seconds whizzing by. The Traveler felt himself gaining control over the vision. He was able to move his perspective outside the hull, where the massive starship floated in space, surrounded by some sort of wreckage. The most recent *Enterprise* was a distinctive spacecraft, beautiful in its own right yet clearly the successor to a noble line.

His joy at seeing his mother's ship was quickly tempered when he noticed more debris, oddly flickering running lights, and the craft's stricken appearance. Then he heard one voice above the others in the hum of the trees. This one was not carbon-based but silicon.

"Autodestruct sequence in progress. Abort impossible in five more seconds," said the computer. "Ten, nine, eight—"

"Mom!" shouted Wesley. He knew she was aboard the ship. There was no question: *All* of his shipmates were on the *Enterprise* at that moment, and time was ticking down.

"Five, four, three," intoned the computer matter-of-factly. *No one could stop it now!*

"Wait!" he cried helplessly.

Wes reached for the *Enterprise* as if it were a toy vessel floating upon the black water. Before he could save it, the starship erupted in a monstrous fireball, spewing glittering rubble into the far corners of his vision. The Pool of Prophecy blazed like a sun going nova; then it was dark again, except for a sparkling cloud of glitter that expanded ever outward. That shimmering dust was all that remained of the mighty *Starship Enterprise.*

The Traveler roared in grief and plunged his hands into the water. At once, the vision shattered into a million neon eels, all squirming to escape from the murky pool.

"What do I do?" he wailed, turning to look for his mentor . . . or anyone. But he was alone in the golden forest, kneeling at the edge of a muddy pond. "How can I save them?" he begged to the heavens.

That was like asking, "What is zero subtracted from zero?" There would never be anything he could do to save them, because he was just a witness. With shock, the Traveler realized that every trial and every vigil he had suffered during his training had only been to prepare him for this moment. If he could resist misusing his powers now, he would be a trusted member of this unique society. That felt more like a curse than a comfort.

Crouching by the Pool, the newly born Traveler buried his face in his hands and wept for his dead mother, fallen comrades, and lost innocence.

Chapter Two

"COMING OUT OF WARP," reported Lieutenant Kell Perim from the conn of the *Enterprise.* "We're five thousand kilometers from gateway three."

"Proceed with caution, half impulse," ordered Captain Jean-Luc Picard as he rose from his command chair and approached the viewscreen. He had heard so much about the Battle of Rashanar and the vast graveyard left behind that he felt as if he'd been here already, only this was their first pilgrimage. The image on the overhead viewscreen showed what looked like a nebula; however, it didn't consist of stars, planets, and celestial bodies, but a swirling cloud of destruction. "Magnify that view, Mr. Data," he ordered.

"Yes, sir," answered the android at the ops station.

His fingers darted across his console. The images on the viewscreen became bigger . . . and more disturbing.

Sundered, scorched warships from a dozen different worlds hung in confusion like the contents of a child's toy chest dumped into space. Energy beams rippled between the silent hulks, making them look alive and still lethal. Surrounding these derelicts was a shroud of smaller debris, which glittered in the glow of a distant sun. Deep within the battle site were bright power spikes and giant arcs of energy, side effects of all the ruptured faster-than-light engines. The scuttled wrecks were reported to be in orbit around a mysterious gravity sink at the center of the graveyard. At the outer ring, most of these orbits were slow and stately, however some were fast and erratic. Most of the orbits were collision courses.

A few large chunks went crashing around the wreckage like pinball spheres. Picard could see dangerous plasma clouds glowing in the distance. There was also supposed to be an antimatter asteroid lurking somewhere in the spherical junkyard. To Picard, it looked like an immense snow globe filled with confetti, lightning, and hellish mobiles made from disemboweled starships.

"And this is supposed to be one of the *safe* entry points?" asked Commander William Riker, standing behind the captain. "I'd feel better if we stayed out here and explored with shuttlecraft."

"I second that, sir," came a voice from the rear of the bridge, at the tactical station. Lieutenant Christine Vale was a spare, compact woman who wasn't given to offering unsolicited advice to the captain.

Picard's lips thinned as he gazed at the mostly unexplored debris field—remnants of the deadliest battle in the Dominion War. Every ship that took part in the Rashanar engagement was destroyed. Not one single ship limped away to tell the tale. There were stories and superstitions about this place, and its legend continued to grow in the years since the end of the war. Despite the dangers, the lure of salvage and secrets often attracted the wrong sort of visitor. Military historians had yet to figure out what had happened here, and unraveling that mystery was the only part of this assignment which appealed to Captain Picard. Normally, he wasn't eager to catalog so much death and destruction.

"This access point has been charted and cleared of immediate dangers," said Data helpfully. "The *Enterprise* is within parameters for entry and is cleared for incursion to warning buoys, level three. However, sensor readings will be unreliable, and it is advised to raise shields."

"Make it so," said Picard with a glance at Lieutenant Vale. "If we're going to spend three months excavating a mass grave, we might as well jump right in and not be squeamish."

"Shields up," answered Vale, working her board.

"Entry in one minute," reported Lieutenant Perim at the conn. "I'm using the suggested coordinates and course, although the debris has shifted."

The captain stepped toward her. "That's to be expected. Take us in."

"Yes, sir," replied the unjoined Trill.

"Captain," said Riker, "how many away teams and shuttlecraft do you want to send out?"

"Enough to recover bodies, work security, and run

our science missions," answered Picard. "We don't think we'll be able to use transporters, so—"

"Pardon me, Captain," said Vale, "we're being hailed. Captain Leeden of the *Juno.*"

"Oh," answered Picard, mustering a smile for the captain with the longest tour of duty at the Rashanar Battle Site. "Put her onscreen."

Although he was smiling, his counterpart who appeared on the viewscreen was not. Jill Leeden, the dark-haired, dark-skinned skipper of the *Juno,* said, "I suggest you stop right there, Captain. Don't enter the boneyard."

Although confused, the captain lifted his hand and said, "Full stop."

"Aye, Captain," responded Perim.

Still trying to be charming, Picard said, "I didn't realize we would have a welcoming party. Is there some danger we don't know about?"

"There are *thousands* of dangers you don't know about. We don't either, and we've been here a year." Her image began to break up with static, and her next words were inaudible.

The captain turned to Christine Vale. "See if you can amplify their signal."

"Too much interference," said the human, shaking her short brown hair. "The *Juno* has broken off contact, but I've got them on sensors—they're headed out of the field toward our position."

Riker gave Picard a quizzical expression. "What was that all about?"

"I trust we'll find out soon," answered the captain,

turning back to the grim reality on the viewscreen. "The 'boneyard,' she called it."

"It looks more like a haunted house to me," said Riker.

They watched as a jagged beam arced dramatically between two derelicts, one Klingon and the other Jem'Hadar. A moment later, the hulks collided in a shower of sparks. For a moment, it seemed the two ghost ships were still battling each other. Then they slowed down as a chunk of a large nacelle went hurtling through the wreckage, banging around like an entrant in a demolition derby. It finally coasted on its way, altering course with everything it hit.

"Where did that nacelle come from?" asked Riker.

Data shook his head and wrinkled his brow slightly. "Unknown, sir. Its presence did not register on sensors until we made visual contact. All of the debris seems to be affected by the gravity source at the center. It appears to be unstable. This is assuming that our sensor readings are correct, when they may not be."

"Captain, the *Juno* is within transporter range," announced Vale at the tactical station.

Everyone on the bridge turned to see a stately *Excelsior*-class starship emerge from the scorched hulks in the graveyard. The warship cruised slowly to a distance that brought it nose to nose with the larger *Enterprise*.

"Sir," added Vale, "Captain Leeden requests permission to transport for a brief meeting with you."

"We'll meet her in the conference room next to transporter room three," answered Picard as he nodded to Riker and headed for the turbolift. "Mr. Data, you have the bridge."

The two officers arrived in the conference room slightly ahead of their visitor. The captain hoped that after a year in this unique site, she would be able to enlighten them and help their investigations go smoothly.

A moment later, an ensign escorted a tall, lanky woman with dusky skin and hair to the conference room. She looked very regal in her black-and-gray uniform, if a bit younger than Picard had anticipated from the static-filled images.

"Captain Leeden," Picard said warmly, stepping forward to shake her hand. She gave him a firm grip but very little expression. "This is my first officer, Commander Will Riker."

"It's a pleasure," she said flatly. Picard motioned to the table. The skipper of the *Juno* strode purposely to a chair and sat down.

Picard and Riker sat down across from her, and the captain said, "I'm curious to know why you stopped us from entering. We had our shields up and were obeying the known protocol. Is there some new hazard?"

"It's very simple, Captain," said Leeden. "No ship enters the boneyard without clearance. That means my approval. If you read your orders, you'll see that I'm the fleet captain of this lost outpost. There are usually half a dozen authorized starships plus their shuttlecraft working the site at any one time, and we can't cover all of it. We've been deluged with impostors, even ships impersonating Starfleet vessels."

She counted on her fingers. "We've got Pakleds, Androssi, Orions, Hok'Tar, Ferengi, Kreel, and a dozen other syndicates actively trying to loot this graveyard.

As you can imagine, the Dominion spacecraft have been magnets for them. In the last two months, we've had four scavenger ships destroyed, and also we've had major damage to two of ours."

"Now that we're here," Picard assured her, "I think we can alleviate some of your workload. So, security is your biggest problem?"

Captain Leeden replied gravely, "Our primary mission is to recover the dead, which I consider to be a sacred responsibility. I come from a lengthy military family. We follow the creed of 'leave no man behind.' We're too late for some of these crews, but we're doing the best we can. The scavengers don't care about the bodies and they interfere with our duty."

Riker cleared his throat and asked, "How were the scavenger ships destroyed?"

"Commander," said Leeden wearily, "you'll find that there's no shortage of ways to die here in Rashanar. You're spending three months in the boneyard—by that time, you'll just be learning your way around, if your ship hasn't taken too much damage to be useful."

"We've been in difficult situations before," Picard said. "I will admit that you have more experience than we do at this site, but we have our orders too. We've had several scientific investigations approved by the admiralty."

He glanced at his first officer and saw Riker nodding in approval.

"Scientific investigations," echoed Leeden. "Well, *that's* useful to the galaxy as a whole. If you want to help me, keep those scavengers off my back. I'll retrieve the bodies, which is a tricky job under these conditions. It would take you a long time to learn to do it safely. I know the *Enterprise* can fight, so fight them off. But I warn you, they don't always leave if you ask nicely, not even after a warning shot across their bow."

She sighed and said, "I hate to cut this short, but we just cracked open a Vulcan ship, and we've got it tractor-beamed. There are delicate protocols we have to follow with the bodies. In twenty-two hours, we should be finished . . . if we don't have to chase scavengers. Welcome to Rashanar." With that, Captain Leeden rose from the table, assuming their business was concluded.

Commander Riker sat upright in his seat and said, "Captain, before you go, we wanted to ask you about the anomalies. The gravity sink, the antimatter asteroid, the weird discharges? Aren't you studying them?"

"Studying them?" asked Leeden. "We're trying to *avoid* them. The gravity sink is getting stronger, and it's causing a vortex. Believe me, you don't *want* to find that mobile mass of antimatter, and heaven help you if you do."

"But these phenomena have to be categorized and explained," insisted Picard.

Captain Leeden shook her head. "We've had plenty of science vessels come through here, and most of them ran screaming into the night. You don't understand, gentlemen, there is stuff in that battle site that you won't find in any physics text, and it changes by the second. It's not a normal junkyard . . . it's truly haunted. I hope you won't regret coming here."

With that ominous warning, the captain of the *Juno* strode toward the door and left the conference room.

Picard and Riker followed her out and down the corridor into the transporter room.

"Captain, one more question, if you please," asked Picard as Leeden stepped onto the transporter pad. "How could every ship in the Battle of Rashanar be destroyed? Do you know?"

Leeden sighed for a brief moment, her face showing the pain of all she had seen. "On every ship, we've seen evidence that they fought to the death . . . weapons exhausted, shields out, life-support gone. Surrender didn't seem to be an option for anyone. Enter with care, Captain Picard, and stay in contact. Most of the buoys are subspace relays, and we usually find that delayed subspace works better than RF when inside the boneyard, despite our close proximity."

The impressive woman motioned to the operator. "Energize."

Picard and Riker watched the captain of the *Juno* leave their ship in a swirling column of crystalline particles.

"Hmmm," said Captain Picard, his lips thinning. "That didn't go as planned, did it? However, this *is* her turf and we do have more to learn from her than she from us."

"I seriously think she needs a break from this assignment," commented Riker. "I'd like to arrange a meeting between Deanna and Captain Leeden—nothing official, maybe a social occasion—just to get the counselor's opinion. If we want to do what she says would help her the most, we should scan for looters and send shuttlecraft to patrol the perimeter."

"Do that, along with everything else we planned to do," answered Picard. "I want to use all the resources of the *Enterprise*—full duty shifts, every shuttlecraft in flight. Let's bring ourselves up to speed as quickly as we can."

As the door whooshed open, the captain allowed himself a slight smile. "Take us in as far as the warning buoy six. Then I want my new yacht prepared to launch."

Riker's jaw clenched as he stepped into the corridor. "Captain, I don't need to tell you how dangerous it is out there. While you're off the ship, there may be difficulty with these wildcat salvagers."

"I trust you to handle them, Number One," said Picard confidently. "Don't be concerned, I'll keep the shields up. Someone needs to take readings on that gravity sink, plus there's a *Galaxy*-class starship that went down in the same area."

"The *Asgard*," said Riker, nodding somberly. "Yes, we have the coordinates for it. A recovery team has already gone over that ship, but it's classified as dangerous and in an erratic orbit."

"I'll take Commanders Data and La Forge with me," decided the captain. He met Riker's concerned gaze and said, "We haven't got much time to make a difference here, so let's do everything we can."

"Yes, sir," agreed the first officer.

The captain's yacht, *Calypso,* was a step up from a standard shuttlecraft, with an elliptical shape, low warp drive, and more opulent passenger room. It was a copy of his last one, the *Cousteau,* which had been destroyed at the Ba'ku planet. The yacht could dock outside the

Enterprise, allowing a quick launch without going through the shuttlebay.

Beside him in the pilot's seat, Data swiftly ran through the prelaunch checklist. Geordi La Forge sat at an auxiliary console that he had already configured into a science station. It might have been selfish to take three senior officers on one mission, mused the captain, but understanding this gravity sink was essential to the safety of the crew. If it was relatively benign, they wouldn't have to devote much time or many personnel to it, but if it was as dangerous as had been suggested, then they had better start planning how to deal with it with the best personnel possible.

On the small overhead viewscreen, one of the warning buoys was suddenly engulfed in ripples of wild, arcing energy. Picard was reminded of the story of Benjamin Franklin's kite braving the lightning storm. The roving web of energy then moved on and surrounded the blasted hull of a Klingon bird-of-prey, making it look like a green mountain in the middle of a tropical storm. Nearby, other derelicts bobbed in space like balloons from yesterday's birthday party. Clouds of plasma and ozone throbbed with unclassified energy. Geordi La Forge glanced at the captain, then at his readouts, and shook his head.

"I don't know, Captain," said the engineer. "The *Enterprise*'s shields have been hit six times by energy discharges since we stopped here. I can't advise dropping shields, even briefly. These discharges are totally unpredictable. With shields down, one strike might start a chain reaction. The *Enterprise* may be safe if we just sit here, but to launch all the shuttlecraft we have planned, we'll need to back off to a safer spot. Maybe go outside the site."

"The *Calypso* can launch quickly enough to leave from here," said Data. "But I agree with Geordi—extended operations without shields would be unwise."

Picard nodded grimly. "For now, we'll be the only craft launching from here. Are we ready?"

"Yes, sir," answered Data.

The captain tapped his combadge and said, "Picard to bridge."

"Riker here," came the swift reply. "Are you sure you can't be talked out of this? I haven't made my usual effort."

"No," answered Picard with a smile, "but I will allow that we can't launch any other craft from here. Lower shields on my mark, raise them as soon as we leave. Then pull back to the gateway before you launch any more shuttlecraft."

"Aye, sir," replied Riker. "If we lose contact, we'll try the subspace frequencies. We'll just have to put up with the delay. You're cleared for launch."

Picard glanced at Data, who nodded vigorously. "Mark," said the captain.

"Shields are down," reported Geordi.

With the sure hands of the android at the controls, the yacht, which looked like a miniature *Defiant*-class vessel, dropped from its dock and glided cautiously into the boneyard. With mysterious flashes of energy all around them, it felt like cruising an ocean storm. Deftly the android guided them between the blasted hulks and glittering clouds of debris, but rubble still sizzled against their shields. It was sobering to see so much destruction and waste close up. Picard's disheartened mood deepened.

"Data, head to port ten degrees," said La Forge as he studied his sensors. "I'm already picking up the gravity surge."

"I see its location," answered the android. "I am correcting course."

Picard had little to do but gaze out the front viewport at the depressing array of stricken spacecraft. For a starship captain, it was impossible not to envision the *Enterprise* as one of these derelicts. *If we had participated in the Battle of Rashanar, would we have fared any better than these others?* wondered the captain. Suddenly the musty hulk of a Cardassian *Galor*-class warship swiveled slightly, as if touched by an invisible hand.

"I saw one of the wrecks moving," Picard pointed out.

"The gravity effect is definitely stronger here," said La Forge. "This entire graveyard would be spread out over a larger area if it weren't for the gravity."

"I am slowing down," reported Data. "I do not think we should get much closer—the source is less than one kilometer away."

"I don't see anything," said Picard sharply. "Can you pinpoint its location and size?"

Geordi shook his head. "Not unless we triangulate using sensor arrays. That might take a while . . . and be inaccurate. It's the equivalent of looking for a black hole—we wouldn't know it was there except for the effect it has on other objects. But the debris isn't in a stable orbit. Objects are crashing into each other, falling apart, getting zapped by discharges."

With his ocular implants, La Forge peered through the viewport into the boneyard. "That gravity dump is out there, and given these readings, I have a theory where it came from."

"Please enlighten us," said Data with interest.

"Well," the engineer began, "almost every ship in both fleets was equipped with artificial gravity. On Starfleet vessels, the gravity generators are redundant and are among the last systems to fail. I believe it had to be the same with most of these starships. As the battle wore on, more hulls were ruptured in close combat. The gravity generators on some ships continued to work; then the graviton stream extended into space. It's possible that enough of the gravitons cohesed to produce this mutant gravity source."

Data cocked his head. "Although your theory is intriguing, Geordi, proving it would be difficult. It would be impossible to reproduce these circumstances for an experiment, and even a computer simulation would be insufficient."

"I know," said the engineer with a sigh. "That's why I'm telling you, but probably won't be putting it into my report. But we've got clouds of plasma, antimatter, and who knows what else running loose here. Why not gravity?"

"It's the closeness of battle that's a mystery to me," mused Captain Picard as he surveyed the carcasses of lost starships. "Yes, a few badly damaged vessels might slug it out toe-to-toe, but all these ships—it's like they were paralyzed with indecision until it was too late."

Data shook his head slightly. "Captain, this site has been much disturbed. The gravity sink has caused a collapsing effect. I would not place much credence in the current positioning of the ships."

"Perhaps not," said Picard grimly. "Whether they were here or ten kilometers from here, this was a bloodbath. As Captain Leeden told us, something kept them all fighting until the death. But what?"

"I have an interesting visual," said La Forge. "I don't want to get any closer, but I'll put it on the viewscreen."

Picard turned his attention to the small overhead viewer, where he saw what looked like an out-of-control merry-go-round. When he got a better look, he frowned. It was really blasted hulls and broken nacelles circling swiftly around a dingy mass of debris. This whirlpool of junk was illuminated briefly by spikes and spits of energy, making it look more hellish than it already was.

"A vortex," said Picard grimly. "Captain Leeden mentioned it."

"There are level-five warning buoys around it," said La Forge.

"I am compensating for increased gravity," reported Data. "I suggest we withdraw a few kilometers."

"Is the gravity sink going to be harmful to our operations?" asked Picard with grave concern.

"Not if we stay away from it," answered La Forge,

"which would be my advice. We're still tracking the orbits of the biggest shipwrecks."

"I concur," said Data. "We could study it further, but that would be risky and might only add to the inconclusive data we already have."

"These sensors are a mishmash," complained Geordi, shaking his head in frustration. "I'm actually getting life-sign readings. We know that can't be possible. One thing I've confirmed—our secondary target, the *Asgard,* is off to starboard about two kilometers."

The captain nodded. "Commander Data, proceed to the *Asgard.* Mr. La Forge, I hate to see us give up on a good theory. Is there any way we can use probes to show that gravity generators were the cause of this anomaly?"

"I'll ready a shuttlecraft with some probes when we get back," promised La Forge. "We're approaching the *Asgard*—I'll put it on screen."

The viewscreen showed the crippled *Galaxy*-class starship about a minute before they could view the entire spacecraft with the naked eye. Seeing this blasted derelict, which was intact enough to resemble the old *Enterprise*-D, tugged at Picard's guts. It was missing one nacelle, and the underbelly was ripped so badly that it looked disemboweled; still it was a grand wreck, one of the most impressive in the entire boneyard. Somberly Picard recalled how he had lost his *Galaxy*-class ship in the Veridian system while fighting Dr. Soran's murderous plans. The *Enterprise*-D had been a total loss, split in two with the saucer section crashed on the planet and the rest destroyed by a Klingon bird-of-prey. Fortunately, most of his crew had survived.

As the captain surveyed the husk of the *Asgard,* he decided that destruction was preferable to leaving such a morbid monument. The forlorn ship wasn't even in a place where anyone could safely visit it. It was not only a tragic memorial but a neglected one as well.

"The bridge appears mostly intact," said Geordi. "Of course, we'll need environmental suits to get around. I'm still getting faint life-sign readings, but I don't trust any of these sensors. What would you like to do, Captain?"

"Let's suit up and go over," answered Picard. "Can we use transporters?"

"I wouldn't advise it," answered La Forge. "But the previous recovery team put in a new shuttle dock for their use, so we won't have to do an EVA to get aboard. Data, it's a lifeboat hatch on the starboard dorsal."

"I see it," answered the android, skillfully piloting the captain's yacht toward the only working dock on the massive derelict. "Five minutes until docking—you may suit up."

On their approach to the saucer section, clumps of debris sizzled against their shields, and nearby energy arcs ripped through the blackness of space. This made Picard uneasy, and he tried to ignore the feelings of déjà vu as they cruised under the familiar-looking hull.

Data finished the docking procedure and rose to his feet just as Picard and La Forge put on their helmets. The android, needing no environmental suit, strode ahead of the two lumbering humans. Data opened the airlock, turned on his handheld light beam, and strolled into the hatchway. He shined his light around the corridor, becoming the first to board the *Asgard* in many months.

"I'm going to secure this hatchway," said Geordi, his voice sounding hollow in Captain Picard's headgear. "We may shift while we're docked. I don't want the *Calypso* breaking free."

"Make it so," agreed Picard. La Forge punched in commands on a panel by the airlock. After the two humans stepped into the corridor of the *Asgard,* the engineer used his tricorder to complete the security precautions. The sheen of a forcefield spread across the opening for a moment, as his tricorder beeped in response. La Forge slipped the device into a pouch on his waist and nodded to Picard.

In their bulky suits, Picard and La Forge walked down the corridor like two toddlers. The captain's light beam caught an access port that had been emptied, leaving nothing but ripped wires. Ahead of them, Data paused to let his comrades catch up, and he consulted his tricorder while he waited.

The android turned his light on an unblemished bulkhead and activated his built-in communicator. "There are no signs of hand-to-hand fighting or boarding parties. However, many of my readings are inexplicable."

"I put my tricorder away," said Geordi. "In this place, I'm not trusting anything I hear, and only half of what I see. You know, if we stay on this level in this same direction, we'll reach someplace familiar—Ten-Forward."

"Let's take a look," said Picard grimly. They lumbered onward.

Data had to force the doors open to allow them to peer into the ship's biggest observation lounge. When Picard looked over the android's shoulder, he caught his breath. The spacious room was a blizzard of broken glassware, dishware, foam, and furniture, all in pieces and floating in suspension. They couldn't even see the big observation windows at the forward part of the hull. This widespread destruction was like a microcosm of the Rashanar Battle Site itself, mused the captain. It brought a sense of futility to their mission.

"I don't really want to go in there," said Geordi, echoing the captain's thoughts.

Picard nodded somberly and pointed to an access hatch above their heads. "That Jefferies tube will take us to the bridge, won't it?"

"Yes, sir," answered Data. With a gentle leap, the android soared through the low gravity to the hatch, got a handhold, and pulled the hatch open. He climbed into the access tube, while Picard turned off the magnetic field in his boots, jumped, and floated upward to join him.

The three of them had nine decks to climb; it was easy going in the low gravity. The Jefferies tube afforded access to several internal systems, and they could see evidence of burned-out circuits and hasty, ultimately futile repairs. Picard tried not to think about the bodies that had been recovered here, in Ten-Forward, the bridge, and every other part of the *Asgard.*

"Why couldn't they get away in escape pods?" he asked no one in particular.

"According to the *Asgard*'s last message, all their computer systems failed," answered Data as they climbed. "They reported that Breen thermal-pulse weapons damaged every sensitive system on the ship. We are unsure what happened after that, because all logs and visual records were stolen by looters."

"Stolen?" Picard shook his head grimly and sighed. What did he expect to find here that teams of investigators and looters had overlooked? It was almost as if the crew of the *Asgard* had lowered their shields and allowed their most crucial systems to be taken out, mortally wounding the ship.

Suddenly, a strange clang sounded on the other side of the bulkhead—on level three. The visitors stopped to listen and glanced puzzledly at one another; Data let go of the rungs of the ladder long enough to check his tricorder.

"My readings are inconclusive," said the android. "Should we investigate deck three?"

"We'll check there on the way back," answered Picard, who had seen many pieces of junk floating through these ghostly corridors. "For now, let's keep moving."

Delving into a ghost ship was like exploring a tomb, he thought, only this tomb had been plundered by grave robbers.

A few minutes later, their light beams were probing the eerie darkness of the *Asgard* bridge, illuminating the scorched circuitry, uprooted seats, and smashed access panels on the bulkhead, deck, and consoles. For the first time, Picard saw clear signs of looting, or possibly very careless recovery of sensitive components. The captain was drawn to the command chair, which was charred and splattered with blood but still rooted to the deck. Data divided his attention between the ops station and his tricorder, while La Forge went to his old post at the conn and wiped the dust from the membrane surface.

"There's still static electricity on these controls," observed Geordi. "No power, of course. Why didn't they consider towing this ship out and retrofitting it?"

"It could be retrofitted, but that would be inefficient for a ship of older design with no crew," said Data bluntly. "As long as you are assembling and training a new crew, it is more efficient to assign them to a new vessel."

Picard wanted to protest and say there was value in an old warhorse like the *Asgard*, but Data was right. Without a crew to lovingly put her back together, as his crew had done many times with the *Enterprise*, it wasn't going to happen. Like it or not, the *Asgard* was an elaborate mausoleum at best, scrap metal at worst.

The android consulted his tricorder. "I am receiving fewer inexplicable readings here than in the Jefferies tube. Is there anything in particular we should look for, Captain?"

Picard waved his hand in his bulky suit, realizing how pointless this venture had become. The mysteries of the Battle of Rashanar would probably never be solved, at least not with a cursory examination of a ship that had been picked clean like a Christmas turkey.

Suddenly they heard a very loud noise, like a small explosion, and the tricorder on Geordi's waist began to beep. The engineer consulted the device. It was easy to see his pale eyes widen through the faceplate of his helmet.

"Somebody is trying to steal the yacht!" he said in alarm.

"Permission to intercept them?" asked Data, moving swiftly to the Jefferies tube.

"Yes, go!" answered Picard.

The android vaulted for the access panel, grabbed the handle, and propelled himself headfirst into the Jefferies tube.

The captain tapped a button on his wrist to activate a com device in his helmet. "Picard to *Enterprise,*" he said. When there was no answer, he repeated, "Away team to *Enterprise.*"

The silence told him they were on their own, and somebody was trying to steal their only means of transportation.

Chapter Three

DATA FLEW WEIGHTLESSLY down the Jefferies tube on a perpendicular path through the decks of the *Asgard*. When he emerged from the hatch on level ten, he kicked off the bulkhead like a swimmer making a turn in a race and shot down the corridor, his hands at his sides. The android saw flashes of light and fleeting shadows ahead of him, and he heard voices and footsteps. They weren't actually footsteps, he corrected his impression, but the kind of scuffling, pulling, and gliding motions a humanoid had to use to move in a weightless environment.

As he neared the hatchway where the yacht was docked, Data entered a cloud of rancid gray smoke. From this haze emerged a hulking figure. The android stopped to do battle with the intruder. He caught the foe's arms as the limp environmental suit crashed into him, and Data immediately realized that his attacker was unconscious and badly burned, as were the hatch and portions of the corridor. The foe must have tried an explosive device on the forcefield, Data surmised, with disastrous results. He continued to hear scuffling sounds, and he concluded that a second intruder was making his escape.

Data would have gone after him, if not for the wounded being in his arms. By the time he stabilized his prisoner's weightless body and reached for his combadge, Data heard his companions gliding down the corridor at breakneck speed. Picard zoomed into view slightly ahead of Geordi; as soon as the captain stopped himself, Data gently pushed the unconscious being into his arms.

"Captain, this one needs medical attention," he reported. "A second one is fleeing, and perhaps I can catch him."

"Make it so," agreed Picard. "La Forge, let's get this person on board and give him some first aid."

"Where did he come from?" asked the incredulous engineer. "Don't tell me there are squatters on this wreck!"

The android pushed off the bulkhead and streaked after the fleeing intruder. As he glided down the corridor on sheer momentum, Data consulted his tricorder, knowing that the ghostly life signs they had detected were more real than previously thought. A flash grenade suddenly exploded just a few feet ahead of him, forcing the android into the bulkhead and causing him to drop his tricorder. For a moment, he was disoriented. He proceeded to run diagnostics on his positronic brain and neural network.

The tests were interrupted by the chirp of his combadge. "Data," came the captain's voice, "we heard that explosion. Are you all right?"

"I am reasonably well," answered the android, retrieving his tricorder and finding that the readings had returned to gibberish. "After using a flash grenade, the second intruder escaped. I am returning to your position. Data out."

By the time the android got back to the yacht and artificial gravity, the captain and Geordi had removed their prisoner's helmet and had placed the unconscious being on a fold-out examination table. The female humanoid had a slender, almost delicate face with sepia-hued skin and long brown hair tied in a ponytail. Picard took off his own helmet and grabbed a medical tricorder from the first-aid kit.

"Androssi," said Data.

"That was going to be my guess," replied Picard. "La Forge, make sure that hatchway is secure. We don't want any more unexpected visitors."

"Yes, sir. I'll set up a sensor array, too," answered the engineer, moving to obey the captain's orders.

"She is breathing at regular intervals," observed Data, leaning over their dazed patient.

"Yes," said Picard as he studied the tricorder. "I don't think she's in severe danger, just suffering from shock, concussion, and a few burns. I don't want to leave the *Asgard* and let her associates escape. We could revive her and question her."

Data nodded. "A low dosage of tricordrazine would stimulate neural activity."

"Go ahead and prepare a hypospray," said Picard. "I'll use the restraints to keep her on the table."

A minute later, they were prepared to revive their prisoner, and Picard administered the hypo to the Androssi's neck. Within seconds, she blinked awake and stared at them with amber eyes that were almost the color of her skin. Immediately she began to struggle against the restraints. Her wiry strength was impressive, but the bindings held firmly.

"You're not going anywhere," said Picard. "Besides, you're injured, so I wouldn't try to struggle too much."

Still seething over her misfortune, the Androssi female glared at the captain. "Am I under arrest?"

"Considering that we found you in a restricted area on a Starfleet vessel without permission . . . yes," answered the captain. "If you answer our questions, we'll release you as soon as possible. Where did you come from? Were you *living* on the *Asgard?*"

The prisoner shifted her eyes back and forth, surveying her surroundings and assessing her chances of escape. La Forge joined them. The prisoner seemed agitated when the engineer gazed at her with his ocular implants. Then she stared frankly at Data, who gave her even more of a start.

"Androids? Cyborgs? What are you?" she asked.

Picard scowled. "We're asking the questions, remember? You were on the *Asgard* when we arrived. Were you living here?"

"We're a forward reconnaissance team," she answered. "Keeping track of the movement of Starfleet spacecraft."

"Fascinating," said Data, cocking his head. "You have spotters embedded among the derelicts in order to safeguard and coordinate your operations. We have seen one of your associates. Are there only two of you on the *Asgard?*"

"I think I've said enough," answered the Androssi warily.

"You were trying to steal this shuttlecraft, weren't you?" asked La Forge.

"We're salvagers!" she answered, "Not thieves. We thought this tiny craft was salvage, the same as the rest of the vessels in this junkyard. It *was* deserted when we found it, and forcefields can be automated."

Picard shook his head. "You nearly killed yourself trying to get in."

She said indignantly, "There's only one difference between you and us. We consider this area to be free space, open for salvage. You've decided to illegally restrict access and hog its wealth all to yourselves."

"Wrong," snapped La Forge. "We're trying to recover the bodies of our fallen comrades and foes. You're only interested in profit off the misfortune of others."

The Androssi sniffed. "We don't care about dead bodies. If you want any more information, you'll have to torture me."

"We don't torture our prisoners," said Picard carefully. "However, we do make deals, and I know the Androssi are not averse to making a deal. Couldn't we convince you to wait until we finish recovering our bodies and making our investigation? Then perhaps we could open up this site for salvage."

"You can't make that deal," the prisoner replied. "We're already operating under a contract."

"The Androssi do not have a strong centralized government," remarked Data. "It is unlikely we could strike an agreement they would all observe."

"What he said," answered the Androssi, staring curiously at the android. "But if you gave us a humanoid machine like *him,* we could make a trade that would be very beneficial. We recently came upon a Romulan cloaking device. I believe we could adapt it to a Starfleet spacecraft."

Data felt a bit flattered, but Picard scowled at their guest. "Commander Data is considerably more valuable than a Romulan cloaking device—he's the equal of any of us. In any event, we have treaties with the Romulans precluding our use of such technology."

"Sounds like another super Starfleet deal," scoffed the Androssi.

"Do you have a name?" asked Data, intrigued by their visitor.

"Ghissel," she answered, accenting the second syllable. "That's the last question I'm answering."

"Very well," said Picard. Tight-lipped, he turned to his comrades. "Find the other one and bring him in. I'll stay here and watch our 'guest' while I try to reach the *Enterprise.*"

"The *Enterprise,*" echoed Ghissel, sounding impressed. "What a prize that would be."

"Don't get your hopes up," said Geordi. "Data, I set up a portable sensor array in the hatch. With two more, we could triangulate the location of any life signs we find."

"Good idea, Geordi," replied the android. He turned to the Androssi and said, "We will find your companion, but we do not wish for anyone to be harmed. How many of those grenades does he have?"

"Plenty," she answered with a smile.

Exasperated, Commander Will Riker pounded his fist on the arm of the command chair and stared at the chaos on the bridge. A wild spike of energy had just struck the *Enterprise* as she disgorged her first contingent of shuttlecraft. They were in the *supposedly* safe gateway. Several bridge consoles had blown out, and the ship's computers had switched automatically to red alert, complete with blaring klaxons and red emergency lighting. They had gotten three shuttles launched before disaster had struck. As fetid smoke filled the bridge, Riker seethed at taking damage from a random incident. He'd rather a real foe.

Christine Vale announced from the tactical station, "Unidentified raiders at bearing three-hundred-thirty mark twenty-two."

"Conn, do we have impulse?" asked Riker, trying to sound calm.

"Half impulse at best," answered Lieutenant Perim. "I've set course."

"Are shields holding?" asked the acting captain.

"At sixty percent," replied Perim.

"Computer, cancel red alert—go to yellow alert," ordered Riker. "Conn, set course to intercept the intruders. Tactical, inform all launched shuttlecraft to pursue them, too. Ops, tell the shuttlebay that we are canceling all shuttle launches until further notice, and get me a damage report."

His orders elicited a chorus of "Yes, sirs," and Riker finally settled back in his seat as security personnel worked to put out the hot spots on the bridge.

"Damage report, Commander," said Jelpn, a lanky Deltan who was filling in for Data at ops. "Our deflectors prevented the most serious damage, but the transfer conduits and electroplasma sublimators overloaded and failed at an average of thirty-two percent shipwide. We should expect power irregularities. Engineering estimates that impulse engines will be at full in twenty minutes, and shields will be full strength in ten minutes."

Riker was just about to congratulate himself on dodging a bullet when Lieutenant Vale interrupted. "Sir, I've received a message from Captain Picard on a subspace frequency. He's been trying to contact us and requests assistance."

"Tell him we're chasing intruders and repairing damage, with a full report to follow," answered Riker. "How urgent is his situation?"

"Just a moment, I'll find out," said Vale as she relayed the message. Impatiently, Riker grabbed a spare fire extinguisher and helped the security personnel put out the smoldering remains of a power conduit.

Yellow alert, normal lighting, and a modicum of order had returned by the time Vale said, "Captain Picard's situation is not urgent, but he has encountered hostiles and has a prisoner."

"Tell him we'll dispach a shuttlecraft and security team as soon as we can," replied Riker, returning to the command chair. "Ops, ask Counselor Troi to report to the bridge."

"Yes, sir," answered the Deltan.

Since they were clearly in more danger than they had anticipated, Riker needed another senior officer on the bridge to take over . . . in case he got injured. The Betazoid's presence was always calming, both to himself and others, and he wanted her to be present if he had to talk to Captain Leeden, which seemed likely.

"Shuttlecraft *Hudson* has sustained enemy fire," announced Vale from the tactical console.

"Tell them to break off," said Riker angrily, sitting up in his chair. "Can we get a fix on these enemy craft?"

"Onscreen," answered Vale, working her console. "The quality will be poor."

Static and lines of interference obscured most of the image, but they could see a small green cruiser go darting under two hulks locked at the stern and twirling like a propeller. A Starfleet shuttlecraft appeared for a moment, but it broke off rather than follow them into the maze of derelicts.

"Are they Orion?" asked Riker.

Vale nodded. "That's the warp signature I got, but Orions have been known to sell cruisers to other worlds." The lieutenant sighed and shook her head. "They're gone from our sensors, and we have limited range right here. Shuttlecraft *Cortez* says they can follow the last one and keep them in visual contact."

Not liking this as the only option, Riker grumbled. "Tell them to pursue but keep out of weapon range. If the Orions stop, the *Cortez* is to get their location and back off."

While the tactical officer relayed orders, the turbolift door opened, and Deanna Troi strode onto the bridge. The counselor's dark eyes took in the smoking remains of one console and a team of technicians making repairs at another. Her gaze finally drifted to Riker, and she gave him a sympathetic smile.

"Troi reporting for duty," she said. "What happened, Will?"

Riker heaved his big shoulders and told her. He ended with the observation, "This is like chasing off vandals from a sacred house . . . before they can break all the windows. Considering the danger, I needed another senior officer on the bridge."

"Understood," answered Troi.

Riker turned to Jelpn at ops and asked, "How is the *Hudson?*"

"They reported only minor damage. They still have impulse engines."

Riker nodded, thankful for small favors. "Lieutenant Vale, send them Captain Picard's location with orders to assist him."

"He's docked at the *Asgard*," said Vale as she worked her console. "Sending orders."

The commander took a breath and gazed at his beloved. He whispered, "In case you thought you were going to be bored on this cruise, we have plenty to amuse us."

She gave him a seductive smile. "I haven't been bored since we left the Ba'ku planet."

"Shields back to ninety percent," reported Jelpn.

Riker nodded. "Good."

"Will," said Troi, "while it's quiet, I meant to ask your opinion on something. Almost every member of our crew lost someone they know in this battle. This mission has been unsettling for them. I would like to add a few memorial services to the ship's calendar of events."

"Good idea," said Will. "I just hope we'll have the time to attend them."

"Commander!" called Christine Vale. "There's an Ontailian ship, the *Maskar*, near the gateway, and they request permission to enter the battle site."

Riker allowed himself a smile. "They must have us confused with Captain Leeden and the *Juno*. Put their ship onscreen."

A moment later, a sleek blue warship appeared on the viewscreen; parts of its hull were so slender that it looked like a paper airplane, and there was a distinct lack of markings. The *Maskar* looked about half the size of the *Enterprise* and far more suited for operations inside the graveyard than the larger ship.

"They joined the Federation just as the Dominion War was breaking out," said Deanna. "This battle was partly to save their homeworld, which is one light-year away. Their planet has low gravity, and they're not humanoid."

"I'm glad you're here," said Riker with a chuckle. "Vale, put their captain onscreen."

As before, the image was less than perfect, but it was still rather startling to see interconnecting trellises made of tubes and pipes, with vines growing in profusion. More than the bridge of a starship, this chamber looked like a narrow jungle gym, or perhaps a greenhouse. As the image improved, Riker could see that the vines were really the long limbs of very slender creatures, which came in a variety of colors. Like sloths, the Ontailians crept through the structure, hanging and swinging from beam to beam on their wiry limbs. Looking carefully, Riker spotted a lumpen head and slim torso on one of the creatures, at the junction of its appendages. The Ontailian was so graceful that he moved with the silky ease of an octopus, and several of his fellows manipulated tools and worked controls on the tubes. It was a true bridge, and these remarkable creatures were running the elegant starship *Maskar.*

Although Riker had stepped forward to greet his counterpart, no such representative of the Ontailians emerged from the workers. Some sharp chittering sounded, and Lieutenant Vale explained, "It's taking a while for the Universal Translator to catch up."

"We are the *Maskar,*" a synthetic voice finally announced. "Hello, Federation *Starship Enterprise.* We know of your exploits. We have business inside the sacred field, assisting the *Juno.* May we obtain your blessing to enter?"

Riker hovered momentarily over the Deltan at the ops station. "Have we verified their warp signature?"

"Yes, sir," answered Jelpn. "It's quite unique. They've been assigned here for almost ten months."

Riker mustered a smile. "Please enter the sacred field with our blessing. I remind you to be cautious—it's dangerous in there."

"It is an honor to be here with the sacred," said the crackling voice. *"Maskar* ends transmission."

The image on the viewscreen shifted to the angular blue starship, which sliced through the debris of the boneyard like a knife through butter. Within seconds, the sliver of a ship had vanished among the hulking wrecks and sparkling spits of energy. The battle zone looked relatively quiet for a moment. Every crisis had been dealt with.

Riker turned to see Deanna Troi frowning with concern. He had almost forgotten about his *Imzadi* until then. He recognized that expression well enough. Something was wrong.

"What is it?" he asked.

Her brow furrowed, Troi shook her head. "I had the strongest impression that they were hiding something. Like they slipped past customs with contraband in their luggage."

"Have you ever met Ontailians before?"

"No," she admitted. "My feelings may be incorrect."

"We had better get used to them," said the ops officer, Jelpn. "There are five Ontailian ships working this site on a regular basis, more than anyone else."

"Conn, take us out of the boneyard," said Riker, making an executive decision. "I'm not going to drop shields to launch any more shuttlecraft until we're five thousand kilometers away."

Geordi La Forge stared at the remains of a meal, two tattered blankets, some gel packs, and cables, all of it stored weightlessly in the space under a food replicator in a break room near the laboratories on the *Asgard*. What was more impressive was the portable generator that had been left behind, which Data was inspecting for booby traps. The food replicator blinked at Geordi, giving every indication that it was working. Owing to the low gravity, the squatters had performed several crude alterations to the replicator, including one that added an oxygen line out. *They're using the replicator to refill the oxygen in their suits,* thought the engineer. Pretty clever. In this one little corner of the expired starship, life still struggled for survival.

"They *were* living here," said La Forge in amazement. "Living off the land."

"Forward observers," remarked Data as he studied his tricorder. "From some residual tachyon readings, I believe they had more equipment than this."

"A transmitter?" asked Geordi, pushing himself off the bulkhead and floating in his suit like a big balloon in a holiday parade.

"Perhaps a portable subspace transmitter," answered Data. He shined a light into the cabinet where La Forge had been looking and found some ripped wires and still swirling dust. "The layer of dust from static electricity has been disturbed," he pointed out. "Ghissel's companion was here and removed the transmitter. We must find him before he can call for help."

Bobbing just above La Forge's head was a heavy-duty crate that contained a portable sensor array; he retrieved it, leaving a second one undisturbed. "I'll set up one array here—you find another position for the third, then we'll triangulate. Even with the interference, we should have a strong sign where he is."

"Very well," nodded Data, "I will proceed to the port side of the saucer section."

"Just don't take long." La Forge glanced around nervously.

"Are you afraid?" asked Data, cocking his head.

The human nodded. "Yes, this is a creepy place inside a spooky place. Don't turn your emotion chip on, unless you want that old-fashioned tingle."

"I will leave it deactivated," Data assured him, "although I had assumed this was an atmospheric situation."

"So let's get rid of the bogeyman," said La Forge. "We may not be able to get through on the com channel, so once you get a clear reading from all three arrays, don't wait for me—just go there. I'll do the same."

With a nod, the android grabbed the second sensor array, pushed off the bulkhead, and glided from the room into the corridor, where he executed a turn to the right.

La Forge shook his head and checked his own tricorder. Life-sign readings were still vague, as if there were scattered pockets of cockroaches on the ghost ship, but linking the three sensor arrays should give a clear picture of where the uninvited guests were. Just to be safe, he checked his hand phaser and found it to be fully charged and set to stun, although he was no fast draw in the bulky suit.

While keeping a watchful eye on the doorway, the engineer placed adhesive pads on the feet of the scanning device, stuck it to the deck, and began to activate it as quickly as he could.

On the examination table in the cramped quarters of the yacht *Calypso,* the slender Androssi female writhed in her restraints. That was after making sure that Picard was watching her. It was a good thing he had left her compact environmental suit on, because she didn't appear to be wearing anything underneath. The captain had paid little attention to Ghissel since his companions left, having spent his time contacting the *Enterprise.* That had been a sobering experience, since they were suffering their own assortment of setbacks. But at least he had gotten through to them, and a shuttlecraft was on its way.

"There's no sense struggling," he told the Androssi female. "Your suit can handle your needs until we are finished here."

"I'm stiff and sore," she complained. "I have burns. Isn't there any other way to restrain me?"

The captain checked his readouts to make sure the sensor array was working. So was one of the remote arrays, and he hoped the other one would be active soon.

"Captain Picard!" she whined. "This is how Starfleet gets a reputation for being so brutal!"

"You know, I liked you better when you refused to talk," said the captain with a sigh. "It's quite common for a person with burns to be in restraints temporarily, and you've been treated to the best of my ability. You could have been more cooperative, but you preferred to act as if you're guilty. So let's wait and see what happens."

Ghissel began to whimper. "I haven't been in gravity

like this for a long time. *Something* is digging into my back. Please take a look at my belt and see what it is."

Picard stopped watching the readouts and turned to his prisoner, who was wearing a fairly substantial tool belt. "I'm just looking, but you have to promise to be quiet."

"I will," she breathed.

The captain rose from the pilot's seat and walked across the short bridge to the examination table in the galley area. The Androssi stopped struggling and released the tension in her body, lying passively on the table for the first time since awakening. Ghissel gazed hopefully at him with her frank amber eyes.

"Thank you," she said in advance.

"I haven't done anything yet," muttered Picard. He studied the unfamiliar environmental suit, which was burned through in a few small areas but otherwise intact. The helmet was resting on a countertop. He heard a crunching sound and glanced up to see Ghissel chewing something. She opened her mouth and expelled a misty sneeze in his direction.

Picard coughed once, and the compartment began to swirl all around his blurred vision. He grasped the side of the examination table and felt as if he were swaying on a boat . . . and about to get seasick. Picard remained on his feet as long as he could, but his legs gave out. He slumped to the deck in what seemed like slow motion, and a moment later he was conscious but paralyzed.

Ghissel activated something on her utility belt, and it shimmered with a burst of energy. The captain could hear latches snapping open.

Rubbing her wrists, Ghissel sat up and smiled at him. "It's only a muscle toxin. It knocks out some species, but apparently not you . . . and has no effect on us. You won't die, Picard, but you won't be able to move for several minutes. And thank you for sending your android away, or this would have been difficult."

As Picard looked on in helpless rage, his escaped prisoner ran to the hatch and worked the console. It took her several seconds, but she was a quick learner. As soon as the door slid open, another suited figure stepped in from the airlock. He set a transmitter on the deck, spotted Picard, and drew a Klingon disruptor from his belt.

Jean-Luc couldn't scream or even twitch—he could only lie there, waiting to die while the spittle drooled from a corner of his mouth.

Chapter Four

"No, HE'S A CAPTAIN," said Ghissel, grabbing the thug's weapon hand before he could shoot Picard with his disruptor. "Such as you can't kill him. Besides, we don't want Starfleet to get *too* mad at us. Put that away and check the controls."

Grudgingly, the Androssi in the environmental suit put his weapon away and strode toward the pilot's instrument panel. While Picard lay helpless, the female Androssi found his helmet and slipped it back onto his head, making sure it sealed with the neck of his environmental suit.

"I hope you're breathing," said Ghissel, grabbing her own helmet. "We'd like to take you with us, but prisoners aren't as easy to deal with as hardware—and they're worth less."

Showing surprising stength, the slender Androssi dragged Picard's dead weight through the airlock and into the corridor, where he became weightless. She grabbed the portable sensor array that La Forge had set up in the hatchway, then left Picard there, floating helplessly.

A few moments later, he felt faint vibrations and heard the whine of impulse engines. That would almost certainly bring Data and La Forge running back, but it would be too late to prevent the *Calypso* from being hijacked. The explosion, the burns, the unconscious Androssi bobbing in front of the hatch—it had all been staged for their benefit. They knew Ghissel would be hauled inside to be treated and questioned, and her booby-trapped belt would be unfastened at some point. The Androssi had no intention of breaking in with force when stealth and guile were much more efficient. Plus they had stolen the craft without even putting a dent in it.

Really a job well done, thought Picard. *I suppose I should be grateful that she spared my life.*

Some feeling was just coming back in his left foot and right thumb when he heard La Forge's shocked voice shout in alarm, "Captain! Data, do you have the tricorder?"

"I'm alive," croaked Picard in a slurred voice. His comrades probably couldn't understand the words, but the fact that he spoke at all proved his point. He tried to relax and allow his nerves and muscles to come back to functionality.

Data studied his tricorder and said with understated

frankness, "The captain is alive, and the yacht is gone."

Picard moved a little bit in the bulky suit, feeling like a creaky marionette hanging from invisible strings.

"Shuttlecraft is coming," he managed to say through clenched teeth.

Data nodded. "That is welcome news."

"I never liked that style of yacht, anyway," said Geordi cheerfully. "It wasn't like you used it much. They'll get you another one—a better one. Finally there's a new class of them."

Picard grumbled something unintelligible. His standing in Starfleet was safe enough to survive an incident such as this. He was really concerned about telling Captain Leeden.

Three hours later, in Captain Leeden's ready room, Picard sat as his counterpart paced in front of him, very agitated. "Now we've got a perfectly legitimate Starfleet vessel running around the boneyard, and it's full of Androssi," she complained, shaking her head.

"It's a rather unusual class of ship," said Picard.

The slim, dark-skinned woman paused and nodded. "Yes, that's a blessing. The problem is, we won't recognize it in a few days—after the Androssi modify it. They're experts at this, kludging from one technology and adding to another. Or maybe it will look like a common cruiser when we next see it, because they're also good at camouflage."

Captain Picard had come aboard the *Juno* alone, leaving Data, La Forge, and their rescuers in the shuttlecraft *Hudson.* He felt he owed it to Captain Leeden to give her a personal account of what had happened.

She shook her head sadly. "I will have to report this to Starfleet."

"As will I," agreed Picard. "The Androssi are very clever, and I won't underestimate them again. We made several fundamental mistakes today. We could use more information about this sort of threat."

"I know you and the *Enterprise* have distinguished yourselves countless times," said Leeden, "but this is unlike any place you've ever been. None of us know what we should be ready to face."

She scowled. "We went into that Vulcan ship and saw that it had been torn apart by scavengers. There were body pieces everywhere—mummies so dry and brittle they break off like weak foam. So this hasn't been an easy day for me."

"We're going to scale back on some of our operations," Picard promised, "in order to concentrate on security to allow you to do your job."

"Thank you," she said sincerely. "We'll be here two days longer than anticipated. I presume you'll be on the periphery."

"Yes," answered Picard.

"Picard, I've had a feeling of dread for months now. The longer you stay in the boneyard, the more you realize we're at their mercy."

"Whose mercy?" asked the captain.

"This place!" she said in exasperation. "The looters, the squatters, the scavengers . . . and the ghosts. I can't explain it, but the war still goes on here. I've asked for more help, but Starfleet is spread so thin. Rebuilding. I asked Starfleet for a specialized task force, and they sent me the most decorated ship in the fleet. So, Picard, are we going to let this place go to hell, or not?"

"No, we're not," he answered.

"You must be vigilant!" warned Jill Leeden with thunder in her voice. "Because, Picard, we don't want to add to the ghosts."

The veteran nodded gravely as he turned and left the wiry figure in the black and gray uniform contemplating the mystery of the boneyard.

Dr. Beverly Crusher peered closely at Captain Picard, who was stretched out uncomfortably on an examination table in her sickbay. She opened a drawer that contained tricorders, hyposprays, probes, and other medical implements, and counted them as if she intended to use every single one.

"Is this really necessary?" complained Picard. "I feel fine."

The redheaded doctor smiled charmingly as she stood up. "According to Data's report, you inhaled an unknown toxin that paralyzed you. According to Geordi, you had a near-death experience, and you've avoided me for the better part of a day. Thus, Jean-Luc, you are getting the whole treatment."

He tried to relax and take this extra punishment as bravely as he could, because he knew Beverly was just doing her job. She was as gentle with him as possible, and several minutes later, she nodded at him but didn't look satisfied.

"You're a little anemic and dehydrated," she said. "It might be from stress or an extended time in that environmental suit. For a couple of days, double your liquids and dietary supplements."

"Yes, Doctor," breathed the captain with relief as he sat up and pulled his tunic over his wiry frame. "Am I free to go?"

Beverly's calm demeanor cracked a little. "Do you have a few minutes to talk?"

"Yes," he answered, realizing that he had been so preoccupied lately that he hadn't paid much attention to his oldest and most intimate friend aboard the *Enterprise*. "Is there something wrong?"

The doctor rose from her seat and paced the quiet corner of sickbay. "It's just that I've been having vivid dreams lately . . . of Wesley. They're so real, it's as if I could touch him. I swear, last night I looked up and saw him standing at the foot of my bed. Of course, it was only a shadow, or maybe I was still dreaming. I don't know—"

Her green eyes grew misty as she peered at him. "It's been years since I've seen Wesley, but he seems closer than ever."

Picard gave her a sympathetic smile. "It's natural for you to be thinking of Wes, and I'm sure he's thinking of you."

That's pabulum, thought the captain, *but what can I tell this woman to relieve her mind? After seven years of no contact with her son?*

Beverly bit her lip and looked pensively at him. "Do you suppose it could mean . . . he'll be coming home soon?"

"How can any of us predict that?" answered Picard, taking her hands in his. "Listen, why don't we find time for a quiet dinner tonight? Or even a noisy dinner, if you want to be around people. Anything you like."

She smiled knowingly. "You really think no crisis will call you away? After the day you've had?"

The captain frowned and said, "We seem to be in a routine now—running around the fences, chasing off prowlers like an old Doberman pinscher. We're too slow to catch any of them, but we keep their comfort level down."

"Well, it's only for three months," said Crusher, managing a smile. "If we're in a routine, perhaps you should ease up a bit, read a book, practice your flute. This whole crew is still suffering trauma from being here. It's like reliving the war, and you're no different."

"More vitamins and read a book," answered Picard, jumping to his feet. "I feel better already, Doctor. Shall we say nineteen hundred hours for dinner? My place?"

She nodded gratefully. "I'll be there. Don't push yourself too hard, Jean-Luc."

"Good-bye, Beverly." The captain moved swiftly out the door and into the corridor, secretly relieved that he had passed his physical. He was still in a sour mood but getting better, and he told himself that the loss of the *Calypso* was an unusual happening. How could they know that the *Asgard* was inhabited by forward spotters for the Androssi? Their sensors were no help anymore.

Still, no matter how often he repeated these facts, it

was painful to admit that he had given the enemy a Federation ship—and a barely used one at that.

Picard thought briefly about going to his quarters instead of the bridge, but he knew he wouldn't be able to simply relax and play his flute. Until today's incident became history, it was best to work as hard as he could to prevent anything else from going wrong.

His combadge beeped, and a familiar voice said, "Bridge to Picard."

"Yes, Number One?"

"An Ontailian ship near buoy sixteen is putting out a distress signal," said the first officer. "Data says the *Enterprise* can reach them first."

"Was it enemy fire?" asked Picard. "A spike?"

"Unknown," answered Riker. "Should I set course?"

"Yes," agreed the captain, increasing his stride. "I'm on my way."

About a minute later, the captain walked into the command center of his ship. He found that the glances directed his way lingered a bit longer than usual. *Yes, I'm the idiot who let my shuttlecraft get stolen by a pretty alien,* he wanted to say to them. *Nobody's perfect.*

He brushed off these concerns and gazed at the viewscreen, seeing one of the unique Ontailian ships, with its lines like a three-bladed kitchen knife. It rippled strangely as it floated in front of an indeterminate blob of wreckage; perhaps it was just a thick debris cloud, but it glittered gold and blue in the blackness of space.

"Arrival in twenty seconds," said Lieutenant Perim at the conn. "How close do you want to get, Captain?"

"Transporter range," he answered.

"Captain, we have been advised not to use transporters," Data pointed out.

Picard held up his hand. "Yes, I know, but we're not going to get too close until we know the nature of this emergency. Lieutenant Vale, hail them."

"I have been, sir," answered the compact woman at tactical. "There's no answer, and they've stopped putting out their distress signal. There's no sign of salvagers or any other ships in the vicinity."

Data shook his head. "Our sensor readings are unreliable, sir, but I do detect life signs on this spacecraft. It should have a crew of about seventy-five, but there are fewer than that."

"They're not humanoid, Data," Riker reminded him. "More like very slender sloths. Your count may be off."

"I am not placing much faith in these sensor readings," replied the android, lifting his face to gaze at the viewscreen, although the image was clearly distorted.

"Data, ready a tractor beam," ordered Picard. "Maybe if we get them away from that cloud, we can contact them. Number One, prepare a boarding party."

"Yes, sir," answered the first officer, crossing the bridge to an auxiliary console.

"Set course back to the gateway," ordered Picard, crossing behind Kell Perim. "As soon as the tractor beam is locked on, proceed at one-quarter impulse."

"Sir," called Data, looking curiously at his instruments. "The structural-integrity field of the tractor beam is failing. I will try to compensate."

Before anyone could answer him, a beep sounded, and a familiar voice broke in, "Engineering to bridge."

"Picard here."

"Sir, the warp reactor is overloading," reported a frantic La Forge. "Field suppressors are failing, and we're losing compression in the antimatter stream."

"Antimatter?" asked Picard, turning to look at Riker. Their eyes connected with alarm, and the captain whirled around to his subordinates. "Drop the tractor beam! Full reverse!"

While Data and Perim worked their controls, the cloud of glittering debris began to turn black, as if seeping with ink from within. A second later, it had turned into an opaque and abject void, with a million miniature fireworks popping and sizzling inside. Black tendrils reached out for the sleek Ontailian ship, and the tranquil section of the boneyard exploded with a ferocious blast that shook the escaping starship and blotted out everything on the viewscreen.

Picard was thrown into his command chair. He looked up, hoping his ship was still intact. It was, but the image on the viewscreen was hellish, unbelievable—like a new sun being created and destroyed every other second. This eerie fireball expanded and contracted to nothing ten times in the blink of an eye, making Picard doubt his senses. Finally it blasted outward, shaking the *Enterprise* again and making the screen go dark.

Thankfully, Perim had the starship in full retreat, as safely as could be executed in the graveyard of lost ships. "Damage report?" asked Picard.

After a moment, Data answered, "None to us, but the Ontailian ship was destroyed."

"I presume that's the antimatter asteroid we heard about," said Riker. "Were the Ontailians studying it, or had they just found it?"

"We'll ask them when we report this," Picard decided. Then he wondered who should do the reporting. "Perhaps we should go through Captain Leeden first, since she knows them better. Lieutenant Vale, send a brief report to the *Juno* on subspace. Data, when it's safe, take scanner readings. Look for survivors, and see if you can track that thing's path."

"Survivors?" asked the android, shaking his head. "If it was a matter-antimatter annihilation, there will be nothing left but trace elements."

Picard rubbed his eyes and tapped the com panel on his chair. "Bridge to engineering."

"La Forge here."

"Are your systems back to normal?"

"Yes, sir," answered the engineer. "What was that?"

"It's called an antimatter asteroid, for lack of a better term. Just one more unique feature of the Rashanar Battle Site. Tell everyone on duty in engineering to contact the bridge immediately if they see fluctuations like that again."

"Understood, sir."

"Captain," said Vale. "Captain Leeden has responded and wishes to know if we need assistance. She is contacting the Ontailians for us."

"No assistance needed," said Picard. "I'll copy her on my report later. Anything, Data?"

The android shook his head. "Some trace elements of neptunium, which indicates a transmutation reaction. Captain, how could an orbital accumulation of antimatter survive after annihilation? This might be a one-time phenomenon, but it should not be reoccurring."

"I presume that's why it's a mystery," answered the captain with a frown. "Clearly it's not a legend—it's a real danger."

"Captain," said Vale with a puzzled tone to her voice, "I've received another message from Captain Leeden. But it doesn't make any sense."

"Read it aloud," ordered Picard.

The lieutenant consulted her screen and read, *"Enterprise,* be advised that the Ontailians report that all of their ships in the region have reported in. None have been lost. One crusier did briefly put out a distress signal, but Ontailians responded. Perhaps you are suffering sensor malfunctions or viewscreen phantoms. If you actually saw the antimatter, you were lucky to get away. Signed, Captain Jill Leeden, *U.S.S. Juno."*

Picard gently pounded a fist into the arm of his chair. "That's ridiculous," he said evenly. "We all saw that ship blow up, and we felt the impact. Data, are there any logs we can send them?"

"I am afraid not, Captain," answered the android. "Our sensor and visual logs have been classified as corrupted and unverifiable. If they choose to deny this incident, we cannot produce anything to refute them."

"Captain," said Riker, stepping to his side. "Troi sensed something wrong with the first Ontailian ship we contacted . . . like they were hiding something. But she hadn't had any experience with them before, so she wasn't sure."

"Was this the same ship?" asked the captain.

"Possibly," answered Data. "The first vessel was the *Maskar,* which is listed as still on duty. They are the same class, but we could not identify the ship which was destroyed."

"The more we see, the less we know," muttered the captain as he rose to his feet. "Number One, you have the bridge. I'm going to be doing research in my quarters. Take us back to our primary patrol route. Thank you, everyone, you handled that emergency well." His shoulders a bit more hunched than usual, Captain Picard walked off the bridge of the *Enterprise.*

"You just relax, I'll get them," said Beverly Crusher as she walked across Picard's sitting room to his food replicator to fetch the plates of sushi, their second course of dinner after miso soup. Jean-Luc settled into his seat, poured himself a cup of tea, and allowed his attractive dinner companion to serve him. He glanced around his tasteful quarters to make sure nothing was amiss, and he noticed the model on his desk of the old *Stargazer,* his first ship as captain. Thus far, they had avoided discussing the problems of the day while reminiscing about old times with Jack and Wesley. Jean-Luc had been part of their extended family back then, and they had made him feel like a crucial part of their existence. He had never forgotten that kindness. Now the extended family was bigger, but real family was shrinking in both their lives.

"And you thought you were going to be demoted

after the Maxia Zeta attack," said Beverly, picking up the thread of their conversation. Demurely, she delivered their plates to the table, then sat across from Jean-Luc. "Instead you got handed the pride of the fleet."

"I was certain of my demotion," admitted Picard with a sheepish smile. "You never really know how your actions will be perceived by history and your superiors. Like today!"

With a sigh, he picked up his chopsticks and poked at his replicated rice and soy seafood. "Now that I've read a lot of the reports, I realize that this site was mishandled from the beginning. Resources were scarce, there was an overemphasis from Starfleet on retrieving bodies, and scientific research was done the way we've done it, catch as catch can. Please remind me why I asked for this assignment."

"Do you want an honest answer?" asked Beverly.

"Of course," nodded Picard. "Don't I always?"

She cocked her head and winced, as if he wasn't going to like her answer. "Because you're sometimes arrogant and think you can do things other people can't. Coming here, you thought you could explain what happened at the Battle of Rashanar—what destroyed all these ships when some should have escaped—but this place doesn't want to give up its secrets. Sometimes there are good reasons for a mystery to stay a mystery."

"I suppose," grumbled Picard. Of course she was right, but she had cut to the quick swiftly and painfully. "I thought we were on a forensic mission . . . I let my guard down and it cost us."

"Trouble went looking for us today," replied Beverly, spearing a piece of sushi and eating it. "Say, the consistency of the *mekajiki* has improved."

"Doctor, do you think I've become jaded in this job?" he asked, only half in jest. "Have I been sitting too long in that chair . . . issuing orders that are followed without hesitation?"

Beverly frowned deeply, giving his question a serious mulling. "Since you addressed me as a doctor," she finally said, "and not your friend, I'm obligated to give you a professional opinion. You have spent twice as long in the command chair as a typical Starfleet captain. You probably should have become an admiral when it was offered to you. Of course, none of us would exist if you hadn't been there to insure first contact. You could retire and rest on your laurels, and probably keep busy enough with your hobbies. You would make a wonderful admiral."

She sighed. "But since the war, we've got more admirals than experienced captains. Even if you have done everything, and suffered enough traumas to break a normal man, Starfleet needs you. You're going to have to be the one who decides to retire, because I don't foresee Starfleet giving you the boot."

"No matter how many yachts I lose?" he asked with a pained smile.

"You could start listening to Will and let others lead the away teams," suggested Beverly, popping a tidbit into her mouth. "In other words, be a little more careful. As your doctor, I would definitely approve that idea."

"So I'm too arrogant, too old, and too careless," concluded Picard cheerfully. "But I should stay on the job anyway?"

"Yes," she answered with an amused smile. "Do you notice, you're starting to feel sorry for yourself, too. Even with all your horrific faults, you're still better than anyone else Starfleet has."

"What a ringing endorsement," replied Picard, lifting his cup of tea. "Shall we make a toast to the long years of mediocre service I have ahead of me?"

Crusher laughed and lifted her glass of *sake*. "May we grow old on this ship together."

The immense Romulan warbird drifted silently in space, dwarfing the other wrecks around it. Even in repose, the warbird looked deadly, rapacious—a true predator with a beaked bow, curved wings, and long graceful lines. The energy spikes and ripples that raked the other derelicts seemed to have no effect on the monstrous, green-hued hulk. Various scorch marks, fissures, and gaping holes hardly diminished the magnificence of the spacecraft, which was ninety percent intact.

"That's the target, the *Rom'drex,*" said Ghissel from the pilot seat of the *Calypso,* the latest addition to the Androssi fleet. Half a dozen slender Androssi overseers gathered around the viewport and nodded their heads sagely. All of them wore the requisite number of five nose rings. Since Ghissel had stolen a brand-new craft right from under Starfleet's nose, she had risen in importance among the loosely knit clan of salvagers. Yesterday she was a mere forward spotter, living in obscurity; now she was a captain with the best-disguised ship in their ragtag fleet.

"*D'deridex*-class," she added. "Just commissioned before the war. The latest-generation cloaking devices, singularity warp reactor, interphase generators, disruptors, shields—even a working still to produce Romulan ale."

The assembled overseers nodded appreciatively. "I have a buyer for that," said one.

"And it's never been cracked," said Ghissel, her amber eyes glittering. "It's been guarded closely. The Federation is waiting for a Romulan team to process it. The ship has many alarm systems. In fact, we only have a few minutes before a Starfleet vessel comes by. It would be pointless to try to salvage this ship here, and that's why I need your assistance. We must combine together to tow this ship out intact."

Her associates grumbled a bit. This was a large undertaking, fraught with danger. But they all knew how difficult it would be to mine this resource under Starfleet's nose. Better to process the warbird at their leisure in a safe site.

"For an equal share of the profits?" asked one.

"Yes," answered Ghissel. "I'll need all of your tractor beams, and there are technical details to work out. Plus you have contacts I don't have. We'll need to make a concerted effort to pull this off."

A veteran leader with a braid of white hair asked, "Do you have a plan?"

"Of course." A smile stretched across the Androssi's impish face. "How many tugs would it—"

"Overseer," interrupted her copilot, "our spotters say the patrol ship will be here in thirty seconds."

"Take us back to base," ordered Ghissel.

The *Calypso* banked gracefully for a shuttlecraft of its size, then darted between the Romulan warbird and another dusty relic, using them for cover as a Starfleet cruiser glided into view.

Chapter Five

DEANNA TROI SAT in the command chair of the *Enterprise,* spending some time on the bridge while Will and Captain Picard went over duty rosters in his ready room. On this second day of their stay in the boneyard, the duties had become more demanding and more hazardous, and virtually every member of the crew was involved in the effort. They were occupied by shuttlecraft patrols, the *Enterprise*'s own guard duty, and had three teams working with the *Juno* to learn the tricks of body retrieval from the mobile wrecks. On top of that, researchers all over the ship tried to bring themselves up to speed on the various elements they faced here.

While she was acting captain, Troi's attention was on her crew and the viewscreen, but some part of her mind kept harking back to the Ontailians. Their tapered cruisers were spotted several times throughout her shift, but they never exchanged any greetings. Two of the Ontailian vessels were on regular patrol, according to Captain Leeden's schedule, but the others engaged in business that was puzzling to the counselor. They buzzed back and forrth lazily, like honeybees looking for a flower in wasteland. Sometimes they ignored the scavengers they were supposed to be keeping at bay. Granted, the *Enterprise* could not respond to everything either, but the Ontailians were helpful only because of their numbers and sheer presence.

Since the *Enterprise* was constantly on the move, Troi had no opportunity to monitor the Ontailian ships for more than a few minutes around each encounter. Then the silvery slivers were off again to their mysterious purpose among the shipwrecks. She seldom had suspicious feelings about another Federation member, but the Ontailians seemed to be avoiding anything but the most cursory communication.

After warning a Pakled ship to back off and go home, Deanna ordered the *Enterprise* back to their primary security route. The energy ripples seemed to be relatively quiet tonight. The storm seemed distant, on the other side of the metal mountains. The boneyard was depressing, but also oddly beautiful in its display of the random way that nature reclaimed something built by mortals and reverted it to the primitive. The skewed wrecks reminded Troi of adventure stories her father had told her—of ruined temples overgrown by thick jungle vines.

The Ontailians didn't seem to have much interest in the derelicts themselves, and they seldom docked with any spacecraft. Still they seemed to be searching for something. *Are they treasure hunters?* she wondered. *Is that the secret, a buried treasure in this ships' cemetery which only the Ontailians know about?*

No matter how much reading she had done, Troi never learned much about the benign, slothlike beings. First contact had been made less than fifteen years ago, when it was discovered that a class-L planet with no humanoid life-forms was launching elegant spaceships. The Ontailians were always cordial, but they permitted no study of their culture, which appeared at a glance to be much more primitive than it was. Heavy gas clouds covered their homeworld, so not much could be learned without their cooperation.

Then the Cardassians had landed, and the Ontailians discovered that they were in the expansion plans of the Dominion. They requested immediate membership in the Federation. It wouldn't have been granted so quickly without the saber of war hanging over all their heads. Maintenance of the Rashanar Battle Site was virtually the only project on which the Federation and the Ontailians cooperated. They had expressed no interest in studying other Federation worlds or being studied. They were still an enigma, if a friendly one.

At last, Will and Captain Picard emerged from the ready room, just off the bridge, and Deanna Troi rose to attention. She tried not to smile too broadly when Will winked at her. They were planning to slip off for an intimate breakfast. Captain Picard, on the other hand, looked grim and haggard, and she could sense his uneasiness. After the escapades of the day before, they were all on high alert.

"Status?" asked Picard.

"We had a discussion with a Pakled ship, which decided to move off," she answered. "There are nine shuttlecraft and teams launched, three with the *Juno*. We've seen the usual traffic of Ontailian ships, and we're on schedule, on primary route."

"Very well," answered the captain. "I believe both of you are on break now."

Riker held out an isolinear chip and said, "I'll post the new schedules and orders before I go." The first officer strode to an auxiliary station.

After Will had moved off, Troi lowered her voice to ask, "How are you sleeping, sir?"

He gave her a wry glance. "Don't tell me I'm under your scrutiny, too."

"Always," she answered with a charming smile. "Everyone on this ship is. I know you had a trying day, and I was hoping you were able to sleep it off."

Picard gave her a wan smile. "Let's say, I'm not quite at the point where this assignment allows me to sleep easily."

"Captain Picard, large ship approaching," said Vale, frowning at her tactical readouts. "We haven't seen one of these before—it's an Ontailian battle cruiser, the *Vuxhal*."

"I believe it is their flagship," added Data from the ops console. "The *Vuxhal* has been away from this site for four weeks, getting repairs."

The viewscreen showed a dramatic silver fin, which

had to be fifty decks high but as narrow as a two-lane street. The warp nacelles were paired vertically on the top and bottom, and they blended in with the aesthetic lines of the vessel. As the sleek starship glided past them, they could see rows of impulse thrusters aligned vertically along the stern. They fired in a sequence that made the tail of the silver behemoth look like a flapping fin.

"Audio message coming in," said Vale.

The tactical officer punched her panel, and a synthesized voice came over com link. "Honors be to the *Enterprise,* guardian of the sacred. We are the *Vuxhal,* and we are here to resume our hallowed vigil over the bones of the sacred. With respect, we pass you now and enter the honored space."

"Regards to the *Vuxhal* from the *Starship Enterprise,*" said Picard simply. "Be cautious on your journey. *Enterprise* out."

"Captain," blurted Deanna Troi, "let me follow them."

"What do you mean?" asked Picard. By that time, Riker had finished his task and had rejoined their conversation, and both men look puzzledly at the counselor.

"I've been watching them come and go, and I can't figure out what half of their ships are doing," she answered. "Plus there was the incident with the Ontailian ship that was destroyed, then never existed. I know they're hiding something—let me find out what it is. I'll be careful."

The captain frowned. "Spying on our allies doesn't sound like a very efficient use of our time. Even if we do have questions about them."

"Captain, it can't hurt just to see what they're doing," added Riker. "I'm off duty now, I'll pilot her."

"The shuttlepod *Wasp* is back from maintenance and awaiting assignment," said Deanna. "Please, sir."

The captain said, "Go on, but think up a good cover story in case they catch you."

With an adventurous grin, Riker nodded to his beloved, and the two of them dashed for the turbolift door.

"I found the *Vuxhal*," said Troi, studying her readouts at the secondary console of the shuttlepod *Wasp*. There was only enough room for the two of them in the cramped cabin. "Bearing one hundred sixty-seven mark ninety-two."

"Changing course," replied Riker from the pilot's seat beside her, "but I'm not going to make straight toward her. I'll take an elliptical route. Maybe it won't tip them off. Hey, this isn't exactly how I thought we'd spend the morning."

Deanna gave him a nervous smile, although now that they were out here among all this mammoth junk in a tiny tin can, she was beginning to think she had made a terrible mistake. One chunk of a bronze Cardassian ship came bouncing off a green hull and hurtled straight toward them. Will steered them to safety without batting an eyelash.

"Can you tell what they're doing?" he asked.

Troi stared at her readouts and shook her head. "They're cruising deeper into the boneyard. They just passed a level-four buoy, which is a lot deeper than the *Enterprise* would go. So what's our cover story?"

"We're inspecting level-four buoys," answered Riker with a smile. "Are they headed toward the gravity sink?"

She shook her head. "No, they're going to miss that. Wait a minute, they just changed course."

"Do you think they spotted us?"

"We're close enough to see them with the naked eye," answered Troi, putting her finger against an upper corner of the viewport. In the distance glinted a silver triangle, looking like a sailboat among a harbor full of hulking gray freighters. "Shields are up?" she asked.

"You bet," answered Will. "Why?"

"I'm getting some funny sensor readings," she answered. "I know that's typical, but I'm getting slush deuterium readings. They've slowed way down. Is there something wrong with the *Vuxhal*'s plasma vents?"

That was a rhetorical question, and she didn't really expect Will to know much about the exotic craft. Riker never took his eyes off his controls as he answered, "She's stopping near a Jem'Hadar battle cruiser in slow orbit. I'm going to cut our impulse engines and drift, which is a good idea if they're venting plasma or deuterium. Maybe we'll just look like a piece of wreckage to them."

A moment later, it was oddly quiet inside the tiny manned pod as they drifted in the cover of the burnt and blistered hulk of a Cardassian warship. Every few seconds, rubble sizzled against their shields, and Troi jumped, startled.

"Calm down," said Riker with a smile, putting his arm around her. "We're not going to hit anything too big."

"Although something might hit us," said Troi nervously. She contented herself with the fact that her pilot managed to keep one eye on his readouts even while he kept an arm around her shoulders. She wasn't going to let him get too romantic, though, even if this was like a surreal carnival ride.

She checked her own sensor readings and frowned. "They're launching a ship . . . or something."

"Let's see," said Riker, pulling back his arm and working his controls. Now the Ontailian silver fin was magnified in the center of the small viewscreen overhead. A small pod was moving away from the Ontailian ship, obviously just ejected; it glinted in the sun as it tumbled gently. Suddenly the *Vuxhal* unleashed a tractor beam, which caught the falling object and stopped its outward journey. The object bobbed in space two hundred meters or so beneath the heavy cruiser.

"Whatever they dropped, it's even smaller than this shuttle," said Riker. "Maybe they're just laying buoys or probes. Or alarms. That's not a bad idea, although I don't think anyone would want that Jem'Hadar wreck."

Troi shook her head and brushed back a strand of raven hair. "Again I sense they're not doing this out of altruism. They're hiding something . . . but maybe it's so minor that it doesn't make any difference."

"In the long run," mused Riker, "how can they make this place worse?"

Suddenly both their boards lit up, and they looked at one another in alarm. The Ontailian ship was putting out a distress signal, just as the smaller cruiser had the day before.

"All right," said Riker, sitting back in his seat, "do we answer that?"

"I hope it's not because they saw us," said Troi, "although that would be a strange response."

As Riker sifted through radio chatter and interference, their romantic little shuttlepod was no longer so silent. Finally he shook his head and said, "I *think* one of their ships is responding."

As abruptly as it had started, the distress signal ended, and the sleek Ontailian ship fired thrusters and slowly glided off. It left the small pod behind, drifting among the clouds of space dust. Deanna and Will glanced at one another, neither able to offer a theory as to their ally's behavior.

Once the Ontailians had moved out of sensor range, Riker rubbed his hands together and said, "Let's check it out." He started the impulse engine and streaked toward the object so quickly that Troi almost yelled at him to slow down. The Betazoid had a feeling that time was running out on this spy mission, and someone else could be coming.

As they drew closer to the mysterious pod left behind by the Ontailians, both of them let out a breath of disappointment, because it was unremarkable. It looked like a large octagonal storage barrel, painted in rather garish yellow stripes. There were no antennas, deflectors, or markings on it.

"They came a long way to dump *that*," said Riker. "Can you get a sensor reading?"

"Only because we're right next to it," answered Troi. Her brow furrowed when she actually checked her readings, and she gripped Will's arm. "Massive magnetic fields. I'm surprised we're not sticking to that thing. It's turned on, ready to go . . . for what?"

"What's it made out of?" asked Will.

"Tritanium." Deanna double-checked the readings, but they were strong and clear at this close range. "That's an exotic alloy for a garbage can."

Riker suddenly looked stricken. "That's no garbage can!" He began working his controls furiously.

"What is it, Will?"

He swatted at his board. "I can't get a reading beyond the shielding, but the magnetic fields, the tritanium—that looks like an antimatter storage pod to me."

"They're dumping that in *here?*" asked Troi, aghast. "What about the antimatter asteroid?" She felt a tingling on her neck, and she gazed out the viewport to see the kaleidoscope of junk all around them start to move. Within seconds, it was spinning, and the junk was crashing into everything else. When the shuttlepod began to spin, she realized they were in the middle of a vortex. Her instruments were failing, and so were her eyes.

She gripped her companion's arm. "Will!"

"I'm trying to get out of here!" he rasped, struggling with the instrument panel. "Engines aren't strong enough. I can't compensate—we're out of control!"

Suddenly the rubble in the vortex began to disappear, as if eaten away by a black rust from within, and Troi could swear that she saw the antimatter pod begin to rip apart at the seams. There were loud thuds as chunks of debris blasted through the failing shields to strike the helpless shuttlepod.

Certain they were going to die, Deanna gripped her mate. "I love you, *Imzadi*."

He grunted something and reached for her, just as the pod was turned upside down and yanked from the melee at incredible speed. Troi blinked her eyes open, certain the little craft ought to be in pieces; in the corner of the viewscreen, she saw the triangular Ontailian cruiser backing away from them. A shaft of light withdrew with them, and she wondered if it was a tractor beam. The vortex was all but gone, and so was any trace of the antimatter storage pod, if that's what it was. With a blip, the Ontailian ship was also gone.

"Did they just leave at warp speed?" asked Riker, sounding amazed that anybody would try such a thing. "Or maybe they're cloaked."

"Will," breathed Deanna, "they just saved our lives."

Riker cleared his throat and smoothed back his ruffled hair. "And they didn't want to wait around to be thanked. What about their pod?"

"It's gone," answered Troi quietly. "The dust has been kicked up, but otherwise there's just the Jem'Hadar wreck. Do you think they knew we were spying on them?"

Riker entered commands on his console and breathed a sigh of relief. "Like you say, they knew we were here. We've got full impulse and full navigation again, so we can get home. I don't suppose there's anything worthwhile on the sensor logs?"

Troi consulted her scientific readings and shook her head glumly. "It's like the usual gibberish we get this far in. You know, Will, they're going to deny this happened, and we haven't got any proof."

"Yeah, but at least we're alive," he said with a grin. "Next time, let's have that quiet romantic breakfast instead."

Captain Jill Leeden leaned back in her chair in her ready room on the *Juno*. "I don't care what you say, Commander Riker," she began, "the Ontailian command center claims that there was no pod—antimatter or otherwise—and that they saved your shuttle from destruction."

"Yes, they did," agreed Riker. "We'd be dead without them. Then again, do they have any explanation for what we encountered? Or what *they* were doing there?"

Leeden shook her head and looked at the other two *Enterprise* crew members who were visiting the *Juno,* Captain Picard and Counselor Troi. Deanna felt sorry for the skipper of the *Juno,* because she could tell that Leeden was under tremendous pressure to hold together that which could not be held together. Order was not going to be imposed on the Rashanar Battle Site.

"It was reported there were Ontailian prisoners on that Jem'Hadar ship," explained Leeden. "They have long wanted to recover the bodies, but it's a likely ship to be booby-trapped. Not only that, but a Kreel ship blew up in that same area four months ago. Commander Riker, you once asked me how the scavengers died . . . well, one of the ways almost took you."

"I'm not demanding anything further be done," Riker said, "and I'm grateful for their timely rescue. But Captain Leeden, you should know that the Ontailians are engaged in secret operations here."

"Since the beginning, the Ontailians have been the ones most intent upon recovering bodies, and I've never had a problem with them. All of us are going to get spooked by the weird anomalies out there, but we've stuck together. Now you show up and, after two short days in the boneyard, tell me that they are working against us?" asked Leeden, exasperated.

Riker started to reply, but Captain Picard grabbed his subordinate's arm and stepped forward. "Captain Leeden," he said, "you have admitted that you don't know a lot about what is going on here. There are mysteries and oddities here, and we want to shed some light on them. There are rational explanations for the gravity sink, the wild antimatter, the Ontailians' actions, and we should go find them. We may fail, but we can no longer take 'oh, it's haunted' as an explanation."

"If that is what you believe, then I guess we have no more to talk about." Captain Leeden rose to her feet. "If you decide to pursue a reckless course, I wouldn't count on being rescued every time."

"We'll still perform our agreed-upon security duties," Picard assured her. "Good-bye, Captain Leeden."

She pressed a panel and opened the door for her visitors, and security officers snapped to attention on the other side. Leeden said softly, "Picard, I wish you luck in explaining these phenomena, but don't trust your eyes or your sensors."

Troi led the way out. Neither Riker nor Picard had much to say as they strolled down the corridor, and it was a silent walk to the transporter room, accompanied by security officers.

When they finally stepped off the transporter platform and back onto the *Enterprise,* Captain Picard managed a wan smile. "Number One," he remarked dryly, "when you said you were going to arrange a meeting between Counselor Troi and Captain Leeden, I didn't think you would go to such lengths."

"I can see why Will wanted me to meet her," said Troi. "Her stress levels are very high. So is her determination. She thinks she's right, and she's certain she has told us the truth."

"Then let's hope she's wrong," replied Picard.

Chapter Six

FOUR DAYS LATER, Captain Picard strode onto the bridge of the *Enterprise,* feeling refreshed and energized after a full night's sleep. Their first two days in the Rashanar Battle Site had been difficult; since then, the mission had gone much more smoothly. They had found a routine that worked, even under adverse conditions, and they were fulfilling their security obligations while stepping up scientific inquiry.

The captain glanced at the viewscreen and saw three unidentified craft speeding away from the *Enterprise* in three different directions.

"Status?" he asked.

"We had to fire two warning shots, but the Hok'Tar finally dispersed," answered Commander Riker. "I would send shuttlecraft after them, but those scout ships can outrun anything we have."

The first officer glanced over Data's shoulder at the ops readouts. "We now have six shuttlecraft out on patrol and no serious problems to report. The *Juno* is only about three hundred kilometers away, inspecting a Centaurian ship. It's been a relatively quiet morning."

Picard nodded with satisfaction. "Let's keep it that way. Mr. Data, any word from the probes we sent into the gravity sink?"

"None of them are responding," answered the android. "Or perhaps the anomaly is acting as a dampener. Commander La Forge and I would like to take a shuttlecraft to investigate further. The *Hudson* has just come out of repair."

The captain looked around his bridge and saw plenty of competent officers waiting to step in as needed. They kept a full bridge complement these days; it was like the height of the Dominion War. "Very well, Mr. Data," said Picard. "As soon as you and La Forge are able to free yourselves, take the *Hudson.*"

"Yes, sir," answered the android.

"Permission to leave the bridge, sir," asked Riker.

Picard smiled. "Yes, Number One. You might want to try to rest on your off hours. You're looking a bit ragged."

"Our first team has retrieved bodies from the *Orlando,* and I'd like to check on the arrangements," said Riker. "But I promise to rest." With a nod, the first officer hurried toward the turbolift, leaving the bridge to the veteran captain.

With confidence, Picard turned to the viewscreen, and wished he hadn't. No matter how cheerful his mood upon reporting to the bridge, seeing a field of dead starships always soured it. Today was no exception. To starboard was a Klingon bird-of-prey that had been cut in two pieces, which were now spinning and locked by gleaming arcs of energy. To port was the saucer section of a great starship. It had been squashed until it looked like a garbage-can lid. A line of crushed hulks stretched into the distance, although Picard knew this was an optical illusion, due to Lieutenant Perim's deft piloting along the primary patrol route. Still it was an endless reminder of the death and destruction of the last war, and the captain knew why the locals called it the boneyard.

"Permission to leave the bridge," requested Data, jarring Picard out of his reverie.

"Good luck," said the captain, checking that Data's replacement, Jelpn, had taken his seat. "It would be nice to find an answer or two out there."

"Understood," said the android. "I will contact you from the shuttlebay when we are ready to launch."

A second later, he was gone, and the captain turned his attention to the viewscreen, where a flash of light caught his eye. "What is—"

"An Ontailian cruiser just catching the sun," answered Vale from tactical. "I told them about the Hok'Tar, and they're giving chase to make sure they leave."

"Very good," said Picard, glad that his bridge crew were taking the initiative to make this assignment work. With this kind of cooperation, perhaps they would eventually find a happy medium between security and scientific inquiry.

Captain Picard sat down in his command chair, feeling confident about the shift ahead.

"Patrol ship has just passed out of sensor range," reported Boenmar, Ghissel's new copilot on the *Calypso.* He was a first-class pilot and an accomplished spacefarer, unlike the usual lower-caste riffraff she worked with. He was also very slim, young, and handsome. She had her new colleagues to thank for his presence.

"Signal the task force to get into position," ordered the Androssi. She struggled with a lump in her throat from all the excitement. "Get ready to dock with the *Rom'drex.*"

"Yes, Overseer," replied Boenmar as he plied the controls of the stocky shuttlecraft.

While four larger ships in their ragtag force maneuvered off the bow of the hulking Romulan warbird, the *Calypso* slipped under her main hull, searching for the extendable docking port, which they had scouted two days earlier. It didn't matter if the dock was fully intact and functional, as long as they could latch on and appear to be part of the *Rom'drex,* at least to a casual scan.

Boenmar gnawed his lower lip as he attempted the tricky docking maneuver. It took two failed tries and some scraping of fresh paint off the hull, but he finally made a solid connection. With a click, the docking clamps took hold, and the pilot sat back in his seat.

"We're on," he reported. "Seal holding."

"Well done," said Ghissel. "Go ahead and start the warp-drive diagnostics. Vent a little plasma, and blow the injectors. Make it look convincing. I'll contact the other ships."

She sat at the copilot's seat and sent an encrypted subspace message that required no response, except for immediate action. One by one, the four Androssi ships off the bow turned on their tractor beams, and the shuttlecraft was jostled slightly. It took several minutes for them to coordinate their efforts, but they finally locked on to every square centimeter of the great green wreck, plus the small passenger clinging to its underbelly. While they did this, two more Androssi ships scouted ahead on their projected route, using tractor beams to move derelicts out of the way as needed.

The ships off the bow of the *Rom'drex* blinked their running lights, which was the next signal, and Ghissel twisted her delicate bronze hands. "If we're hailed, I will answer it," she said.

"As you wish, Overseer," said the pilot, checking his readouts. "Our warp signature is active."

Again they were jostled, more forcefully this time. "We've begun to move," reported Boenmar, studying his board. "One-quarter impulse . . . tractor beams holding . . . dock holding."

Ghissel let out a pent-up breath, thinking, *Maybe it will all go as smoothly as this.*

*   *   *

Vale squinted at her readouts and said, "Captain, I'm picking up activity near buoy thirty-two. There's a Starfleet vessel apparently chasing four Androssi ships through a heavily littered area. They have not requested help."

"What vessel?" asked Picard, crossing toward his tactical officer.

She shook her head. "That's difficult to determine with these partial sensor readings, and I can't get a visual. It's a large ship, and it's definitely a Starfleet warp signature. The Androssi have their usual kludged-together hodgepodge of technology. It's a slow chase, so I assume the passage is difficult—but they are making for the outside. Shall I hail them?"

"What's our distance from them?" asked the captain.

"Less than fifty kilometers. The *Juno* is holding her position, so it's not her. This area is on regular patrol because of some allied wrecks."

Chasing four of them, thought Picard. *That's rather ambitious.* He strolled in front of the conn and said, "Lieutenant Perim, make in their direction, half impulse."

"Yes, sir," answered the unjoined Trill, diligently working her instruments. As they picked up speed, glittering junk and festive energy spikes danced across the viewscreen, belying the dangers in the debris field.

"Lieutenant Vale, send them a general hail to let them know we are available," ordered the captain. "And inform the *Juno* why we're leaving our route."

"Yes, sir," answered the human with a curt nod.

The turbolift door opened. Deanna Troi walked onto the bridge. Picard hadn't asked for the counselor's presence, but he was glad to see her. With a nod to him, she went to the secondary chair and took a seat. Picard often wondered if Troi had a sixth sense about danger, because she often came of her own accord just before she was needed. *They really are an attentive crew,* he thought to himself, *and I'm lucky to have them.*

"Captain," interjected Vale, "I've gotten subspace from an Ontailian ship, the *Maskar,* which is also in pursuit of the four Androssi. They say we can break off."

The captain nodded thoughtfully. "Very well. Conn, break off pursuit and return to our primary route."

"Yes, sir," came Perim's response.

The captain returned to his command chair, and Troi gave him a sympathetic smile. "Is it still pick-and-choose what to respond to?"

"With faulty sensor readings," added the captain, "so we never quite know what's going on. We're like *targs* with a *ta'ra* bone—we bark at everything that moves and chase it if it doesn't move fast enough."

"Captain," called Vale. "Captain Leeden wants to know why we broke off chasing the Androssi."

"Explain to her that two other ships are in pursuit," said Picard. "Tell them to contact the *Maskar* for more information."

Vale didn't respond; instead she stared puzzledly at her readouts. "Sir, I've just brought up our duty roster, and the *Maskar* is not listed as being in Rashanar. They suffered an accident yesterday and went back to their home port for repairs."

"An impostor?" asked Picard. "Can you run an analysis of that message from the *Maskar?*"

Vale nodded. "Yes, sir, but it may take some time to track the subspace routing. We use no special encryption with the Ontailians, and that came over a standard subspace frequency. Without any analysis, I can tell you— Wait a second, sir, I'm getting a subspace message from the *Juno.*"

The captain clenched his hands as he waited, because he knew Captain Leeden wouldn't want the scavengers to get away.

"Captain," reported Vale, "the *Juno* is going in pursuit of these mysterious ships, and they want us to follow as backup."

Picard's lips thinned, and he nodded. "Set course to intercept, but proceed with caution."

"Yes, sir."

"Just a little farther!" said Ghissel, nervously pounding her slender fist on the instrument panel of the Starfleet shuttlecraft formerly known as *Calypso.* "When can we go to warp?"

"Not for another thirty minutes at least," answered the irritated pilot Boenmar. "The sweepers haven't done a very good job of clearing the way. That's the second wreck we've had to go around."

It wasn't easy for their four cobbled-together ships to tow the mammoth Romulan warbird around obstacles, but they had made it so far. Ghissel's eyes narrowed at the unfamiliar readouts. She was too excited to try to decipher them. Something caught her attention, and she glanced out the viewport in time to see a blackened nacelle come hurtling past at too close a range.

"It's always changing there—that's normal," the Androssi declared, trying to mask her anxiety. "We're still on schedule."

"There are two Federation starships headed after us," said Boenmar with a scowl. He pointed to the readouts she had ignored. "Those two have been hailing us—the *Juno* and the *Enterprise*. Given our start, we might still make it, but it will be close."

"We only need one ship with a tractor beam to get to warp," answered Ghissel, stressing the simplicity of their plan. Of course that was after they were free of the boneyard. "If we've been discovered, do we need to stay docked to the *Rom'drex?*" she asked.

The youthful pilot raised a wispy eyebrow and gazed at her with rust-colored eyes. "That's a good question, Overseer. You're the one in charge."

"We may have to break off and fire at the Federation ships," announced Ghissel.

The pilot blinked at her and asked, "How?"

"Hit and run. We have four short-range torpedoes—we installed them yesterday." The Androssi gazed at her readouts, suddenly inspired to decipher them.

"Every other ship in our armada is occupied," she pointed out, "the two sweepers and the four tugs. We're free to cause some problems with these watchdogs. If we can get them to chase after us, the others can escape with the *Rom'drex.*"

Ghissel composed a subspace message to the rest of the fleet.

Boenmar raised a slender finger and said, "Tell them that if they cut engines and hold perfectly still among the derelicts, they might escape sensor detection."

"They already know that," she answered. "All right, the message has been sent. There won't be a response—we'll just stop. When they lower the tractor beam, go."

"Yes, Overseer," answered the young pilot. He concentrated all his attention upon his instruments, while Ghissel watched the distinctive Androssi spacecraft just ahead of them. She saw their thrusters firing to slow their momentum at the same time that Boenmar went through his prelaunch checklist.

They were going out to do battle with the mighty Federation. This was a considerable risk. Maybe after this haul, she would retire from such dangerous duty for a while, although the excitement was compelling.

The dust suddenly became clearer outside the viewport, as if a haze had melted away. "We're free," announced Boenmar as he worked his controls.

"Run!" she shouted, although her urging was hardly needed.

With a bump and a click, they disengaged from the enormous green wreck and dropped underneath her scorched hull. The yacht swiftly banked away from the convoy, and Ghissel could see a tractor beam glimmer on behind them. A second later, they were streaking toward their pursuers, while the convoy plodded toward the exit from the thicket of old relics.

"We will set an ambush. If we wear our suits, can we deactivate life-support and all telltale systems except torpedoes?"

"I think so," answered the young pilot. "Since we just added them, the weapons systems are stand-alone."

They watched each other as they stripped down, and she could tell from the blushing stripe down his back that he was aroused. It was with reluctance that they pulled on their golden environmental suits, which were as thin as normal clothing for most species. When helmets were in place, they communicated by internal com link, and their voices sounded shrill and disembodied.

"Now let's find a place to blend in," said Ghissel as she returned to her seat. "They should think they're still chasing the same number of ships."

The pilot brushed against her as he sat down. He studied his instrument panel, while she gazed through the viewport, inspecting each wreck visually. She finally spotted a mustard-colored tubular ship with sweeping orange wings. The starship was shredded from stem to stern with awful gashes, and a cloud of mauve gas floated near her stern, giving this old relic the illusion of traveling under her own power.

"That Benzite wreck," she said, pointing to the mustard vessel, "do you think you can fly us into one of the gashes and fire the weapons from in there?"

"Yes," answered Boenmar slowly and thoughtfully. "The difficulty will be in getting out again."

They drifted lazily. Boenmar was already shutting down running lights and as many systems as he could. He revved the thrusters and shot through a sparkling curtain of debris to reach the Benzite tube ship. The elliptical shuttlecraft fit fairly well into one of the big gashes to port, and he had to turn lights on again to look around. To their relief, the ship had been disemboweled. There was plenty of room for the yacht to maneuver. They spotted a similar huge gash on the starboard side of the craft, so they had both a weapons slot and an escape route.

Boenmar steered the yacht carefully into position, and Ghissel could only imagine that he would be a patient and attentive lover. Their bows pointed a few centimeters out of the gash, but it looked like just another jagged tear in the hull of this once-noble starship.

"Plenty of clearance for the weapons and the viewport," said the pilot with satisfaction. He continued to work his board, nodding to himself as the cabin of the pod grew dark. "Since almost everything will be shut down in a few seconds, we'll have to have visual contact. From the navigation console, I can target and fire separately."

"I'm looking for them," replied Ghissel breathlessly as she peered out the window at the parade of junk that glided past their hiding place. A dense cloud of silvery bits hung over their position for several seconds, and it seemed like a lifetime. Finally the Androssi spotted a hull and saucer section that was moving, and she pointed excitedly just as a wild energy spike rippled across the starship's path.

In that same instant, Boenmar fired his first torpedo, which streaked from the torn hull of the Benzite derelict toward the pursuing Starfleet vessel. It struck her forward shields at the same moment that another energy arc exploded behind the mammoth spacecraft, and a chain reaction of explosions rippled up and down her gleaming hull.

Ghissel screamed with excitement and grabbed her pilot's forearm. He was trembling, because this attack was going to do much more than merely slow them down. The starship actually spun around, as if caught in a vortex, and a funnel of blazing energy beams lifted the saucer section and pulled the ship off course. Out of control, the behemoth careened into a tattered Klingon attack crusier, and the two ships locked in screaming metal and fiery bolts of energy.

"That was an excellent shot," rasped Boenmar.

"Yes and no," answered Ghissel, her voice barely a whisper. "They'll be looking for us now. Go back the other way—deeper into the boneyard."

"Are you sure?" asked the pilot, igniting the engines and bringing the small craft back to life.

But the Androssi female couldn't talk anymore; all she could do was gape at the massive destruction they had caused as energy beams rippled between the dead ship and the dying one. It was almost like a sexual experience, and she was panting.

"Going into retreat," whispered the pilot as he piloted

the yacht within the gutted hull of the Benzite wreck. They cruised cautiously out the gap on the starboard side and streaked away from the scene of the disaster.

The bridge of the *Juno* was aflame. Smoke and sparks shot from every console and access panel. It was all Captain Leeden could do to hang on to the arms of her command chair as she coughed uncontrollably for several seconds. Emergency klaxons blared, and the computer's voice droned on with various warnings. The overhead screen was broken and sizzling, but the view with the naked eye through the observation window was horrific enough. Everywhere she looked, they were engulfed in rampant energy outbursts, which were feeding off their own labored power sources.

Leeden gulped down the smoke and finally found her voice. "Conn!" she shouted. "Get us out of here— full reverse."

"The helm is not responding," answered a harried Coridan officer. "Shields are failing, impulse engines are overloaded, and communications are out. Every deck reporting damage—repair teams have been dispatched."

"If we don't get away from here, there'll be nothing left to repair!" Captain Leeden looked in vain for help and cried, "Where the hell is the *Enterprise?*"

Chapter Seven

ON THE BRIDGE of the *Enterprise*, Captain Picard looked grimly at the *Excelsior*-class starship trapped in an inferno of pulsing energy. What looked like lassos of lightning were racing around the stricken starship, and the *Juno* couldn't pull back. She had rammed a Klingon shipwreck and was locked at the hull, taking tremendous damage with shields down. If he didn't act fast, they would be adding to the grisly toll of Rashanar.

He stepped smartly from one bridge station to another, issuing orders. "Conn, get us to tractor-beam range and prepare to lock on. Tactical, tell transporter rooms to stand by and notify the Ontailians to cut off that force of Androssi ships. Ops, alert sickbay that we may be taking on injured. Any answer to our hails?"

"No, sir," answered Vale.

Picard crossed down to the ops station and asked, "Did we get a read on where that torpedo came from?"

"No, sir," answered the Deltan Jelpn, shaking his bald head and working his board. "However, there was a shuttlecraft in the area. I don't have much data on it, but I'll double-check everything."

"Make it fast," said Picard. "Counselor Troi, will you contact Data and La Forge on the *Hudson* and let them know what's happened. Tell them to abort their mission at the gravity sink and get back here."

"Aye, sir," said the Betazoid, scurrying to an auxiliary station.

"Captain, we're in tractor-beam range," announced Perim at the conn.

"Drop shields and lock on," ordered Picard, "and get the *Juno* out of there."

"Aye, sir," answered the Trill with grim determination on her face.

"Captain," said Vale, "with shields down, we might take—"

They were rocked by a blinding energy spike, and Picard staggered on his feet and answered, "Damage. Yes, I know."

"Locked on," said Perim, deftly working her board. Just when Picard thought they would be moving, she said, "I can't isolate the *Juno* with the tractor beam! We have to separate them from the wreck."

Every second, the blackness of space erupted with blazing, twisted flashes of light, and the *Enterprise* shimmied eerily under Picard's feet. It seemed as if the two living starships would never extricate themselves from the white-hot lightning . . . or the jagged clutches of the Klingon derelict.

"Ready a test torpedo," the captain told Vale. "No charge. Target the bridge of that Klingon cruiser."

"Aye, sir," she answered, working her controls.

The *Enterprise* was jarred several more times, and a power conduit exploded at a spare console. "Fire when ready," said Picard.

"Torpedo away," announced Vale, lifting her eyes to look at the viewscreen.

The captain looked, too, and they saw their dummy torpedo hit the jutting bridge of the wrecked ship, only a few meters above the hapless *Juno*. The attack cruiser crumpled from the impact and recoiled a few meters. That was just enough to put some distance between the *Juno* and the once-proud relic of the Klingon empire.

"Locking on with tractor beam," announced Perim. "Reverse half impulse."

The energy ripples grasped the *Juno* for a few more seconds until they cleared about a kilometer between them and the wreckage. Then most of the errant discharges veered to a closer clump of debris.

"Well done," said Picard to Vale. "Ambassador Worf couldn't have done it any better."

"Thank you, sir," she answered with a satisfied smile.

Picard turned his attention to the conn. "Steady as she goes. On my mark, cut the tractor beam and put up our shields. The *Juno* can drift while we reposition."

"Yes, sir," answered Perim.

He waited until a lull between the crackling bows of energy, then barked, "Mark!"

Suddenly the larger starship broke free and veered off, as her shields deflected a sparkling burst. The crippled *Juno* drifted toward a void in the graveyard, finally free of the lightning that had bedeviled her.

"Captain," said Jelpn at ops, "there was a Starfleet shuttlecraft in the vicinity, but its ID marker was deactivated. I'm going to lose them soon, but they're leaving this area and flying toward the center."

Before the captain could respond, Counselor Troi interjected, "Captain, I'll tell the *Hudson* to look for them."

"Make it so," replied Picard, turning his attention back to the stricken starship on the viewscreen. "Any answer to our hails?"

"Not from the *Juno*," answered Vale, "but the Ontailians have responded and are blocking the escape routes on this side. They've got five vessels en route to help them, including two of our shuttlecraft. The scavengers will have to double back or try to break out."

The captain nodded with satisfaction, then asked, "Are you sure all those messages are legitimate?"

"Yes, sir," answered Vale with a sheepish smile. Suddenly her eyebrows lifted, and she made a triumphant fist. "Sir, I've got Captain Leeden onscreen!"

The captain let out a breath and turned toward the screen with a smile on his face. When he saw the smoke and chaos on the *Juno*'s bridge, his grin started to slip, but Captain Leeden hardly looked ruffled by her ordeal.

"Thank you, Captain," she said. "I would like to know why you initially broke off pursuit of the Androssi."

"We detected one Starfleet vessel chasing them, and an Ontailian ship reported that it was also in pursuit. If this was a mistake, we're sorry, but this looked like one of a dozen chases we break off every day. How badly damaged is your ship?"

She shrugged and grinned. "We'll probably be in pursuit of them before *you.*"

The captain tried not to react to her gibe; instead he focused on the task at hand. "We detected a photon torpedo—is that what hit you?"

"As far as we can tell, yes," she answered. "They got lucky. It hit us just as our shields were dealing with a massive energy spike, and it started a chain reaction. We're going to find whoever attacked us."

"Shortly after the attack, a shuttlecraft headed away from here toward the center of the boneyard," added Picard.

He glanced at Counselor Troi, who nodded in confirmation of her recent actions. The captain turned back to the viewscreen and said, "I've got Commanders Data and La Forge on the *Hudson* pursuing this mystery shuttlecraft. And the Ontailians have cut off the escape routes, to force the Androssi back."

"Very well," said Leeden. "I'll bet you five buckets of deuterium that the *Hudson* will find your missing yacht."

"Let's hope so," answered Picard. "But my yacht doesn't have photon torpedoes."

"Don't underestimate the Androssi," warned Captain Leeden. "I'd like to capture them alive, but it isn't necessary. By the way, Captain, that was quick thinking with the dummy torpedo, although you had us scared for a moment."

An underling handed the *Juno*'s captain a padd, and her face sagged as she read it. "We can handle our wounded, but we're going to need some spare parts and several technicians."

"We're at your service," answered the captain with a polite bow.

"Hmmm," mused Geordi La Forge as he read the latest missive from the *Enterprise;* it had been sent by subspace even though they were only two hundred kilometers away from the *Enterprise.* "Somewhere out there is a Starfleet shuttlecraft with no ID," he told Data, who sat beside him in the cockpit of the shuttle *Hudson.* "And we have to find it. They think it could be the missing yacht, and it may have attacked the *Juno.*"

Data cocked his head quizzically. "The *Calypso* does not have a weapon system."

"I'm just repeating what Troi told me," answered La Forge. "I wish she had told us where it is."

The engineer lifted his head and stared out the window of the shuttlecraft into the grim spectacle of the ships' graveyard. To his ocular implants, the dusty hulks were blue shapes of cold metal, and the pulsing arcs and spikes were vivid streams of orange fire. The myriad gas clouds and dust particles lent a transparent pastel filter to the scene, and he could make out more of these wispy features than even his companion, Data. But he didn't see anything that looked like a living, working shuttlecraft, except for their own.

"We go from searching for a needle in a haystack to searching for a toothpick," he muttered.

"Is the *Enterprise* certain they were headed this way?" asked the android.

La Forge nodded. "Toward the center, and that's where we came from. It's too bad we didn't have time to finish our experiment—I think those probes are still active, but their signal is being dampened."

"When we find this suspected Androssi ship," said Data, "what are we supposed to do?"

"Since they have weapons and we don't," answered Geordi, "I say we keep them under surveillance until the *Enterprise* gets here. But we have to find them first."

Data nodded sagely. "If they attacked a much larger ship and are fleeing, then they will be taking evasive actions, even hiding."

"Right," answered La Forge, not sure where his android friend was headed with this line of reasoning.

"They will be looking for shuttlecraft looking for them," said Data, "and if they spot us first, we will lose them. I suggest we shut down all systems, except for sensors, and drift as if we are part of the debris."

"All systems?" asked La Forge hesitantly. "Including life-support?"

"Yes," answereed Data, "I am increasing our speed

to get momentum before I cut engines. You may put on your environmental suit."

Geordi nodded. "All right, just give me a moment."

A few minutes later, they were immersed in darkness, except for the frequent flashes of wild energy and the occasional glint of starlight off a nearby derelict. Data had placed the auxiliary station on audible alert status, to signal whenever a warp signature, impulse engine, or power source was detected. The android had put them on as safe a course as he could, away from the larger chunks of wreckage, but they were still without shields. It was disconcerting to Geordi to hear rubble pepper the hull of the *Hudson,* but Data was oblivious. The android kept his fingers on the controls to correct course the moment something too large headed their way, but it was still a nerve-racking glide through the boneyard for the human.

Although they were able to talk as they sailed along, the environmental suit inhibited La Forge. Stuck in this now-dark and powerless metal can, hearing nothing but the hollowness of his own breathing inside his helmet, the engineer began to feel like a part of the debris as they drifted within it. He had seen lifeless starships abandoned in space many times before, but the sheer number and wretched condition of these derelicts put them in another category. It felt as if he were in an art gallery of abstract sculptures, crafted and hung by giants in some long-dead civilization. There was a timeless, ageless quality that made this feel like a graveyard from eons in the past, not just a couple of years ago.

Finally, the eerie silence was broken by a sharp

beeping at the auxiliary station. Both La Forge and Data turned their attention to the sensors.

"You fly the ship," said La Forge. "I don't want to run into anything."

Before he could even get a good look at the screen, the beeping stopped. The signal was gone. Geordi frowned and said, "There was a blip at bearing thirty-four mark one hundred ten, but it's gone now."

Data sat back in his seat without touching his controls.

"Aren't you going to change course?" asked La Forge.

"No," answered the android. "They are apparently drifting with no power, as we are. If they have detected us, they will flee, and we will have difficulty keeping them in sensor range. If we have not been detected, we are still getting closer to them. The last thing we want to do is to be detected before we can locate them."

"Make them blink first," said La Forge.

Data cocked his head. "I do not believe the Androssi blink."

"Just an expression," said La Forge, gazing through the faceplate of his helmet at the quiet view of decimated starships. "It may have been just a sensor phantom, or it could be a legitimate Starfleet shuttle on legitimate business. You know how they come and go here."

"I do," answered Data. "It is like Grand Central Station in here." He gave Geordi a quizzical smile and added, "An old Terran transporter nexus."

The beeping sounded again, making Geordi jump, and he turned his attention to his suddenly active screen. "They're on the move," he reported. "Bearing thirty-five mark one hundred twelve."

"If we can track them long enough to determine their course, we can intercept them," said the android.

"I'm getting a fix," said Geordi, studying his read-outs. "They're on a course that will take them near the gravity sink. They must be trying to get to the other side of the boneyard, or they're going to try to hide in that same sensor dead spot that got our probes."

"Either way, we will be able to follow them," said Data, "because we will become harder to detect when we—"

From nowhere, a bolt of energy flashed across their bow, jolting the shuttlecraft and whirling it like a gyroscope. La Forge was thrown against the bulkhead by centrifugal force, and Data furiously worked his controls to compensate. When he activated the shields, most of the energy spikes were deflected elsewhere, and the android finally regained control of the small craft.

When Geordi staggered back to his feet, he went immediately to his controls, which registered nothing but gibberish. "We lost them," muttered the engineer.

"Then we will have to catch them," said Data. At once, he reactivated the shuttlecraft, and it streaked through a sheen of glittery rubble and plunged deeper into the boneyard.

"Captain Picard," said Vale from her rear station on the bridge of the *Enterprise*. "I've just received word from the Ontailians."

The captain stopped his pacing and turned to face his tactical officer. "Good news, I hope."

"Mostly," answered the lieutenant. "Near gateway

four, they intercepted the Androssi convoy and found them towing a big Romulan warbird, the *Rom'drex.* Apparently, they were trying to make off with the whole ship."

"That was ambitious," said Picard with begrudging admiration. "What happened?"

"One Androssi ship opened fire on the Ontailians and was destroyed," answered Vale. "The other three Androssi ships abandoned their prize and fled back into the boneyard. Now they're headed in our direction again. Our shuttlecraft *Cortez* is with a task force that is pursuing them toward us. The Ontailian battle cruiser, *Vuxhal,* is also with them."

"Now we know what their plan was," said Picard. "And that we stopped them."

Vale looked intently at her console for a moment. "Captain Leeden is hailing us."

"Put her onscreen," answered Picard.

Looking gaunt and harried, the captain of the *Juno* appeared on the overhead screen. Behind her, the bridge of the *Juno* was teeming with activity, with technicians at every station. Half of them were from the *Enterprise* crew.

"Captain Leeden," said Picard, "you seem to be making headway in your repairs."

Jill Leeden replied, "Yes, but not nearly fast enough. We're still five hours away from being mobile again. Did you receive the message from the Ontailians?"

"I did," answered Picard. "They stopped the Androssi."

"For now, but they're still at large," she said. "We're

dead in the water, so it will be up to you to stop them if they come this way."

"Understood," said the captain. "With any luck we can finish assisting you first."

"There's no time to wait for that," she answered. "Even though you have a lot of personnel on the *Juno,* you need to break off from us and pursue these scavengers."

Picard's face expressed his concern. "You'll be helpless . . . a sitting duck."

"Let me worry about that." Leeden picked up a padd and gazed at it for a moment, then said, "We're supposed to have shields within the hour. When we do, you can go."

Picard agreed with her assessment of the situation. He also realized that he had a short time to be prepared to deal with the Androssi ships headed his way. It had already been several hours since the attack on the *Juno.* An hour from now, he should be ready to meet them.

He nodded curtly. "We'll be ready to go as soon as you regain your shields. Anything else, Captain?"

"Yes," she said grimly, her dark eyes burning. "Get those bastards. What about the ship that attacked me?"

Picard replied, "We spotted them. Unfortunately our shuttlecraft was hit by a discharge and lost them. But we're back in pursuit."

"Don't let them get away again. The dead need to rest in peace," she said. "Leeden out."

Picard let out a sigh, and his shoulders slumped.

He turned to gaze at the crippled *Juno* just off their bow; it looked uncomfortably akin to a number of derelicts visible in the background. He let out a worried breath. The last thing he wanted to do was add to the death and destruction of Rashanar. He was beginning to think that perhaps they should leave the bones to the vultures. It was better than wasting time shooing them off, or shooting them. Unfortunately, the stolen yacht *was* his responsibility, and he knew that particular craft had to be recaptured or destroyed, even if the other Androssi ships got away.

He turned to tactical and asked, "Any word from the *Hudson?*"

"None, sir," replied Vale. "Shall I try hailing them?"

Picard shook his head. "No, I'm sure they'll report when necessary. Keep your sensors trained toward gateway four. We should be getting hostiles from that direction."

"Yes, sir," answered Vale with determination. "We'll spot them."

Captain Picard nodded, thinking he had done all he could for the moment. Still he experienced an odd feeling of dread, not unlike that which Captain Leeden often talked about, and he felt a twinge of sympathy for the embattled captain of the *Juno.*

"Sensor readings are getting squirrelly again," complained Geordi La Forge as they neared the region of the mysterious gravity dump in the middle of the boneyard. "The shuttle is going to be hard to find in here."

"Perhaps we should let them find us," said Data. He cut power to the engines. They began to drift among the ruins and wrecks, some of which were moving swiftly this close to the gravity. Thankfully, the plasma explosions and errant energy bolts seemed distant, although La Forge knew those deadly storms could find them quickly.

The human sighed and reached for the helmet to his environmental suit, which he was still wearing. "Are we going to play dead again?"

"Until we can think of a better plan," answered the android. "From our recent readings, we know they are in this vicinity, and no other ships are present. They will have to move eventually, so we are back to whoever blinks first."

"If only we had a way to flush them out," muttered Geordi. Then his eyebrows lifted. He turned to look at the rear compartment of the shuttlecraft, which was filled with silver cases. "Wait a minute, we've got more probes!"

"But they are not weapons," Data pointed out.

The human smiled. "But the Androssi don't know that, and the sensor problems will disguise what they really are. By the time they spot them, they'll look like quantum torpedoes."

Data cocked his head and said, "Impressively devious."

La Forge moved closer to the controls. "You load a couple of probes for launching, and, based on our last sighting, I'll try to pick the best place to rustle the bushes."

After two minutes of work in the lower hatch, Data reported that two probes were ready for launch, and La Forge nodded with satisfaction. "There's half a Breen warship over there," he said, pointing a gloved hand to a severed green-gold starship visible in a corner of the viewport. "It's putting out slightly stranger readings than the rest of them, including its other half over there, and it has a stable orbit. They might be hiding behind it. If we hit it head-on, maybe we can get some fireworks."

"I am not sure fireworks are advisable in this site," said Data, returning to his seat. "But I do not have a better idea. The probes are set to look for heat, so there is a chance they will tell us something."

La Forge sat back, holding his hands up to let Data take over. "I suggest we double the shields, in case they fire back."

"Very well," answered the android, working his board. The *Hudson* banked around and took a forward angle at the sundered Breen ship. The shuttlecraft vibrated slightly, and a probe shot from her belly and streaked toward the derelict. "Probe one away," said Data. "On target."

A moment later, the Breen wreck was blasted off its lazy orbit and spun around as a spike of wild energy arced across space to strike it in the stern. The chain reaction was mild and lasted only a few seconds, but a living craft suddenly darted from a debris cloud in the area and flew away at breakneck speed. Geordi was thrown back into his seat as Data took off, and the *Hudson* was soon in hot pursuit of the captain's stolen yacht.

"The criminal always returns to the scene of the crime," said Geordi. "We're going to pass the *Asgard* in a few seconds."

Sure enough, they streaked past the blasted *Galaxy-*

class starship, where the *Calypso* had been hijacked only five days ago. The shuttle suddenly veered toward the center of the boneyard. Ahead of them, their prey also swerved erratically before they disappeared behind a pinkish plasma cloud.

Data quickly compensated, saying, "I hope the Androssi have a good pilot, because we are dangerously close to the gravity sink."

"I should send our position to the *Enterprise,*" answered Geordi, opening a subspace channel. "There's no doubt that's the *Calypso,* is there?"

"Her actions are very suspicious," answered Data. "Now that the target is coasting without power, we have lost her from sensors and visual again."

"But she can't go far," said Geordi, grinning that his ruse had worked. He completed his message to the *Enterprise* and sent it via subspace, then gazed into the junk-filled heavens. "We've got a much tighter area to search for her . . . plus more probes. If they thought we were unarmed, wouldn't they come out to fight?"

The android cocked his head, taking the question seriously. "Androssi are treacherous and clever but avoid direct confrontation. The way they stole the *Calypso* is more typical."

For several minutes, they cruised the area with sensors wide open and shields up, since the debris was fast-moving and erratic down here. In the distance, they saw the deadly vortex, a churning pinwheel of broken nacelles, hulls, and unrecognizable chunks. La Forge shivered. The vortex could well be the future of every relic in the Rashanar Battle Site.

Suddenly his console began to beep steadily. Before Geordi could turn around in his bulky suit, Data said, "Distress signal. Perhaps our prey has run afoul of some wreckage."

"You can pinpoint their location?" asked La Forge excitedly.

"Without problem," said the android, "but we must be careful. It could be a trap."

"At least they're not going to go anywhere," said La Forge, hoping that was true.

Battling the gravity pull, which seemed to ebb and flow like a rapid tide, the *Hudson* cautiously drew close to a smashed, rust-colored hull that might have been Tiburonian. La Forge could do little but peer out the viewport and trust Data not to take undue risks. Certainly, they couldn't see anything that looked like a shuttlecraft about to fire weapons at them, so they slowly circled the rusty derelict with Data's fingers poised on his controls. When they approached a huge gash in the sundered hull, Data stopped the shuttle and backed off a few meters.

"Are they inside?" rasped La Forge.

"That is the only possible explanation," answered Data, "but we do not want to expose ourselves to give them a clear shot at us."

"No," agreed the engineer.

The android suddenly jumped to his feet and walked toward the rear of the shuttlecraft. "I am taking an EVA to the relic. Please maintain our position here."

La Forge took a deep breath. "Don't be gone long—I wouldn't want to leave you here."

The android nodded and quickly pulled on a jet pack

that had been modified for use without a suit. Data popped the hatch at the the rear of the shuttlecraft and hurled himself into space. Even though Geordi had seen him do this before, it was never less than astounding, and he watched as the unprotected android used thrusters on his backpack to maneuver himself to the smashed hull. At the helm, Geordi had his hands full keeping the shuttlecraft close to the moving wreck without exposing himself to the ragged gash, where the enemy must be lurking. He adjusted course and backed off a few meters just as Data disappeared into a crater in the hull.

La Forge monitored his sensors. None of the readings were distinct, except for the distress signal, which was still broadcasting from a short distance away. A subspace message came in from the *Enterprise,* saying their message had been received. From the terse quality of the missive, Geordi figured the *Enterprise* was hip-deep in some sort of excitement.

In between nervous course corrections, he stared out the viewport, looking for Data or the signs of a fight within the dusty hulk. He expected to see the *Calypso* come bursting through the gash and zoom into space. None of those things happened. Finally, he spotted Data emerging from the wreck with several pieces of equipment in his arms. As the android flew toward him, La Forge lumbered to the hatch to help him in, along with his collection of equipment.

"This is a communications module," said Geordi, looking at Data's souvenir. "And power cells. Wait a minute, is this all that was in there?"

"Yes," answered Data, taking off his jet pack. "We were tricked, and we have lost valuable time. The Androssi are quite inventive, and this was a clever way to elude us. However, now we can prove it was the *Calypso,* and they no longer have the ability to send distress signals or false messages."

The android strode to the pilot's seat, while La Forge rushed to close the hatch. Data announced that shields were up and a course had been laid, while Geordi scurried back to his seat. A second later, the shuttlecraft *Hudson* roared off into the graveyard of lost ships, looking for the only spacecraft that was trying to stay lost.

Ghissel laughed and slapped her slim thigh, gazing longingly at her pilot and lover, Boenmar. "We have done well, haven't we?"

But the pilot of the yacht formerly known as *Calypso* was still intent on his instruments, looking unconvinced that the Starfleet spacecraft had been thrown off. "I might want to drift again without power," he said.

"That's fine." Ghissel caressed his bald skull and the braid of black hair that hung down his back. They had snatched frantic bouts of lovemaking when they were hiding out, and the dangers lurking all around them had heightened the intensity, making Ghissel almost forget her grandiose plans and well-connected associates. Who cared if they hauled off some old Romulan wreck, when the lithe Androssi was having the time of her life? The thrills, the excitement—this was why she had joined the Androssi salvage fleet.

Boenmar brushed her hand away in order to concentrate on his board. "You're insatiable," he said with a smile. "They didn't tell me this job would have such fringe benefits."

"They didn't know," purred Ghissel, leaning forward to kiss his neck. He suffered the nuzzle while still working his controls. They veered slowly into a fairly empty section of the boneyard and began to drift among clouds of silver and golden debris, like so much space junk.

Boenmar cut the engines, then turned to devote some attention to his mistress. They embraced hungrily, kissing and fondling, oblivious of the rest of the universe. Suddenly, the colorful stretch of space in front of them began to shimmer and waver, coalescing as if it were an illusion about to reveal its true appearance. Ghissel noticed this anomaly first, and she uncharacteristically pushed her ardent lover away.

"Boenmar, what is *that?*" she asked, pointing toward the wispy curtain forming in front of them. It almost looked like the wall of a holodeck before it changed into an impossibly beautiful vista from some famed vacation spot. Before the pilot could answer her question, every system on the ship shut down, and they were plunged into blackness, except for the shimmering scrim that loomed before them.

"Where's our power?" asked Ghissel, thinking she had better get her environmental suit back on. Suddenly a high-pitched whine sounded in her ears, and she bent over in pain. "What . . . is it?"

"Aaagghh!" screamed Boenmar. The Androssi gripped his head to try to suppress the agony, and when that didn't work, he reached for his controls. But his hands trembled uncontrollably—he wasn't able to even touch his board. As the piercing tone grew worse, both of the Androssi gripped their ears and tumbled out of their seats onto the deck.

Mercifully, both of them were unconscious a few seconds later, and they didn't see the glittering cloud of space dust as it slowly engulfed the darkened yacht.

Chapter Eight

"ANDROSSI VESSEL DETECTED at bearing three hundred mark twenty-six," reported Christine Vale from the tactical station on the bridge of the *Enterprise*. "Heading our way."

Captain Picard rose from his command chair and walked behind the ops console. "Mr. Jelpn," he asked, "do we have all of our technicians back from the *Juno?*"

"Yes, sir," answered the Deltan. "The last shuttlecraft just entered the shuttlebay."

Picard nodded with relief. "Shields up. Lieutenant Vale, hail Captain Leeden on the *Juno* and tell her we're pursuing the Androssi ship. Lieutenant Perim, set a course to intercept that spacecraft."

"Yes, sir," answered the Trill, sounding energized.

All of them were tired of sitting around nursing the *Juno* back to health.

Vale broke into his thoughts. "Sir, Captain Leeden says, 'Good hunting.' She expects to have impulse engines online in one hour."

"I hope so," replied the captain. He turned to his conn officer and said, "Engage as soon as you have your course."

"Intercept course laid in," answered Perim. "Half reverse."

Under Perim's careful guidance, the immense starship backed away from the crippled spacecraft and executed an abrupt turn. A few seconds later, the *Enterprise* was streaking through the boneyard, rubble frying against her shields and dust clouds scattering in her wake.

"The *Vuxhal* is in pursuit too," reported Vale. "We're right on course to intercept both of them, but we should get to the Androssi freighter first."

"A freighter?" asked Picard curiously.

"From its dimensions, I believe it was once a Cardassian troop transport," answered Vale, "outfitted with a new warp reactor and tractor beam."

"They probably stole it from here," remarked Deanna Troi, who was seated in the second-in-command chair. The counselor was looking at the viewscreen, and she suddenly jumped up and pointed. "There, I think I see it."

In the distance, a boxy golden-hued freighter glinted in the sun for a moment before it made a bank that looked impossible for a ship that was so ungainly. Picard was about to order the image magnified when Jelpn anticipated his command, and the hexagonal hull of the Androssi freighter filled the viewscreen.

"I'm hailing them on all frequencies," reported Vale, "but there's no answer."

Picard nodded grimly. "Target a quantum torpedo for standard warning round. Suppress fusion."

"Yes, sir," answered Vale, as she armed a torpedo that would light up the boneyard and get their attention, even if it was all show and no bang. They had fired so many warning shots on this mission that they had optimized the standard for firing in the battle site.

"Torpedo ready," she reported.

The captain lifted his finger to signal her, but before he could execute the command, the lumbering freighter vented a glowing stream of plasma. This cloud caught an errant discharge and erupted into a wild arc that smacked a blackened derelict, which exploded into a spider vein of radiating bolts.

"Full stop!" ordered Picard, but they still caught part of the discharge, which jarred them but didn't cause serious damage to the delicate bridge circuits.

"Shields holding," said Vale, "but the Androssi are getting out of range."

"Fire that torpedo," ordered the captain, knowing that it was more of a gesture than a real threat. The foe apparently didn't intend to be captured, because venting that plasma was a desperate and dangerous act under these circumstances. Now this could get tricky, because they couldn't merely let these scoundrels get away with a warning, not after their attack on the *Juno*.

The torpedo streaked into the strobe-lit field of wrecks and energy discharges, adding to the unearthly light show. "Don't lose them, Lieutenant," said Picard.

"I'm on them," answered Perim. They could see from the shifting image on the viewscreen that their prey was still in sight.

"Ready a quantum torpedo, Lieutenant Vale," said Captain Picard grimly. "Target their engines and fire when ready."

"Yes, sir," answered the tactical officer. She worked her board with determination and pounded it with some urgency. "Torpedo away."

This one they barely saw in the streaks of light, but it exploded in the distance like a volcano erupting. And they could see the Androssi ship spin out of control, its stern aflame.

"Ready second torpedo," ordered Picard.

"Captain, wait a second," said Troi, rising abruptly from her seat. "I think they realize they've been caught."

"They *are* slowing down, Captain," said Vale, working her board. "Now they're answering our hail and coming to a full stop."

Picard nodded, hoping that a surrender was imminent.

The lieutenant frowned at her readouts and said, "I'm getting too much interference to put them on screen. The best I can do is this audio."

"Enterprise, we greet you," said a monotone voice. "I am Overseer Undenni of the Androssi. We welcome this opportunity to explain any misunderstandings."

"There is no misunderstanding," replied Picard,

tight-lipped. "You will stand down on your weapons, drop shields, and allow a boarding party to enter your vessel. Any further attempts to flee will be met with deadly force. Do I make myself clear?"

After a lengthy pause, Undenni said, "We wish to negotiate these terms."

Picard scowled angrily. The Androssi were fortunate that they couldn't see him. "You didn't choose to negotiate with the *Juno*—you just fired on her—and we don't choose to negotiate with you."

"Captain, I've lost contact," complained Vale. Then her eyes widened in alarm and she added, "They're powering up weapons."

"Ready phasers," ordered Picard, as Counselor Troi stepped to his side.

"There's something wrong here," she said. "Please hold your fire."

"The Androssi are firing," announced Vale. Picard braced himself, but no phaser beams or torpedoes struck the *Enterprise.* Instead the Androssi's beamed weapon shot far wide, off to starboard, and a brace of torpedoes answered them, streaking from this offscreen location.

"Adjusting view," said Jelpn at the ops console, and the viewscreen showed the sleek silver triangle they had seen many times before—the Ontailian heavy cruiser *Vuxhal.* The fin-shaped vessel fired round after round at the Androssi craft as it weaved through space, trying to escape.

"No!" shouted Troi. She cringed as if feeling every missile strike its target. "They're killing them!"

"Hail the Ontailians!" Captain Picard barked. "Tell them to stop their attack!"

"I have," answered Vale, furiously working her board, "but it's too late. Three direct hits . . . the Androssi are breaking apart."

The captain turned back to the viewscreen to see the disheartening sight of the hapless Androssi ship erupting with bright explosions all along the length of her hull. Various flaming chunks of the vessel shot into space like Roman candles, and a final rupture of gases consumed the ship in blazing flames. Seconds later, the former Cardassian troop transport was just another slowly expanding cloud of death and destruction in the Rashanar Battle Site.

"Ops, search for survivors," ordered Picard somberly. He made a fist and slammed it angrily into the palm of his hand. "Tactical, I want to speak to the *Vuxhal*. We were negotiating the Androssi's surrender—didn't they see that?"

Vale shook her short bob of brown hair. "We don't know what transpired between those two ships."

"That was mass murder," breathed Deanna Troi, slumping back into her chair. Her eyes were wide and her breathing came in short bursts, as if she were still reeling from the impacts herself. "They were going to surrender."

Captain Picard turned to the tactical station, and Lieutenant Vale anticipated his request. "The Ontailians aren't responding to hails," she told him, "but a subspace message is coming from the *Juno*. It seems that another Androssi ship is headed our way—

another one of those who tried to steal the warbird."

On the viewscreen, the great silver fin suddenly sliced away from them, and the *Vuxhal* made a graceful bank and took off for parts unknown. Picard clenched his jaw as he watched the deadly attack cruiser leave the vicinity.

"Before this day is out, I'll want some answers," he swore. "That's enough of this murderous sport for now. Lieutenant Vale, contact the *Hudson* and see what has become of Data and La Forge."

"That does it," said Geordi La Forge, sitting back in his seat aboard the *Hudson.* "I've sent the *Enterprise* our coordinates and told them everything we've done so far." He looked worriedly out the viewport at a murky starscape interspersed with somber wrecks and floating mounds of trash. If there was a more eerie, more depressing part of the boneyard, he hadn't seen it. "Do you think we'll find them again?" asked the engineer.

In the pilot's seat, Data nodded. "Given an unlimited amount of time, yes, but we do not have an unlimited amount of time. I believe that the Androssi have not used their engines for the last forty-three minutes, which may indicate they are committed to hiding."

"Or ambush," Geordi warned him. "Do you want to try another probe?"

"I doubt if they will fall for that ruse again," answered the android. "We must have some good fortune to find the *Calypso,* especially if they are out of sensor range."

"Right," murmured La Forge, "and this place doesn't suggest 'good fortune.' "

The engineer stared into the gloomy space cemetery, seeing the bright primary colors, shapes, and textures that were representative of normal sight but were unique to him. The enhanced images generated by his implants often possessed more detail and relevancy than the scattered reflections seen by a human eye. He could also program his perceptions to see heat and cold, electromagnetic fields, water vapor, and certain types of radiation. Only the black emptiness of space looked the same to Geordi as it did to a conventionally sighted person.

He had no particular idea what he was looking for when he spotted two derelicts hovering side by side, some distance to port. That wasn't unusual in this blasted graveyard, because many ships had died in each other's clutches. But these two were perfectly identical, at least to his specific vision. No two derelicts in this place ought to be identical, thought La Forge, because they were a long way from being fresh out of the shipyards.

"Data," he said, "to port at about ten o'clock, there are two small ships. Do you see them?"

"I do now," answered the android, deftly changing course so that they were making straightaway toward the twin relics. "What is suspicious about them?"

"They're identical," said La Forge. "And they're about the right size to be the captain's yacht."

The android cocked his head and looked at his friend. "Do you mean the same class of ship? How could they be identical?"

"Exactly," said Geordi. "Let's just get there and see what we've got."

The closer they got to the two squat spacecraft, the more eerie the scene became. Geordi La Forge kept expecting to see some minute difference. There was none. Both elliptical shuttlecraft were in slow orbit about fifty meters away from each other, and they looked lifeless, hanging in space. Incredibly, both were the captain's yacht, *Calypso,* and both had had their IDs removed. Crude torpedo bays were prominent on the underbelly of each vessel. The *Calypso* had no such weapons until the Androssi added them. Scratches where the fresh paint had been scraped off were identical on both hulls. La Forge felt a shiver down his spine.

"Do they look the same to you?" he asked in a whisper.

"They are the same," answered Data matter-of-factly. "I never doubted you, Geordi, but it is inexplicable. I detect the same number of life signs on each vessel— two—but very faint."

La Forge had a moment of dread. "It could be a trick," he warned. "They've done it before."

"This is a very impressive trick," answered the android, flipping through screens full of sensor data. "In their present condition, neither one of these ships appears to be a threat to us."

His companion made this observation just a moment before all the lights in the shuttlecraft went out, and both instrument panels went dead. Fortunately, Geordi didn't need light to see. He reached instinctively for his helmet. "What the heck is going on?" he asked. "Data, this is no time for *us* to play dead."

He turned to see the android frozen, staring ahead, his hands hardened like claws over his instrument panel. In panic, La Forge grabbed Data's forearm and shook it, but it was like grabbing a pole covered in cloth. The life was gone.

"This isn't funny," he said, thinking he had better put on his suit or he would freeze to death. La Forge could feel the artificial gravity in the shuttle going. Life-support would not be far behind. As soon as he got his helmet fastened to his suit, he started to work on his console, to see if he could bring the shuttle back to life.

That was when his ocular implants began to fail, and the vivid images he depended upon faded to black and white and finally gray. A minute after the deterioration started, the human was totally sightless. *A distress signal,* he told himself, *I've got to send out a distress signal.* But without sight or even any audible feedback, his hands flailed at the controls.

The instruments aren't responding, anyway, he had to admit to himself. *Blind or not, I'm in big trouble.*

Then a shrill, high-pitched tone sounded in his ears . . . or was it his mind? The whine grew louder, and Geordi doubled over in pain. He gripped the sides of his helmet and cracked it open, but nothing brought him any relief. It was all he could do to stay in his chair, and he wanted to roll into a fetal position and whimper. He looked to Data for help, but the android was no more than a lifelike statue. Finally the horrid hum was more than La Forge's senses could take: blinded, panicked, and out of his mind, he hurled himself against the window, trying to escape from the noise and the fear. He thudded hard and bounced backward, already unconscious by the time he began to float in the weightless cabin of the dying shuttlecraft.

Chapter Nine

"The Hudson does not answer hails or respond to subspace messages," said Christine Vale. "It has been forty-six minutes since their last communication."

Captain Picard nodded somberly as he strode from the tactical station to his command chair on the bridge of the *Enterprise.* He stopped to look at Counselor Troi, whose normally tranquil features were etched with concern.

"Can we break off from this engagement with the Androssi to look for them?" she asked bluntly.

The captain frowned and gazed at his viewscreen, where the ghostly ships continued to revolve silently around the boneyard, like a monstrous mobile caught in a lightning storm. There were only two known Androssi ships still at large, not counting his yacht, and at least a dozen allied vessels were looking for them.

"Set course for the *Hudson*'s last known position," he told the conn. Kell Perim immediately set to work.

A moment later, the Trill reported, "Sir, that will take us past a level-four warning buoy and close to a level-five. The *Enterprise* isn't cleared for going that near the gravity dump."

"Captain Picard," interrupted a voice from the tactical station, and he turned to see Vale looking gravely at him. "Subspace message from Admiral Ross for you, marked personal."

"Patch it to my ready room," answered the captain, straightening his shoulders. This could be about almost anything, but it was likely to be about reports they had received from Captain Leeden. "Commander Troi, you have the bridge. Keep trying to contact the *Hudson*."

"Yes, sir," answered Troi with a glance at Lieutenant Vale, who nodded.

Captain Picard strode into his ready room, crossed to his desk, and dropped into a chair. Taking a deep breath, he turned on his screen to see the concerned but gentle face of Admiral William Ross. Since this was a recorded message sent by subspace, there was no opportunity for Picard to respond in real time, but his fingers were on his keypad in case he needed to take notes.

"Hello, Jean-Luc," began the admiral, his manner grave but conciliatory, "I hope this doesn't catch you at an inopportune time. I have to address the reports I've gotten from the Rashanar Battle Site, culminating in one I received just today. Your account of how you lost the *Calypso* was accepted. However, we found out today that the *Calypso* was instrumental in the Androssi attack on the *Juno*. Of course, we are going to need a few more details . . . and possibly an inquiry when you return."

Admiral Ross cleared his throat. "You also sent us reports of an Ontailian ship that was destroyed, the *Maskar,* when, in fact, that ship is at their repair facilities. I don't need to tell you, Jean-Luc, that the Federation needs to hold on to as many member nations as we can. Since the war, they've been dropping like flies—they perceive us as weak, unable to protect them. Ontailians are a perfect example of the member planets we have to hold on to."

Picard sighed, wishing he could reply to this unnecessary lecture. In his recorded message, Ross went on, "Obviously, Rashanar is a difficult place to operate; however, I thought you would have a leg up with your vast experience. I'm sorry I didn't send an admiral with you now, because the incidents keep happening. In a recent report, Captain Leeden states that the *Enterprise* broke off pursuit of an Androssi convoy stealing a complete Romulan warbird."

"We spotted them first and saved the *Juno,*" muttered Picard to himself.

"According to this chain of events, you might have prevented the attack on the *Juno,*" said Ross in his recorded message. "I'll give you full opportunity to reply with your account, and you could also include reports from any senior officers who were on the bridge at the time. I don't mean to give you a hard time, Jean-Luc, when I know what you've been through, but Starfleet is going to request to have some of these issues addressed. Reply at your convenience, and do try to get along with the Ontailians and Captain Leeden. She's by-the-book, but she's a good officer. Keep safe, Jean-Luc. Ross out."

What I've been through? thought the captain, wondering if Ross was referring to their various missions in the years since the Dominion War. Or maybe he was going farther back to the Borg, the Cardassians, the Maquis, or some other trial that should have broken him. Was Ross trying to tell him that he had commanded the *Enterprise* for too long and was past his prime? Was Ross even thinking that, or was this just bureaucracy at work—one document requiring another document?

His com panel beeped, jarring the captain out of his consternation. "Bridge to Picard," said Lieutenant Vale.

"Picard here," he answered, trying to shake off the message from Ross.

"I have Captain Leeden on screen, and the quality is not too bad," said Vale. "She's requested that we go on another sweep near buoy nineteen."

"Patch her to my screen," Picard ordered, sitting up and straightening his tunic.

A second later, her tired face appeared on his desk screen. "Picard," she said, "I've just received some very unusual sensor scans from buoy nineteen. Would you take another sweep around there and see if it's the Androssi?"

He replied, "Captain Leeden, our shuttlecraft *Hudson* has not reported in as scheduled, and we're getting concerned. That's the shuttle piloted by Data that is looking for the *Calypso.*"

"And failing to find her so far," added Leeden. "I am

concerned that we've only subdued two of the five An-drossi ships."

"We destroyed both of those," Picard reminded her. "That freighter was going to surrender to us before the Ontailians arrived, then they started firing at each other."

Leeden sighed and said, "It was unfortunate, but the Androssi are using deadly force against us. We can't let them get away."

Picard sat up in his chair. "Captain Leeden, I've got to find my missing shuttlecraft. Maybe I'll find the *Calypso* as well. I'm moving my search closer to the center of the boneyard," he answered evenly. "We'll get as close as we can, then use shuttlecraft. I'll keep you posted."

"Please do. We really need your help with those scavengers. With each ship they destroy, a few more of the war dead never make it home and their families are left wondering what happened."

"As soon as I have retrieved my living, I will help you protect the dead," he said. "Picard out."

He immediately tapped his com panel again. "Picard to Riker."

"This is Riker," came the familiar voice, sounding a bit drowsy.

"I'm sorry to interrupt your well-deserved rest," said Picard, "but the *Hudson* is missing with Data and La Forge on board. In about twenty minutes, I'll need a shuttlecraft to look for them."

"I'm your man," replied Riker, sounding very alert now. "I'll be in the shuttlebay when you're ready."

"Thank you, Number One. You might wish to take Dr. Crusher with you, in case there's a medical emergency. Picard out." He tapped his panel again and said, "Picard to bridge."

"Troi here," answered the senior officer.

"Commander, have the conn set course and make way for the level-four buoy closest to the last known position of the *Hudson,*" ordered the captain. "I'll be on the bridge in a few minutes, after I file a report."

"Aye, sir."

Captain Picard rose from his desk and paced the short length of his ready room, determined to get control of this spiraling situation from every aspect. As far as he was concerned, the dead were not as important as the living, and keeping people alive in this dangerous place should be their first priority. As Leeden had said, there were many ways to die in the Rashanar Battle Site, and he wasn't going to add to the number of deadly encounters.

Will Riker checked his instrument panel on the shuttlecraft *Polo* and shook his head. He couldn't see any trace of the *Hudson.* They were at its last known position. Here the wrecks were fast-moving and erratic, tumbling in eccentric orbits that often brought them crashing into each other. He had to keep firing thrusters to compensate for the gravity pull toward the center, where he could see the ghastly vortex. The sensors were next to worthless. How could Data and La Forge have followed any kind of a ship in this swirling haystack? After receiving a message from the *Enterprise,* La Forge had responded that they were on the trail of the Androssi ship suspected of being the *Calypso.* He had detailed the cat-and-mouse game they were playing with the enemy. After that, the *Hudson* had never reported again. The endless vista of twisted wreckage made Riker consider the worst.

He turned to his copilot, Dr. Crusher. "Do you get anything on your science scans?"

"Not much," she answered, peering at her scrambled readouts. "There's a vapor trail up around that Breen hulk. Also, I'm getting strange readings from a cloud of debris off to port."

"What about it?" asked Riker.

"It's expanding," she answered. "Of course, most of the debris in the boneyard is expanding or moving, but it has had a year to settle. This still looks fairly compact and fast-moving."

Riker checked her coordinates, fired thrusters to stop the *Polo* from drifting, then set a new course. Cautiously, they glided deeper into the boneyard, swerving this way and that to avoid flying debris. As seen from the *Enterprise,* the devastation was tragic; seen close at hand from a shuttlecraft, the derelicts took on a mythic quality, larger than life. Seeing the endless field of ruins, it was hard to shake the notion that angry gods, not mere mortals, must have destroyed these two great fleets.

"What's this?" asked Crusher, peering at her readouts. "There's a smaller vessel *inside* that cloud of debris. It could be a shuttlecraft!"

"I see it," answered Riker, making his way toward the glittering ball of rubble, which looked like a multicolored snowball exploding in slow motion. He could just make out the silhouette of a boxy craft at the edge of the debris, where it underwent a constant pummeling. Riker took them so close that the rubble sparkled against the shields of the *Polo,* and some of it was recognizable. He saw part of an access panel go floating past; it had a singed yellow sign that looked like Starfleet markings.

"I've got a life-sign reading!" exclaimed Crusher. "Very weak. It may be a phantom, but I'm going to lock on with our transporter."

"We're not supposed to use transporters," Riker pointed out. "We'll have to lower shields."

"I'll take responsibility. How else are we going to get him out?" Crusher punched some commands into her board; then she grabbed her medical kit and rushed to the back of the craft. She knelt expectantly by the single transporter pad.

While she did that, Riker activated a com frequency. *"Polo* to *Enterprise,"* he said. "We've found what looks like the *Hudson* and the *Calypso.* The *Hudson* is still intact but without power, and the *Calypso* has been destroyed."

There was a jarring thud as debris hit the shuttlecraft with her shields down. Riker heard scuffling sounds, and he turned to see a figure in an environmental suit collapse from the transporter pad into Crusher's arms. She gently laid him out on the deck and began to remove his helmet. Riker restored shields just as more rubble pummeled the small craft.

He turned to see the doctor working furiously on Geordi La Forge. He turned back to his instrument panel and tried to get a sensor fix on Data. Everything mechanical or electrical seemed to be shut down on the doomed shuttlecraft, including the android.

"I've got a pulse!" said Beverly quickly. "I think we can save him, but we've got to get back to sickbay."

A hum sounded on an audio frequency, and the captain's voice broke through the static. "Number One, are you sure it's the *Calypso?*"

"It's either the *Calypso* or another yacht of the same class," answered Riker. "I see the VIP gangplank floating right in front of me, and it's unique to that design. We've got La Forge, but we need to get him to sickbay immediately. Can you get a tractor beam on the *Hudson?*"

"It will take some edging closer, but we'll do it," promised Picard. "Get back to the ship."

Dr. Crusher gave the unconscious engineer a hypospray on the neck; then she sat back on her haunches and wiped her brow. "He's stabilized, but hurry, Will."

"Going to impulse," said Riker, backing the shuttlecraft out of the shimmering curtain of debris. He fired thrusters and executed a perfect bank around a copper-colored Cardassian hulk. Then they soared through space, avoiding clumps of wreckage and glittering energy spikes.

The *Polo* almost passed the *Enterprise* coming from the opposite direction. The starship dropped her shields just long enough for Riker to pilot the small vessel into the shuttlebay. As soon as they were aboard, the doctor tapped her combadge and said, "Crusher to transporter room. Direct-beam me and La Forge to sickbay."

The two of them disappeared in a flurry of sparkling

molecules that looked uncomfortably like the debris field they had just left. With a sigh, Riker rose to his feet and ducked through the hatch of the shuttlecraft. He dashed through the double doors and into the corridor, where he covered the forty meters to the turbolift like an Olympic sprinter.

A few moments later, Riker emerged from the turbolift onto the bridge, panting from his exertion, and he saw the *Hudson* on the viewscreen.

"Well done, Number One," said Picard. "We've got the *Hudson* in our tractor beam and are pulling back to a safer position before we inspect her. Mr. Jelpn, can we get a reading on Data?"

At the ops console, the Deltan shook his head. "Negative, sir. If Commander Data is on that craft, he's completely inert."

Picard and Riker glanced uneasily at one another, not liking the sound of that conclusion. Deanna Troi rose from her chair and walked to Will's side, and she gently gripped his hand. She looked as if she was very relieved to see her *Imzadi* back in one piece.

"As soon as it's safe, bring the *Hudson* into the shuttlebay," ordered Picard. "Number One—"

"I'll go back down there," promised the first officer, heading for the turbolift. "And I'll report back as soon as we crack it open."

"Hurry," said Picard.

Will Riker entered the shuttlebay as technicians were using the tractor beam to draw the crippled shuttlecraft into the hangar. The *Hudson* dropped to the deck with a thud; the space doors closed with a softer noise. Riker and two technicians hurried to the hatch of the shuttle-craft. One of them put an electronic device on the hatch to open the lock. With a whoosh of air entering a vacuum, the hatch blew open.

Riker was the first to stick his head into the cabin, and he was astounded by what he did not find. Objects had been floating weightlessly, so the cabin was a mess—but there was no sign anywhere of Data. He stepped aside to let the technicians enter the shuttle-craft. One went to the pilot's console. The other went to the transporter pad at the rear of the craft.

With a scowl, Will tapped his combadge. "Riker to bridge."

"Go ahead, Number One."

"He's not here, sir," reported the first officer. "Data is not aboard the *Hudson.*"

After a moment, the captain ordered, "See what you can find out from the logs and transporter records. You may have to go back out there."

"Yes, sir," answered Riker. "I'll get the *Polo* ready for another trip. We'll find him, sir." He made the last promise with far more certainty than he felt.

Beverly Crusher stood in front of the sickbay doors with her arms crossed, guarding her inner sanctum. "I'm sorry, Jean-Luc, but you can't see La Forge. He just regained consciousness for a moment. Now he's sleeping again. His implants aren't functioning. Geordi is very weak—we nearly lost him. Only the residual oxygen in the shuttle saved him, and his EVA suit kept him from freezing."

"I know," said Picard with a troubled sigh. "But we've got to have some idea what happened to Data . . . where to look for him."

"I don't think Geordi could tell you that anyway," she answered, unmoved. "When he was conscious for a few seconds, he asked *me* where Data was. He's suffering from shock and maybe partial amnesia. I'd like to find Data as much as anyone, but badgering my patient won't help."

"I don't intend to badger him," said Picard carefully. However, it was clear that he wasn't going to be allowed to question La Forge right now, and needling Beverly was indeed futile.

The captain added, "All we know is that they suffered some kind of power failure near the *Calypso*. It may have been one of the anomalies—we don't know. We don't know when or how the *Calypso* was destroyed, or what became of Data."

"Try back in an hour," Crusher suggested. "He may be stronger then." With that, the doctor ducked inside her sickbay and was gone, leaving the captain standing alone in the corridor.

His combadge chirped. "Picard here."

"Captain," said Christine Vale, "Captain Leeden replied to your message. She wants to know how the *Calypso* was destroyed, and she wants physical proof that it *was* the *Calypso*. Samples of the wreckage, for instance, since other ships that have been reported destroyed were found intact later."

The captain scowled at the request and then said pleasantly, "Please give Captain Leeden the coordinates where we found the *Hudson* and the remains of the *Ca-lypso*. Tell her we'd be happy if she collected samples of the wreckage, but our priority is finding Commander Data. When we do, perhaps he can tell us what happened to both shuttlecraft."

"Aye, sir," she answered. "Captain Leeden also said the *Juno* is back to full impulse power. Vale out."

Leeden was right about one thing, mused Picard: The war still continued in this graveyard of lost ships, where it was hard to put the past behind them. He was beginning to think the Rashanar Battle Site should become a vast funeral pyre. Let it burn to the point where there was nothing left to interest anyone. Nothing left but ashes.

"Mr. Data! Calling Mr. Data! Please report to the Preparatory Center," announced a voice over the loud-speaker in the Starfleet Academy cafeteria. Data looked up with interest from his meal, of which he had eaten a small amount out of politeness. The android rose stiffly to his feet and looked at his fellow entrants in the Preparatory Program—all potential cadets, even if only a small percentage would make it all the way through four years of training. Such a proud, eager group, brimming with optimism, which was the first human quality Data was trying to master. But it was very difficult not to look facts squarely in the face and make a dispassionate decision, unclouded by emotion. He wondered how humanoids juggled these two conflicting objectives: optimism and accuracy.

He nodded to the youthful visitors, half of whom

were not humans but other Federation species. "I must go take my examination," he said.

They mustered friendly smiles for the android, although most of them held him in awe. "Good luck!" called one or two of them. "Nice to meet you!" said others. He couldn't understand how "luck" would help him pass an examination unless he actually knew the answers. They offered him their hands, which he remembered to grasp, limply, so as not to hurt them. He cocked his head, wondering why some of them were acting as if they would never see him again. Of course, he concluded, they weren't sure they were going to pass the entrance exams.

The android walked briskly to the office, ignoring the curious glances sent his way. He was unique, even in a school with a hundred and fifty different species. Data wished to make the cadets and potential cadets feel comfortable with him, but he had no idea how to do so.

Without making a false step in his brisk stride, the android soon reached the domed building in the northeast quadrant of campus which housed the Preparatory Program. He was met in the lobby by Director Edwin Craycroft, a gray-haired civilian who was the link between the general population and the cadets and faculty. Craycroft wasn't waiting to meet Data by himself—he had a female Starfleet admiral with him, albeit a rear admiral with only two pips on her collar.

Data stood crisply at attention. He looked at the two human educators expectantly. "Hello, Director Craycroft."

"Thank you for coming on such short notice," replied Craycroft with a warm smile. "This is Admiral

Alynna Nechayev, who has some interest in your application to Starfleet Academy. Can we go over to my office to discuss this?"

Data cocked his head, because it was obvious that they could. When humans stated the obvious, such as "It's a nice day," that was usually some kind of pleasantry. "Yes, let us go to your office," agreed Data.

The director's office was a shrine to Starfleet Academy, thought Data; it was full of trophies, awards, medals, holophotos, diplomas, and all the paraphernalia of academia.

Director Craycroft went behind his desk and pointed to the guest chairs for his visitors. "Please have a seat."

Admiral Nechayev sat down, as did Data, even though he had no physical necessity to sit down. "Am I to take my entrance examination in your office?"

"No, Mr. Data." Director Craycroft sat behind his desk and folded his hands before him. "From the tests you've already taken, we have no doubt that you will pass deductive reasoning, mathematics, and all the scholastic sections of the exam. What will take the other applicants two days to finish will probably take you two minutes. But the physical and psychological tests are another matter, only because they're not written with someone like you in mind. For example, we try to see how you will handle stress, except you don't get stressed."

Data nodded his head. "I do not understand what purpose stress serves."

"Neither do the rest of us," said Nechayev with a smile. Smiles did not appear to come easily to the youthful admiral, and Data could empathize with her on an intellectual level.

Looking troubled, the director continued, "A lot of the questions would be meaningless to you, asking you to evaluate emotional responses which you don't have. Plus your social development is like . . ."

"That of a child," said Data, supplying the analogy he had heard most frequently.

Admiral Nechayev cleared her throat and sat forward. "May I interject, Director?" With relief, Craycroft nodded and sat back in his chair.

The admiral peered curiously at the android. "At last there's someone around here I can speak to bluntly. Mr. Data, Starfleet has regulations to cover almost everything, but not you. We can dispense with the examinations and admit you to the Academy without them. Did you know that?"

"Yes, regulation two-ninety-four, section six, paragraph two," he answered, "although that regulation is generally invoked only during wartime and times of personnel shortages."

"I see you know about it," said Nechayev. "The entrance committee could do that, plus we would like to put you on an accelerated track with credit for individual study. But all of this would make you different from the others."

Data cocked his head and said, "I am already different from the others."

Suddenly this scene from his memory banks was swirled away in the sparkling, debris-filled darkness of space. Data had the sensation that he was drifting, suspended, and not altogether functional. He tried to run diagnostics on his neural network and positronic brain, but instead he kept revisiting scenes from his past. There was the day he joined the *Enterprise* at Farpoint, and Commander Riker apparently insulted him, although he still couldn't understand the insult. *I* am *machine*, he told himself.

Floating here in the serenity of space, among distant starships that seemed oddly silent, reminded him of the last time he had been abandoned, at Omicron Theta, when Dr. Soong had explained that Data would have to stay on the colony even if it was destroyed by the Crystalline Entity.

"We can't take a chance that you will turn out like Lore," said his creator as he checked the settings on the protective chamber. "Now I'm going to have to turn you off, Data."

"I understand," replied the android, not understanding that he didn't really understand. Dr. Soong looked lovingly at him, a tear rolling down his familiar face. Although Data did not feel anything at the time, he had since gained an emotion chip. This had allowed him to appreciate the pain of Dr. Soong's sacrifice, plus his own feeling of absence. Reliving this core incident made Data realize that in his short but eventful life he had suffered losses similar to those known by humans.

I should not be dismayed now that I am about to be abandoned again, thought the android, *because I have experienced many noteworthy events, from physical love to comprehending a joke. Life has truly been "good."*

As he bobbed in space, the android's positronic brain relived the death of Tasha Yar, an event that had jarred him to another level of understanding. With his emotion chip turned on, it was difficult even to think about her murder. Now he realized that he was experiencing these memories for a reason. The android had often heard of a human's life "passing before his eyes" when he was dying, but he had never thought he would experience it. His neural nets were trying to recover from the trauma he had suffered, which had apparently left him in this predicament. Data decided that his long-term memory was checking itself and seemed to be functional, but in the short term he was deficient.

While scattered memories sifted through his damaged circuits—Lore, Lal, the poker games—the android gazed around at his surroundings. This space had no air but a substantial amount of gravity. Data felt certain he was being pulled toward some large object. He looked for a celestial body that might be exerting gravitational force; all he saw was a blackened nacelle from an *Ambassador*-class starship. The *Seattle,* he thought, remembering ships that had been lost in the Battle of Rashanar. The *Seattle* was a once-retired Starfleet vessel that had been recommissioned for the Dominion War. She hadn't stood much of a chance against hardcore Jem'Hadar, as evidenced by her blasted hull, which spun slowly about half a kilometer closer to the center. A severed Jem'Hadar warship near the *Seattle*'s hull told Data that the *Ambassador*-class relic hadn't gone peacefully.

Yes, the Battle of Rashanar, he thought, realizing that

his memory dump was almost at the present day. The mission, the shuttlecraft *Hudson* . . . Geordi. *Where is my friend?* If Geordi were orbiting out here in the void among these junks, he would be dead, he concluded.

The android twisted his upper body and neck to get a look in every direction. All he saw was tangled metal and nebulas of rubble that had once been great starships. Then a swirl of activity caught his attention just beyond the Jem'Hadar ship, and he peered closer. *The vortex,* Data concluded, *an offshoot of the gravity sink* Suddenly, the Jem'Hadar wreck picked up speed as if it were still active. It swerved toward the whirlpool of spinning remains, drastically altering its orbit. Data watched with fascination as the Jem'Hadar vessel was sucked into the swirling mass of the vortex, where it was shredded into a sea of confetti in a matter of seconds.

We are all being swept into it, concluded the android, *myself and these other abandoned machines, and there is nothing we can do about it.*

Chapter Ten

"THAT'S THE VIP GANGPLANK from the *Calypso*," said Will Riker, surveying a batch of salvage parts spread out before him in transporter room three. Hovering over the table were two visitors to the *Enterprise,* Captain Leeden and her first officer, a hulking Antosian named Oierso. All of them peered and poked at a mess of space junk that had just been transported from the *Juno* and spread out on the table.

"There's nothing to identify it absolutely as being from the *Calypso*," responded Captain Leeden.

"There aren't a lot of shuttlecraft that have VIP gangplanks," said Riker with a boyish grin. He was using his most potent charms on the captain of the *Juno,* but she was impervious to them so far.

"Very few Starfleet shuttlecraft do, but others

might," she pointed out. She reached for a singed nozzle with a melted O-ring around it. "What about this?"

Before Riker could answer, Oierso cut in, "Captain, we've checked that out, and it's a nozzle head from a gas combiner. It could be from the *Calypso,* or just about any Starfleet vessel. That's the same for all this debris, but there were biological components in the wreckage—Androssi DNA, an unknown number of dead."

"There, you see," said Riker. "It had to have been the *Calypso,* although that doesn't explain what happened We may never know—right now, we'd settle for finding Commander Data."

"Well, I'm not settling for that," replied Captain Leeden. "We still don't know if this is the ship that fired on the *Juno,* or whether it is indeed the *Calypso.* All of the Androssi ships are combined from something else, so it's hard to prove anything. Without proof, we're operating on wishful thinking."

"Commander Riker," said his counterpart from the *Juno,* "what have you learned from the shuttlecraft you recovered? And your patient?"

Riker stood to meet the Antosian's height. "That patient is our chief engineer, and we hope to hear something about him before you go. As for the shuttlecraft *Hudson,* it met with some severe electromagnetic shock and had all logs and sensor records wiped. It was as dead as those hulks out there ravaged in the war."

Captain Leeden's stiff command style softened a bit, and Riker thought he saw a glint of hopelessness in her dark eyes. She said, "Commander, you once asked me how ships were destroyed in the boneyard, and you thought it odd that I couldn't tell you for certain in some cases. Now do you realize that I've been telling you and Captain Picard the truth the whole time? There are anomalies out there that have never been seen before or will be again."

"Of course," he answered. "I'm not sure our current policy is meeting the needs of the Rashanar Battle Site."

Captain Leeden threw back her head and laughed. "Apparently, you didn't read the reports I've been writing, going back months. My scientific curiosity passed away a long time ago. Now we're just hanging on to our basic mission as stated by Starfleet . . . to recover bodies before the scavengers can get them. You saw the way the Androssi tried to haul off a whole ship, without any concern for the dead."

Riker's combadge beeped, and a clipped voice said, "Picard to Riker."

"Yes, Captain," answered the first officer, "any news?"

"La Forge is now awake and can talk," said the captain with obvious pleasure. "Are our guests still with you?"

"Yes, Captain, shall I bring them to sickbay?"

Picard replied, "Go ahead, Number One. All should have the understanding that La Forge is weak and cannot undergo much questioning."

Two minutes later, Riker escorted Leeden and her first officer of the *Juno* into sickbay. After perfunctory introductions, Beverly Crusher took over.

"I will cut off this interview the moment I feel my patient needs rest or is overly agitated," the doctor warned them all. "And I'm watching his vital signs."

She turned to Leeden and Oierso and added, "You

should realize that Commander La Forge is blind. He normally has sight with his ocular implants, but they were knocked out along with the shuttlecraft's systems. We can't replace them until he's stronger, so please don't all talk to him at once. If he doesn't know you, you should identify yourself when you speak."

Leeden nodded and said, "Let's see him."

With Crusher leading the way, the two captains and two first officers entered the examination room where the engineer was resting in bed. Bandages were wrapped around his eyes. Upon hearing them, La Forge sat up and asked, "Any word about Data?"

Crusher looked to Riker, who shook his head. "Not yet," Will answered. "How are you doing, Geordi?"

The engineer sat back in bed with a sigh. "I've been better," he answered. "But the doctor says I should be as good as new in a couple of days. It seems she has a spare pair of ocular implants."

"You never know when you'll need them," said the doctor with a fleeting smile.

Captain Picard crossed to La Forge's bed and put his hand on the engineer's shoulder. "Don't worry, we're going to find him. I've got Captain Leeden and Commander Oierso from the *Juno* with me, and I think we'd all like to hear exactly what happened to you and Data. First of all, did you see the *Calypso?*"

"See it?" asked Geordi with a bemused tone. "We saw *two* of them. Two yachts, although they were identical down to scratches on the new paint and photon torpedoes added by the Androssi. When we chased them, everything was cat-and-mouse. That was the first good look we got at the shuttlecraft. We were fairly certain it was the craft that fled when the *Juno* took damage."

Geordi sighed and cleared his dry throat. "That was the last time we saw it, too. Moments after we got close to the two yachts, our power went. Data shut off . . . everything died. I lost my implants. Luckily I was wearing my environmental suit but loosened my helmet."

He grimaced as if recalling something painful. "I remember a high-pitched whine that sent me over the edge. That's all I remember, until I woke up here." The engineer tried to rub his eyes but encountered his bandage. He sighed and sat back in his bed.

Riker looked from Picard to their visitors, but nobody burst out laughing or looked as if they doubted Geordi's story. Leeden and her first mate were both good at poker faces, and they weren't revealing what they thought. Of course, this was the boneyard, and the standard for being normal was fairly low here. Sensors, vision, and one's own mind were likely to play tricks on everyone.

"Geordi," said Riker softly, "when we found you, we found the wreckage for one yacht, but not two. Any idea how it got destroyed or what happened to the other one?"

The engineer shook his head. "Data didn't believe me at first either, but I spotted them from a distance as being two identical ships. I guess we should have approached with more caution, but we couldn't believe it even when we were looking at it. Something around there wiped out all our circuits."

"Commander, this is Captain Leeden," said the captain. "Even if your story is entirely true, there's still an

Androssi ship at large. We have to stay vigilant and get them all. Just to be safe, the Ontailians have dispatched the *Vuxhal* to look for the ship that attacked us, if it's still around. They're also looking for Commander Data."

Riker frowned but didn't say a word. The more ships looking for Data, the better, but the Ontailians were too secretive and trigger-happy for his tastes.

"I don't think there's any point in tiring the commander further," said Picard. "Number One, I'll show our guests back to the shuttlebay. You can stay with Geordi a bit longer."

"Thank you, sir," said Riker.

After they bid cordial good-byes, he and the doctor were alone with Geordi. The engineer shook his head and mused, "I don't know what's going on out there. How could Data get out of the shuttlecraft, when he was turned off and so was everything else?"

"The same way we got *you* out of the shuttle," answered Beverly Crusher. "At a short distance, he could have been transported out."

Riker paced around sickbay, grumbling, "So there were two *Calypso*-like yachts. One blew up, and the other took Data?"

"That theory supports the facts," said Crusher. "We know it's the Androssi, who are very inventive."

"If I were the Androssi," said Riker, "I'd get far away from the boneyard. Captain Leeden and her Ontailian allies are out for blood."

"And Data might be with them, but where?" asked Dr. Crusher. She peered at Geordi's vital signs over his bed, as if the answer could be found in the colorful charts and graphs.

Data felt a burst of heat as he floated in the chill of space. It revived him from another blackout. He didn't know whether to be more concerned about the heat that shouldn't be here or the fact that he had spontaneously turned off once again. Only this time his whole memory wasn't wiped, just the time he had been inactive. Looking around, he quickly understood the cause of both conditions when he saw the captain's yacht, the *Calypso,* hovering only about fifty meters behind him.

It was difficult to turn around while weightless in space, so Data had to crane his neck a bit more than usual. The *Calypso* was just as he and Geordi had seen it in duplicate during their earlier encounter. He ought to remember, because it was the last thing he had seen before ending up here, being swept toward the vortex. Technically, the spacecraft was probably modified enough to be called an Androssi ship, thought Data, especially with the added weapons. He wondered if they had stolen him and then abandoned him, or perhaps they were about to salvage him. Either way, it was some progress in understanding what had befallen him.

Time passed floating in the stillness, with flashes of energy searing the blackness every few seconds. The Androssi ship showed no interest in salvaging him or destroying him. It was just sitting there, minimal running lights and activity. He speculated on whether they were using him as bait to lure a Federation ship. Even armed, the shuttlecraft was no match for anything but the smallest of craft, so that made no sense. Data kept feeling he was unavoidably short of information. If he were human, he would use his intuition to understand what was happening to him. Turning on his emotion chip would put him in touch with those areas of deductive reasoning beyond mere logic, he reasoned, and it might also speed up his recovery.

To do his job efficiently, Data normally left his emotion chip off, but he wasn't exactly doing his job at the moment. He knew he would be afraid once he activated the chip, but reason told him that his predicament was very grave. Fear was an appropriate response and would serve to motivate him. In days, perhaps hours, he would be swept into the vortex surrounding the gravity sink. His only apparent salvation was an enemy ship, and they were ignoring him. Data felt he needed an edge to deal with this situation, and the chip was all he had at his disposal.

He activated it, and was at once flooded with concern for La Forge. He yelled, "Geordi! Geordi! Where are you!" Twisting his torso and head as best he could, the android searched in vain for their shuttlecraft, until he remembered that he had looked before, and it wasn't here. Whatever Geordi's fate, it was different from his own. Yelling in space was the epitome of pointlessness. *Just worry about yourself,* he concluded.

That didn't bring much peace to the android's mind, because he was clearly a goner. If he were a humanoid, he'd be dead already; since he was a machine, he was just like the rest of this abandoned space junk. As he got closer to the gravity sink, he would smash into other wreckage and no doubt be torn to pieces. That would be his fate if the Androssi didn't salvage him and use him for scrap metal. *I've got to get some help!* he decided. He waved futilely at the yacht, but the Androssi must have been looking elsewhere.

A minute later, Data realized where the Androssi were looking. A big Ontailian cruiser—the heavy version, which looked like a shark's fin—came gliding toward the yacht. Debris glistened off its shields like water on the fin of a real shark. He remembered that the only such ship operating in the battle zone was the *Vuxhal.* The mammoth triangular warship dwarfed the *Calypso* in much the same way that the *Calypso* dwarfed Data.

Will the Ontailians fire at the Androssi? Data wondered anxiously. He would no doubt be fried in the crossfire if the two armed vessels went at each other. The android waved and yelled frantically at the Ontailian cruiser, although he knew logically that it was pointless. If they even saw him, they wouldn't care—their attention was on the Androssi.

Finally the Ontailian cruiser fired phasers at the smaller ship, barely missing Data. He screwed his eyes shut, expecting to die, but the hostilities ended abruptly. When he cautiously opened his eyes, he saw that the Ontailian ship was dead in space, no running lights or weapons—nobody home. *Just like Geordi and me on the* Hudson, he thought with alarm.

The Androssi craft edged closer to the Ontailian vessel until they were almost nose to nose. Then a strange beam—broad and whitish blue—issued from the Androssi yacht and engulfed the larger cruiser. The space dust was illuminated in this beam, and it looked like a twinkling cloud was engulfing the spacecraft. Terrified but fascinated, the android watched this beam as it seemingly explored every centimeter of the Ontailian ship, making an exhaustive scan. He didn't remember the *Calypso* having any kind of sensors that worked like that. If the Androssi had such advanced technology, why were they bothering to steal from everyone else?

They are not Androssi, Data thought suddenly, *and not Starfleet either.* He had no proof of this theory, except for their strange actions, but he had confidence in his emotion-inspired intuition. Unfortunately, this brought a new wave of fear rushing over Data, and he tried to curl into a nondescript ball, so as not to be noticed by the mystery craft.

The android was a captive audience for when the yacht began to expand in size. The change wasn't instantaneous; it was like a flower opening its petals— something small and insignificant becoming impossibly grand and beautiful. The potential was there all the time, thought Data, it just needed an idea of what to become. The yacht's red coloring turned to silver, like the hull of the Ontailian cruiser, and its shape twisted into a fanciful fin, just like the cruiser.

It is a mimic, thought Data. Whatever the *Calypso* was before, it had now studied the Ontailian cruiser and was turning into a copy of it, down to the smallest and largest detail. As the android watched this incredible transformation, he began to doubt his senses. He almost deactivated his emotion chip. The fear was mounting, twisting in his gut. *Hang in there,* he told himself, *because this explains how you saw two identical yachts. Geordi and I weren't imagining that either.*

This could still be an illusion, the android cautioned himself. *Maybe it's a gigantic holographic projection to disguise the fact that it's really an Androssi garbage scow under there!* Whether the mimicry was fake or genuine, it was an excellent job, Data had to admit. The process seemed almost mechanical, like the way a scorpion stalked and subdued an insect. Paralyze your prey, absorb it, process it. Was there motivation here or a mindless automation? Why paralyze a ship only to mimic it . . . unless the intention was to take its place?

Or to cause confusion in a battle.

Data was now terrified for the safety of the *Enterprise,* but he was entranced by the marvel in front of him. Despite gnawing dread, he watched until the transformation was total and complete. There were two Ontailian heavy crusiers, identical down to dents, oil smears, and racing stripes. Both appeared dead in space, floating only a few meters apart, like some monstrous mirror image. Once again, he wished he were seeing an illusion.

Data looked away from the jarring sight and tried to reason it out. He and Geordi had come upon this transformation toward the end of the process and hadn't known what they were seeing. The mimic vessel must have found their shuttlecraft uninteresting, or it couldn't change into another form after having just mutated. So it had only paralyzed the *Hudson,* nothing more. It stood to reason that this mimic was responsible for putting him out here in cold space, Data decided. Maybe it identified him as some kind of machine, beamed him out of the shuttle, and studied him; after that, it had deemed him unworthy and cast him out.

He was blinded by a flash of light, and the mimic ship began to move away from its paralyzed prey at the center of the graveyard. Data winced, certain he was going to be destroyed, but the big silvery fin veered away from him and started a long, graceful arc. Once again, he had been spared by the imitation ship. If he survived, he had to be able to tell Captain Picard what he had seen.

The Dominion was the enemy in the Battle of Rashanar, he thought suddenly. *The Founders are shapeshifters. Could they have created a shapeshifting spacecraft?*

That idea only tripled his fear, especially for the *Enterprise.* Getting control of his emotions, Data decided that he might not be able to save himself, but he couldn't let the *Enterprise* fall into this doppelgänger's trap. He began to wave at the Ontailian vessel, hoping that some member of the crew was still alert; he was staring at the triangular ship when a gigantic fireball erupted. The Ontailian cruiser exploded into a billion bits, and all of them seemed to fly at once toward Data. He was pummeled by molten metal and flaming debris, and a large chunk of wreckage smashed into him like a battering ram.

Propelled by fiery rubble, screaming with terror, Data went spinning head over heels toward the swirling maw of the gravity vortex.

Chapter Eleven

FLIPPING END OVER END through space, Data sailed toward the whirling maelstrom that marked the edge of the gravity dump in the center of the graveyard. As the android tore through space, crashing into jagged debris from the *Vuxhal,* fear gripped his throat like a garrote. He thought about turning off his emotion chip, but what good would that do? Emotions or no, he had to act quickly to save himself.

Spinning within his reach was the large chunk of hull that had struck him. The rest of the blasted Ontailian ship flew in a million different directions. This could be a boon in disguise, thought the android. Mustering his superior reactions and strength, Data lunged with both hands and grabbed the spinning chunk of metal; it was like grabbing a whirring propeller. His body was wrenched into a new flight path that was part his momentum and part the rubble's. As he hoped, the spinning abated, and he hung on to the chunk of metal as if it were a giant manta ray dragging him under water.

Data finally tucked the chunk of debris under his arm, which freed his other hand, and he grabbed another good-sized piece flying in the other direction. This altered his course again, and he used the two large pieces as shields to ward off the smaller hits that threatened to puncture him. After getting his confidence, the android performed this maneuver at blazing speeds, moving from one chunk of wreckage to another, changing his course each time. It was like jumping from rock to rock in midstream. He could see his destination just ahead, the blackened hull of the *Seattle,* the only *Ambassador*-class starship to perish here.

He swam through the flow of burning wreckage, grabbing and riding each piece that might help him move toward his goal. The *Seattle* was in an altogether different orbit, slow and stately. Data veered recklessly toward it, propelled by his momentum and burning hunks of the *Vuxhal.*

The scorched hull loomed closer. He could see the debris from the Ontailian vessel silently pummeling the old hulk. Data realized that he was going to pass close to the stern. He would have only a nanosecond to catch a handhold or foothold. As he spotted a twisted flange jutting from the stern, he pushed off his metal shields, twisting and thrusting even while crashing into wreckage. With the tips of his fingers, Data grabbed the jagged flange and hung on to the *Seattle* while sheets of debris pelted him. Since he was weightless, he pulled himself easily along the skin of the charred ruin, ducking from the constant rain of rubble.

Moments later, he reached a jagged hole in the underbelly of the main hull. He pulled himself through it without looking. Once inside, he found himself in a dark corridor filled with a blizzard of sparkling metal flecks. Where he touched them, the sparkly bits shot off in whatever direction he pushed them, just like a miniature version of the flying debris outside. Data let out a sigh of relief, and glanced at his surroundings. A direct hit had fused almost everything into molten lumps, but it looked like the maintenance shaft for the tractor beam emitter.

He made note of emitter panels and auxiliary stations, even though they were too badly damaged to be useful. If his memory banks were intact, he knew the emergency battle bridge was near here—only one deck up. That was one of the better-protected sections of this older-designed ship, thought Data.

He was optimistic as he found a Jefferies tube and climbed to the next deck up. Darkness was no problem for the android. He broke through a dented door to enter the battle bridge. Once inside, Data's hope sank as he looked around at the devastated keep inside the bowels of the starship. It hadn't been destroyed by enemy fire but by illicit salvagers, who had made off with everything of worth. Looking at the ripped-up panels and consoles, he understood how Captain Leeden could call them so many derogatory names.

It looked bad, but it wasn't hopeless. With his internal energy supply and connection ports, all he needed was a link to a subspace relay connected to a transceiver assembly. There had to be a combination like that still intact on the ship. Those circuits were usually buried deep in the infrastructure. It didn't appear as if the scavengers had dug very deeply. They preferred to cut the wiring and connectors, leaving them behind while they took the bare units. Since subspace communications relied on relays to boost the signal at every step, all he needed was enough wiring to reach one relay. With power from his own cells, he could transmit a signal strong enough to reach the nearest buoy outside. Then it would be relayed to the next and the next, getting stronger with each iteration. This wouldn't be a long message, thought Data, just a standard distress call. The *Seattle* was clearly in the *Enterprise*'s records, even if its position had changed.

It took Data several minutes of patient testing to find the circuit he needed to reach the nearest subspace relay inside the ship. Just as he was about to move on to the next crucial step, the ruined hull was jolted hard and swerved roughly to port. Data banged into the bulkhead and felt the unmistakable pull of gravity, which was not a good thing on a ghost ship in the center of the graveyard.

When he found himself getting afraid, Data reluctantly turned off his emotion chip. He'd gotten all the intuition and insight he needed, and now he had to work efficiently. No doubt enough debris had struck the *Seattle*'s hull to change its course and send it swerving closer to the gravity vortex. The android poked his head and shoulders into a ravaged access panel, grabbed a fistful of wires, and set to work.

From the viewscreen on the bridge of the *Enterprise,* Captain Leeden looked suspiciously at Captain Picard and the bridge crew. The *Juno* was just off to starboard, so the standard frequency was strong, with only mild interference. "Are you saying we should stop recovering bodies?" she asked.

Picard maintained a conciliatory tone as he addressed his counterpart, because he knew this was a delicate issue with her. "As you told us when we first arrived," he began, "the Rashanar Battle Site is becoming more dangerous with the passage of time, and we aren't getting the resources we need to do half our job. These derelicts are inherently dangerous, and even more so when you consider the anomalies which we've yet to explain."

"How do you propose to keep the scavengers from walking away with everything?" Leeden asked.

Choosing his words carefully, the captain answered, "I will propose to Starfleet that we have a large memorial service. We would invite all the species who perished in this battle, from both sides. Then we should back off and utterly vaporize every old derelict in the boneyard. That would remove the lure for the salvagers."

Captain Leeden slowly considered the idea. "This mass destruction would be tasteful, I presume."

"It may take days for every species to have their say," answered Picard, "but then we can tear down this haunted cemetery."

"I think that may be the best way out of a hopeless situation," answered Captain Leeden. "However, in the meantime we should both join the Ontailian task force covering the gateways. Let's cut the Androssi off before they can get away."

"We're still looking for Data near the center," answered Picard. "Once we resolve what happened, we will be happy to help."

Leeden shook her head sadly. "You're the one who told me that he was forsaking the dead in order to protect the living. I'm rather disappointed, Picard. Leeden out."

Abruptly the transmission ended, and Picard's shoulders slumped. He supposed that he wasn't following his own advice, but there was a difference between these dismembered derelicts and an officer who had been missing for only a few hours. When that officer was Data, his odds of surviving went up considerably.

The captain watched stoically as the *Juno* pulled back, fired impulse engines, and banked gracefully into a littered section of the boneyard. They were headed for the outer belt, leaving the *Enterprise* as close to the center of the battle site as they dared to go, along with the *Vuxhal* and whatever shuttlecraft were still on patrol.

He tapped his com panel and said, "Bridge to Riker, are you ready to take the *Polo* out again?"

"Affirmative," answered the first officer. "We've got a possible lead with some vapor trails we picked up near buoy twenty-six."

Vapor trails, thought Picard. It felt as if they were clinging to nothing but vapors. "Our records show two more shuttlecraft crews will be reporting for duty in—"

"Captain!" interrupted Lieutenant Vale, staring at her tactical console. "There's a distress signal coming from the middle of the boneyard. The source is on a derelict . . . the *Seattle.*"

He tapped his com panel again and said, "Number One, we've just gotten a better lead—stand by for launch. Picard out." He turned to Christine Vale at the tactical station. "Is the *Seattle* intact?"

"No, sir, it's in several pieces," answered Vale. "It's near the gravity sink and classified as too dangerous to board."

"Conn, set course," ordered Picard, "the last known position of the *Seattle.*" Seeing the shocked look on Vale's face, he added, "Don't worry about the warning buoys—we're not going to be there long."

Cautiously, Data made his way back through the sundered starship *Seattle* to the gash in her underbelly where he had entered. Braving the debris smacking against the scorched hull, he stuck his head out the gash and looked around. The vortex appeared so close that he could touch it. The battered husk of the *Seattle* arced toward destruction on an erratic, decaying orbit. Other hulks raced beside them, banging into each other like fanciful vehicles in a mad race. Data felt like he was inside a tornado with the wind blowing in a hundred different directions with a dozen structures whirling all around. In such chaos, the silence was eerie. He reactivated his emotion chip to experience every moment of this spectacular scene. It could possibly be the last thing he ever saw. He could be emotional about that.

This is life at its best, thought Data, *exhilarating and terrifying!* The unadulterated fear tasted like a rare wine, and he appreciated every drop. He had done all he could to get help; now he was dependent upon his comrades. So Data could only watch and shudder as other wrecks were ground to pieces in the looming maelstrom. He estimated that he had less than a minute before he and the charred hull suffered the same fate, but it had been a good existence.

Something came streaking out of the glittering blackness of the graveyard, which wasn't unusual, but the object had a rope attached to the other end. This high-powered harpoon struck the hull perfectly amidships, and the old spacecraft shuddered as some kind of charge exploded. At once, the wreck changed course and was hauled rudely backward out of orbit. This brought it into contact with a ton of rubble, and Data had to duck back inside to save his head. After a few moments, he took one more peek outside to try to catch a glimpse of his saviors. He wasn't aware of any Federation ship in the area which had such harpoons. That was a salvager's tool.

He caught a glimpse of an ungainly vessel that looked better suited to ride ocean waves than cosmic currents. It was covered with so many harpoon guns, winches, antennas, and valves that it looked like a porcupine. Its winches worked slowly, and the old hulk groaned with every meter it was dragged against its will from the gravity sink. Finally they got about two kilometers away from the vortex. Data was feeling considerable relief. He hoped to be able to personally thank his rescuers, but the exploding barb on the harpoon suddenly compressed and withdrew, leaving the blasted hull to drift on its own. Just as quickly, the salvage spacecraft slipped away into the cover of a cloud of plasma.

A moment later, Data saw why his rescuers had fled: the *Enterprise* glided into view, stopping just outside the worst of the debris field. Still the junk popped and sizzled off the starship's hull, making it look like a fireworks display. He wanted to signal them that he was aboard the hulk, so he propelled himself out the gash and caught the jagged edge with his foot. Hanging upside down to their perspective, the android waved his arms frantically.

Two crewmembers in EVA suits, wearing jetpacks on their backs, emerged from a hatch on the underbelly of the saucer section. Pulling a tether line, they flew across the expanse that separated Data from the *Enterprise,* and they secured the line to his waist. He would be able to hold it, but he cooperated and said nothing. Thus secured, the android was reeled into an airlock, with his rescuers flying protectively behind him. The outer hatch was quickly closed, shutting off the rain of debris pelting the *Enterprise.*

Riker and Deanna Troi rushed forward to embrace Data, and the android grinned with happiness. "We must leave this area," he said. "A mimic . . . a shapeshifter . . . It is out there!"

"Do you have your emotion chip turned on?" asked Troi with a smile.

"Yes!" he answered, looking around worriedly. "Where is Geordi? Is he all right?"

"He's fine," answered Riker. "We can't leave just yet, Data, because there's an Androssi ship in the area. They ran as soon as we arrived."

"They saved my life," said Data. "I would be ground up in the vortex if they had not pulled me to safety. They must have intercepted my distress signal."

Riker nodded somberly and relayed this information to the captain. While they conversed, Deanna Troi put her arm around Data's shoulder and said, "We thought we had lost you for good."

"*I* thought I had been lost for good," he answered with tremendous relief. "What I have seen out there, Counselor . . . it boggles the mind. We are in grave danger."

"We've been in grave danger since we got here," answered Troi.

Data nodded urgently. "Yes, but it is worse than we thought. Are you sure everyone is all right?"

Before Troi could reassure him again, Will Riker ended his conversation with the bridge. "Thank you, Captain. Riker out," he said.

With a smile, the first officer turned to Data and announced, "We'll leave the Androssi vessel alone, although there will probably be hell to pay for that later. We should get back to a level-three buoy, anyway. Are you ready to go to the bridge to brief the captain?"

"Yes! Let us hurry," urged Data, pushing them toward the exit.

*　　*　　*

Captain Picard listened intently to a tale he would have doubted only a week ago, but a week in the Rashanar Battle Site had broadened his perspective. He glanced at the viewscreen on the bridge, hoping that nothing was sneaking up on them. "So the real *Vuxhal* has been destroyed," concluded the captain, "and this replicated ship is out there . . . somewhere?"

"That is correct," said Data with a nod. "We must not come in contact with this mimic ship at close range for even an instant. If we do, all systems will be shut down by what I theorize is a directed-energy weapon. After that, the ship is programmed to scan its prey and duplicate it. Both the *Calypso* and *Vuxhal* were destroyed, but had they been left intact, they would resemble these ships in the graveyard. In fact, the presence of this doppelgänger might explain much that has transpired here, going back to the Battle of Rashanar."

Captain Picard stroked his chin thoughtfully and asked, "Who built this ship? How does it work?"

"I have several theories and no proof," said Data, cocking his head. "I have observations . . . and intuition. It is possible this is a Dominion weapon which has outlived its usefulness. We know the Founders are shapeshifters who can exist in a communal state, the Great Link. Perhaps they created a shapeshifting spacecraft from their own protoplasm. Then again, perhaps this is an illusion generated by holographic emitters hidden inside the wrecks—an elaborate trick to drive us out. In the places this doppelgänger has been seen, sensor readings have been inaccurate."

Data considered another possibility. "Captain, you

called it a 'replicated' ship. Perhaps that is what it is. The transformation is rather slow and may be akin to our scanning and replicating process, only on a much larger scale. If one can replicate a coupling, why not an entire ship? I only know one thing for certain—the directed-energy beam is a genuine threat. It causes very little physical damage but is completely debilitating."

"La Forge has verified that," said the captain. He gazed at the viewscreen to see an energy spike ripple between two wretched hulks, as he thought about the greatest mystery of Rashanar. "Perhaps," he mused, "that is why the combatants all kept fighting to the end . . . why they died at their posts, without using escape pods. If there were one or two of these mimic ships in a large-scale battle, they could wreak incredible damage."

There was a silence on the bridge of the *Enterprise* as the senior staff considered this one answer amid a whole slew of new questions. The turbolift door opened; then Geordi La Forge stepped tentatively onto the bridge, looking down as if he were wearing someone else's spectacles. In place of his eyes were his typical ocular implants, and he grinned broadly when he caught sight of his missing comrade. "Data!" he called.

Data rushed to embrace his friend, and he looked as if he was going to cry. Finally the android regained his composure and said, "It is gratifying to see you again, Geordi."

"They told me you were back," said the beaming engineer. "I begged Dr. Crusher to let me get out of bed. If I stumble around, I'm just getting used to these new implants. Some of my synapses atrophied, so it will take a day or two to adjust."

"Data, bring La Forge up to date on what happened to you," ordered the captain. "Take an auxiliary console and see if you can expand on any of your theories about this mimic ship."

"Yes, Captain," answered the android. He turned to his best friend and said, "It was an emotional experience for me."

"I can tell," replied Geordi with a smile.

Riker leaned close to the captain and asked, "Do you want me to stay on bridge duty, sir?"

"Yes, Number One. You too, Counselor Troi." Jean-Luc Picard turned away from his officers and gazed at the viewscreen. For some moments, he watched the somber wrecks make their lonely treks through the graveyard, like ghosts who visited their old haunts and went up and down the stairs and hallways, pointlessly and for eternity. *Is there any way to exorcise the demons from here and send all these lost spirits to their just reward?* wondered Picard.

"Captain," called Christine Vale from her tactical station, "subspace message received from Captain Leeden on the *Juno.* She says an Androssi salvage ship came this way. Have we seen it?"

The captain glanced at Data, who gave him a hopeful expression. "Tell them the truth," answered Picard. "The Androssi ship saved Commander Data, and we were too near the gravity dump to follow them. So we let them go. Tell them we are investigating an anomaly which may explain the duplicate ships. We'll report to

the *Juno*'s position and let her talk to Data. That's all."
Picard turned toward his navigator and said, "Conn, set
course for the *Juno* and proceed with caution."

"Yes, sir," came the response from Kell Perim, efficiently working her board.

"Captain," said Deanna Troi, "I can't help but feel
that the Ontailians are mixed up in this, whatever it is.
It's not that I sense they're plotting against the Federation or anything, but they're hiding something. They
must know more than what they're telling us."

"Captain!" cut in Jelpn from his ops console. "The
sensor readings are erratic, however there seems to be a
ship on an intercept course with us."

"Put it on screen," Picard commanded, moving toward his front line of personnel, the helm and ops.

The Deltan shook his head. "I can't get a fix on it,
sir. But it's moving too quickly to be one of the shipwrecks. It's on a dead intercept course with us."

"Sir," called Vale at tactical. "The *Juno* and her task
force are making for our position, too . . . but it's not
the *Juno*. This one is coming from bearing twenty-six
mark one hundred seventy."

Picard felt a presence at his side; he turned to see
Data, looking intently over the Deltan's shoulder at the
ops console. "Mr. Jelpn, give up your station to Data."

"Yes, sir," answered the officer. The two ops officers
quickly switched places.

"I will try to clarify these readings," promised the
android, setting to work at blinding speed. Everyone on
the bridge seemed to hold their breath, waiting for the
android to interpret the jumbled sensor readings.

"Captain Picard," said Vale, squinting at her board, "now I'm getting a poor image of the approaching ship. It should improve as we get closer."

The captain motioned, and a static-laced picture appeared on the overhead viewscreen. Among the streaks, it was hard to pick out a spacecraft, but a silver fin glinted in a burst of electrical energy. With another jump in magnification, the fin became the triangular wedge of an Ontailian ship.

Data was the first one to gasp out loud. "Captain, there it is—the replica of the *Vuxhal.*"

"Are you sure?" asked Picard, his jaw tightening. "Whoever they are, hail them."

"I'm trying, sir," answered Vale, entering commands repeatedly. "They don't respond to any hail, RF or subspace."

"Conn, evasive maneuvers, pattern alpha-six," ordered Picard. "Modify it to avoid the wrecks."

"Yes, sir," answered Perim at the helm. The scenes on the viewscreen shifted erratically as the Trill took the *Enterprise* on a zigzagging course between the ghost ships. Every few seconds the screen caught the silver fin still trailing them like a shark. It executed their maneuvers more gracefully than they ever could.

"The mimic vessel has matched our course and is gaining on us," said Data worriedly. "We cannot outrun them in here. I estimate contact in one minute."

"You're sure that's the mimic ship?" asked Picard very calmly. "There can't be any mistake."

"That *is* the duplicate!" Data jumped to his feet. "Captain, I advise you to destroy it. Do not let it get close to us, or the *Enterprise* will be like all these other derelicts . . . dead bodies and smashed circuits."

The captain nodded sympathetically and said, "Data, turn off your emotion chip."

The android cocked his head, looked visibly calmer, and dropped his hand. "I have done so. Is that better?"

"Yes," answered the captain grimly. "Get back to your post and take over helm and tactical. Try to lose them."

"Yes, sir." The android slipped back into his seat and swiftly made modifications to give himself control of all three critical stations on the bridge. During the Dominion War at the height of battle, Data had often taken over all the stations and had executed the captain's commands faster than any combination of officers could do it. To Picard, this felt like those days—going into battle against an implacable, inscrutable foe.

A large chunk of debris glistened against the shields, blowing up with a bright explosion, but Data worked his controls unmindful of collisions large or small. Up and down, back and forth, the *Enterprise* lumbered, doing maneuvers no one had ever planned for a *Sovereign*-class starship.

"This reminds me of a movie I saw when I was a kid," said La Forge, gripping the arms of his chair. *"Mr. Toad's Wild Ride."*

"They are closing the distance," warned Data, "and we cannot lose them. You must destroy them before they get too close, Captain."

Picard frowned and asked, "Did you turn off your emotion chip?"

"I did, sir." Data turned to gaze pointedly at the captain. "My advice is perfectly rational. If this shapeshifting vessel were to successfully imitate the *Enterprise* and escape from Rashanar, it could wreak untold havoc in Federation space."

"Are they answering hails at all?" asked Picard.

Data shook his head. "No, sir."

Everyone on the bridge gazed at the viewscreen to see the silver wedge slicing through the glittering rubble, bearing down on them. A wild spike of energy suddenly cut across the bow of the *Enterprise,* and there was an explosion at a rear console.

"We cannot proceed at full impulse," said Data. He stared intently at the shifting screens of information on his console. "Captain, they will be in close range in fifteen seconds. The *Enterprise* will never be in greater danger than it is at this moment. I urge you to fire upon them."

The captain's lips thinned, and he shook his head. "I've never fired at another ship first—without provocation."

"In another ten seconds, I and every system on this ship will be inoperable," declared the android. "It is your decision, Captain."

His lips thinned, and Jean-Luc Picard watched as the elegant spacecraft bore down on them so serenely, so relentlessly.

"Five seconds until contact," warned Data.

Chapter Twelve

IN THE FINAL ANALYSIS, it was all a question of how much Captain Picard trusted the unique android who had served at his side selflessly and tirelessly for twelve years. Although Data wasn't human, there was no human being Picard trusted more than he trusted the childlike, manlike machine. Data never had hidden agendas or ulterior motives—his only concern was the welfare of his ship and his shipmates.

Making his decision, Captain Picard pointed to the sleek silver fin on the viewscreen. It seemed close enough to touch. "Data, target a brace of quantum torpedoes."

"Yes, sir," answered the android, his fingers a blur on his console. "Ready, sir."

"Fire!" barked the captain. If Data was wrong, they

had just fired upon a fellow member of the Federation without provocation.

It was difficult to spot the torpedoes streaking through the sea of debris and energy spikes, but they could see two bright explosions on the narrow hull of the Ontailian heavy cruiser. The *Vuxhal* duplicate was apparently caught by surprise with shields down, because explosions rippled all along her hull. The bridge crew watched in stunned silence as the elegant spacecraft blew apart, followed by interference and static that obscured the image on the viewscreen.

"Sir," said Data, "we have an audio transmission from Captain Leeden."

Picard replied, "Go ahead."

"Captain Picard!" Leeden's voice sounded shocked and surprised. "Have you gone insane? You just destroyed a defenseless ship which didn't even fire at you. The Ontailians are our *allies,* and we saw you fire on their flagship! This must be reported to Starfleet immediately. Picard, this is going to destroy all of the goodwill Starfleet has built up with the Ontailians!"

Picard was heartsick at the prospect, however slim, that he had made a mistake and destroyed the flagship of a friendly member world. The only justification that he had fired in self-defense was Data's extraordinary story, and they might never be able to back it up with proof.

"Lieutenant Perim," he said quietly, "you have the conn. Take us back to look for survivors and debris."

"Yes, sir," answered the Trill. The bridge was so

quiet that Picard could swear he heard every one of his subordinates breathing.

"Lieutenant Vale, you have tactical again," ordered Picard, marching toward his office. "I'll be in my ready room; patch Captain Leeden to me there. Number One, you have the bridge."

Upon reaching his office, Captain Picard sat down at his desk and tapped his com panel. "Picard here," he began. "Captain Leeden, your reactions are understandable, but we have very good reason to believe that the ship we fired upon was *not* the *Vuxhal*. The *Vuxhal* has been destroyed near the gravity sink—Commander Data was a witness. What we fired upon was a vessel which disables its intended victim with a directed-energy weapon, scans it, and transforms itself into a duplicate of the disabled ship. That is how Data and La Forge saw two identical versions of my missing yacht. I know there will be inquiries and a search for evidence—"

"Oh, there will be more than that, Picard," cautioned Captain Leeden. "While I'm talking to you, the Ontailians have surrounded me and are looking for revenge."

Picard sat upright in his chair. "We're on our way."

"Carefully please!" she asked. "Make your way toward me slowly, so as not to alarm anyone, and I'll try to placate them. This won't be easy by any stretch of the imagination. The Ontailians were already unsure about your participation since you reported one of their vessels destroyed that was in drydock."

"But maybe we've discovered what's been haunting

this place," he countered, "even going back to the war. Commander Data makes a very convincing case."

The *Juno*'s skipper sighed a heavy sigh. "Before anything else happens, I have to inform Starfleet. Leeden out."

Picard rose to his feet. The *Enterprise* was all right, and so were Data and the rest of the crew. However, their reputations would take a beating unless they produced some proof for Data's theory. An investigation would have to wait until they cleaned up the mess they had unwittingly stepped into.

Captain Picard marched back onto the bridge and said, "Lieutenant Perim, we have a change of course. Set course to rendezvous with the *Juno* and proceed with caution when ready."

"Yes, sir," answered the conn officer.

Picard sighed and looked at Riker. "Was there any sign of debris or survivors back there?"

"We're not sure," answered Riker with a scowl. "Sensors have been out of whack since we shot that thing. To tell you the truth, I'm glad we're getting out of this area. I'd love to be getting out of the boneyard for good."

The captain looked up at the viewscreen and saw they were moving at a slow but steady pace. "Data, can you get a visual on the *Juno* and the Ontailian ships around it?"

"I am working on it, sir," answered the android, plying his controls. "This is the best I can do."

Now the overhead screen showed the *Excelsior*-class starship surrounded by four Ontailian wedge spacecraft, which looked uncomfortably like smaller versions of the vessel they had just destroyed. Picard suddenly had a very bad feeling about the direction this chain of events was taking.

"Data, have we recalled all of our shuttlecraft?" he asked.

"Yes, sir," answered the android, "the *Raleigh* was the last one."

"Conn, take it up to half impulse," he ordered. "Tactical, hail the *Juno* and see if you can get at least audio." His subordinates fulfilled his orders without speaking, and an uneasy silence hung over the bridge of the *Enterprise*.

Finally Vale said, "Here's Captain Leeden."

"Picard," came the familiar but weary voice, "my negotiations with the Ontailians aren't going very well. I don't think they'll fire on the *Juno,* but you might want to think about leaving the boneyard."

"We're not turning tail and leaving you alone," replied the captain. "We'll be at your position in a few minutes."

On the viewscreen, two of the silver fins suddenly broke off from the squadron surrounding the *Juno,* and they darted off screen. "Picard," said Leeden in an urgent voice, "they've picked you up on sensors. Get out of here! I'll try to cover your escape."

"Captain Leeden!" exclaimed Picard. "If we can join forces—"

"I'm sorry, Captain," said Vale, "but she's broken off contact."

Events unfolding on the viewscreen explained why the *Juno* had ceased contact. The starship took off after the two Ontailian ships who had flown off moments earlier, and the other two Ontailian ships pursued the Starfleet vessel. The odds were poor for the *Juno*—four against one.

"Try to hail the Ontailians," ordered Picard. "We've got to stop this insanity."

"It must have been like this during the Battle of Rashanar," said Deanna Troi, gazing at the streaking ships on the screen. "The doppelgänger caused mistaken identity . . . deadly hostilities . . . vengeance with no thought of surrender. Ships were disabled by the force beam. Whole crews died while they were unconscious. No wonder there was no record of all this."

"Captain Picard!" called Vale. "Two of the Ontailian ships are within weapons range. The *Juno* is right behind them."

Suddenly a bright beam shot across their bow. This time it wasn't an errant bolt of energy. Both Ontailian ships began to pepper the *Enterprise* with beamed weapons. The craft shook from the pounding.

"Shields at seventy percent," reported Data.

"Hold your fire!" ordered Picard, shaking a fist with frustration. "Keep trying to hail them."

Vale shook her head. "I am, sir. No response."

The *Juno,* which had thus far been unscathed, opened phaser fire on the two Ontailian ships in the lead. In response, the two Ontailian ships trailing the *Juno* opened fire upon the larger vessel. Suddenly, the graceful starship was engulfed in deadly beams coming from four different angles, and the boneyard lit up with bright explosions and blistering ripples of energy.

"Target the Ontailians in the lead," Picard ordered reluctantly. "Fire at will."

"Yes, sir," answered Lieutenant Vale, jumping to the task.

Despite the entrance of the *Enterprise* into the melee, all four Ontailian ships pounded away at the hapless *Juno*. The wedge ships were more maneuverable in the crowded boneyard, and they were difficult to hit, whereas the *Juno* was a large sitting duck. In the space of a few seconds, the older starship took a tremendous beating, even with Picard rushing to its aid. Half of the *Enterprise*'s torpedoes struck decrepit wrecks that were in the way, adding to the chaos and wild arcs of energy. The hulks caught in the crossfire gave the *Enterprise* some protection from the Ontailians, but Leeden's starship was exposed, with nowhere to hide.

"Ready a tractor beam!" ordered Picard, thinking he could tow the *Juno* to safety outside the boneyard and spirit both of them into warp.

"Captain, the *Juno* is breaking apart," said Data dispassionately.

"Alert transporter room," said the captain. "Let's save as many as we can!"

Data shook his head. "Captain, there is too much interference to use transporters, and lowering our shields would be unwise."

Picard stared helplessly at the viewscreen, where he could see the burning starship careening out of control. Had the *Juno* been in normal space, she would have been able to escape to warp; in the graveyard, the majestic vessel collided with two old wrecks moments before she exploded in a fiery haze of destruction.

A stunned silence fell over the frantic activity on the bridge, and Captain Picard's stomach churned like an acid pit. The Ontailians' light cruisers were regrouping for a run at the *Enterprise.*

It was time to steal a trick from the Androssi. "Vent plasma," he ordered, "and ignite it with flares as we go to full impulse. Get us out of here, Mr. Perim, quickest route."

They vented a colorful cloud of plasma and ignited it just as the Ontailian cruisers bore down on them. The resulting string of explosions must have been very dramatic to view from a safe distance, but they turned this section of the boneyard into a conflagration. The entire fabric of space seemed to rip apart and burn, and hulking shipwrecks ricocheted off each other like toddlers on a trampoline.

Beating a hasty retreat, there was no time to consider the ramifications of these events. One of Starfleet's most experienced crews and most decorated ships had been destroyed with all hands on board, and an ally had been turned into an enemy. As they escaped from the boneyard, the captain glanced at the viewscreen to see the crumpled wrecks fading into the distance. Soon Commander Riker would get his wish, and they would be gone from the Rashanar Battle Site.

With a heavy heart, Picard ordered them to go to

warp. The Ontailians fired another volley, but their deadly beams sliced through empty space where the *Enterprise* had been.

"Captain," said Kell Perim quietly, "we need a course."

"Back to Starfleet Headquarters," answered Jean-Luc Picard in a grim tone of voice. "I'm afraid our troubles are only just beginning."

Chapter Thirteen

FROM AN UNSEEN DIMENSION, the young Traveler watched the *Enterprise* flash into warp drive just as the fin ships of the Ontailians opened fire, their weapons searing pointlessly into space. He let out a breath he had been holding for what seemed like days, because his mother and friends had escaped . . . for now. He had heard Captain Picard's words of concern, and he feared the captain was right—depite the terrible loss of the *Juno,* the troubles for the crew of the *Enterprise* were only beginning.

This had been difficult, but at least he hadn't witnessed the vision he feared to see most—the *Enterprise* blowing herself to bits with a self-destruct sequence. However, there was no doubt he would see it, because the Pool of Prophecy didn't lie.

His fellow Travelers had left him alone since his

birth into their unique order. That had been both a blessing and a curse. It had put him at loose ends for the first time since going with the Traveler years ago— a vacation from all the vigils he had been assigned during his training. He had known he could visit the *Enterprise,* Earth, or anywhere else he chose; but he had resisted seeing his old comrades, except for one or two glimpses of his mother. Wesley feared that he would be tempted to try to give up the rarefied existence of a Traveler to return to mundane life as a mere human. At times, he felt lonely enough to do it.

When he had finally caught up with the *Enterprise,* he had been too late to help them. Of course, coming to their direct aid would no doubt end his chance to be a Traveler, but he might still do it—to save the *Enterprise* from destruction. He hadn't acted to help the *Juno.*

Wavering in space, the being formerly known as Wesley Crusher had a major decision to make. Should he return to the protected bosom of the Travelers, or should he follow the *Enterprise* to witness its fate? Maybe this was really the first vigil he had chosen for himself, and he would be able to bear witness and refrain from helping his old crewmates . . . when the time came. He had watched suffering before without taking action; in fact, just a few minutes ago. If he turned his back on his shipmates now, he wouldn't have to make a more difficult choice later. When his mentor showed him the vision in the Pool of Prophecy, Wes knew he was being tested. This was the hardest one he could imagine.

From his vantage point in space and time, the new

Traveler turned to gaze upon the ragged, hollow sphere of wrecked starships, orbiting slowly around a gravity pit that shouldn't exist. The mysteries of Rashanar were waiting to be revealed, and Captain Picard was doing his level best as usual; but sometimes the price to solve a mystery was higher than anyone should have to pay. *This will prove to be one of those cases,* thought the Traveler. *How much can I really do to help?*

The destruction of the *Juno* had brought him the usual feelings of helplessness, despair, and inevitability. He wondered if it ever got easier. Solemnly, he made his decision. *The graveyard can hold on to its secrets a while longer. I'm going to find out what will happen to the* Enterprise.

The Traveler envisioned himself at the Starfleet compound in the Presidio area of San Francisco. He found himself standing on an elevated walkway between two buildings—Starfleet Command and Starfleet Headquarters. Cold, sleeting rain pounded sideways, with a few brave pedestrians who rushed past him paying him very little attention. He was a nondescript ensign in uniform, a role he could play with considerable verisimilitude; a humanoid of medium height. Something about him caused one's mind to blur past his appearance, even though a person could acknowledge that he had been there and was supposed to be there. No two people who tried to describe him would agree on the details, or even have many details to furnish.

Wesley looked at the beige and silver buildings, marked HEADQUARTERS and COMMAND—one for determining policy and the other for carrying it out. That's when he noticed that one of the people hurrying past was wearing admiral's insignia. A spare, erect older woman, she carried a file case under her arm and stared straight ahead; the rain splashed harmlessly off her determined face.

"Admiral Nechayev," said Wesley, rushing up to her. "Here's that file you asked for."

He handed her a nonexistent folder, which she tucked into her case without giving it a thought. "Thank you, Ensign," she said, striding past him.

"Any news on the *Enterprise?*" he asked.

"Thank God, they're on their way back here," she muttered as if talking to herself. "What a disaster that has been—I have no clue what we're going to do about it."

Wes opened an umbrella and held it over her head. "Maybe this will help."

Nechayev finally paused to give him a grateful smile. "Thank you, Ensign—" She looked at his name tag and read, "Brewster. I haven't seen you around here before."

"I'm sorry, sir, but you have. I assisted you last week at the inspection."

The admiral shook her head. "Yes, I guess you're right. Come along with me and take some notes."

"Yes, sir," he replied, falling into step beside the admiral and keeping her dry with what looked like an umbrella but was really his subtle powers to alter time and space.

They entered Starfleet Headquarters. The security officers at the door saluted Nechayev smartly. After a jaunt on a speedy turbolift, they were deposited outside a conference room full of admirals seated at a large table. The sleet smashed against a picture window, while the gray skyline of San Francisco shimmered in the mist. Wes recognized Admiral Ross, Admiral Paris, Admiral Nakamura, and several other Starfleet heavyweights.

Ross nodded to Nechayev as they entered, and the ensign took a seat against the wall, along with several other aides who were making notes and organizing documents. Ross went to the head of the table and looked expectantly at the others, while they found their seats and settled down.

"Well, it's official," announced Admiral Ross with a grim expression. "The *Juno* has been lost in the Rashanar Battle Site with all hands on board. This happened immediately after Captain Leeden sent a subspace message saying that the *Enterprise*—without any apparent provocation—fired upon and destroyed the *Vuxhal,* an Ontailian heavy cruiser. Out of revenge, other ships in the Ontailian fleet proceeded to attack the *Juno* and destroy her, while the *Enterprise* managed to escape from Rashanar. We have no ships there now. It seems the Ontailians have taken over the sector."

Ross scowled and tossed a padd on the table. "The Ontailians have recalled their ambassador and have tossed ours out," he grumbled. "They want to pull out of the Federation immediately. Although they haven't declared war on us yet, that might be imminent. Needless to say, the diplomatic corps is up to their ears trying to save the day, but it doesn't look good."

"Wasn't there some trouble before this?" asked Admiral Paris.

"Yes," answered Ross. "Before today, there were several minor incidents with the Ontailians and the *Enterprise*. In fact, I talked to Captain Picard less than a day ago about his conduct and his crew. And now *this* happens. You could hardly believe the conflicting reports I was getting."

"I could believe it," said Nechayev, "because we've been getting conflicting reports from Rashanar for years now. It's a mess, which we've mostly ignored. We expected the *Enterprise* to be the white knight who would ride in and restore order, yet we left Captain Leeden in charge because of her tenure. As for the Ontailians, they're one of the more closed societies in the Federation. I think we make special allowances for non-humanoids, but that's another discussion. In giving the Ontailians more and more control of Rashanar, we were setting ourselves up for disaster."

Mulling over her words, Admiral Ross pulled out his chair and sat down. "We have a number of problems to address. First of all, what is our response to the Ontailians? I know what the diplomatic response will be, but we have to plan for diplomacy to fail. Do we send a fleet there—ships we don't have—to maintain control of the battle site?"

"Our control of the battle site was minimal at best," said Admiral Nakamura. "It's nothing but a treasure trove for looters. And I've heard stories about the place—" He scoffed and waved his hand dismissively. "Well, those stories can't be true. But I say we don't risk another life in that graveyard—too many have died there already."

There were grumbles of general agreement around the table. Wes figured it was hard to argue against such a stance. He looked to see if Admiral Nechayev disagreed, but she was pensively silent.

"What about the bodies?" asked Ross. "Estimates are that we're only at a fifty-five percent recovery rate. To finish the job, we would have to send a task force anyway."

"Let's not rush into anything," cautioned Admiral Nakamura. "If we're talking about an immediate response, let's not make it worse by overreacting. These aren't the Romulans or Cardassians we're talking about—it's doubtful the Ontailians have any designs on Federation space. Maybe we should do what the scavengers are doing: pinpoint our vessels and those of our allies, then tow them out of there. If we sent a small force for that specific task, the Ontailians might not complain."

This elicited a spontaneous discussion, which Ross had to call to a stop after about ten minutes. "We're not going to decide this right now," he concluded. "Doing nothing would be the easiest course. It may be the best course. But we have to take a long-range view. The Federation Council is very worried that the Ontailians' departure will hasten another stampede out the door, especially among the non-humanoids."

Ross cast an uneasy glance at Nechayev, then sat up stiffly. "The next problem is the inquiry as to the possibility of a court-martial for Captain Picard, which is automatic under the circumstances. Jean-Luc Picard has always been a stalwart officer, but this matter is going to eat up his time and attention, no matter how it turns out. We can't keep the *Enterprise* out of commission for that long."

"Riker can take over the *Enterprise*," said Admiral Paris. "He's more than qualified."

"That's true," Ross agreed, "and he has no apparent responsibility for these events. Picard was in command of the bridge on every occasion."

Ross sighed as if scarcely believing what he was saying. "I don't want to prejudge Picard, but the reports and messages from the site are self-explanatory. As you'll see, we've only gotten partial responses from Captain Picard. The *Juno* tragedy is too recent to be in these documents, but you'll receive updates." There was some shuffling of files, isolinear chips, and padds as all of the admirals made sure they possessed the pertinent documents.

After frowning seriously for several seconds, Admiral Paris cleared his throat and said, "Picard should have a psychological evaluation. He's long overdue for a complete workup. He wouldn't be the first to come back from Rashanar with a problem. Not to mention the other traumas he's had. Under regulations, he would be automatically removed from duty, and we'd have time to set up the tribunal."

"Oh," said Nechayev with a scowl, "we've got our scapegoat already picked out."

Ross bristled and sat upright in his seat. "Admiral, there's no complaint in any of these reports against anyone but Picard. Even his own reports admit his failings, such as when he allowed his yacht to be stolen intact by Androssi salvagers."

"So we're going to throw away a fantastic career for one bad week?" asked Nechayev, aghast. "I want to sit on that tribunal, and I want to make sure the Ontailians come here to testify and present evidence. Because Picard gets to face his accusers, and they're the ones who have to justify destroying the *Juno.* If you don't get the Ontailians to testify, there will *always* be questions about this affair."

Admiral Ross heaved his big shoulders. "All right, Alynna. We'll use the inquiry as an excuse to keep in touch with the Ontailians. If they don't come to testify, Picard will probably be acquitted due to lack of evidence, so something good will happen either way."

"We'll want to schedule a memorial service for the crew of the *Juno,*" said Nechayev softly.

"Yes," murmured Ross, casting his troubled eyes downward. He looked so old compared with the man Wesley remembered from the Academy, but he supposed that a war would do that to a leader. Snapping to, Ross pointed to his padd, and said, "Commander Data was also involved in these incidents. I believe he should be available as a material witness. Admirals Paris and Nechayev will serve with me on the tribunal. We also need to assign capable prosecution and defense counselors. I'll be calling on all of you for help in this matter. If there's nothing else to discuss, we can—"

"Admiral," said Nechayev, sitting upright and coming to a conclusion, "I respectfully withdraw my offer to be on the tribunal, because I wish to represent Captain Picard in his inquiry and possible court-martial."

Ross looked shocked for a moment, and the murmuring in the conference room grew very loud. Calmly, Ross held up his hand and turned a frown upon his colleague. "Let's come to order please. Alynna, you haven't acted as defense counsel in decades. This will take you away from a lot of your work."

"I don't think so," said the veteran admiral, leaning back in her chair. "You have no case unless you can get the Ontailians here to testify, and I don't think you can do that."

"We can take a deposition *there,*" countered Ross, growing testy. He turned to the dignified man seated to his left. "Admiral Nakamura, you will serve on the tribunal in place of Nechayev, who is now the defense counsel."

"I object," said Nechayev sharply. "Although he's a dear friend of mine, Admiral Nakamura has shown himself to be biased against Commander Data. On Starbase 173, he wanted to take Data apart and suppress his rights as a sentient being. He's clearly prejudiced against an officer who may prove to be my client also."

Before Ross could muster any response, Nakamura sat forward, bristling. "Admiral Nechayev," he said evenly, "you may want to reconsider. By Commander Data's own log, he was malfunctioning and had his emotion chip turned *on* during these crucial events, including the destruction of the *Vuxhal* and the *Juno.* I doubt if he'll make a credible witness or defendant."

"So we have *two* scapegoats," said Nechayev, her

eyes scanning her colleagues, many of whom looked away.

Ross, however, returned her gaze. "Mistakes were made at Rashanar, and two Federation starships were lost. Nobody wants to prosecute somebody as loyal and valuable as Picard, but the Ontailians deserve a full hearing. I think our relations with them can be salvaged, and I aim to do that."

Nechayev hefted her case and rose from her seat. "I had better start my research. It's probably best that we not discuss this case any further. I trust we'll treat Jean-Luc Picard as he deserves. I sometimes find him stubborn and overly cautious, but he has saved us all more than once—we owe him more than we can ever repay."

"We'll be fair to him," promised the admiral. "Your defense will be proof of that. Thank you."

Nechayev's nondescript aide also rose to his feet, and accompanied the admiral out the door. He didn't need to read any of the documents, because he had witnessed the events. Like most tragedies, this one had been equal parts stupidity, heroism, and unpredictable forces.

In the corridor, he had to call out to stop the admiral, who had all but forgotten about him. "Admiral Nechayev!" he shouted. "I've got to courier some more documents, but I'll be there when you need me."

"Yes," she said thankfully, "I think you will be. They'll probably want to make a deal. This may require more tough negotiating than lawyering."

"I think Captain Picard's luck has changed," said the ensign. "Good-bye, Admiral Nechayev." By the time the officer had left her presence, she had forgotten both his name and face.

"So you lucked out," said Dr. Crusher to her patient, Ensign Ellen Winslow, who was four months pregnant and married to a civilian engineer in San Francisco. "You get to go home three months early."

"Yes," said Ensign Winslow a bit sheepishly. "I hate to take advantage of our change in plans, but I think I will enjoy seeing Allen and being home for a while before the baby."

Beverly smiled pleasantly as she finished up the examination of the future mom. Business in sickbay was rather slow today, and she saw only a few associates making the rounds. Most of them were working on research projects.

"I won't be shipping out again until the baby can travel," said Ensign Winslow as she slipped back into her tunic. "When do you think that will be, Doctor?"

Crusher shrugged and said, "It all depends on how comfortable you are with giving him up for large parts of the day. Infants do fine on the *Enterprise,* but you know how your work schedule can be. You might want to enjoy your baby without interruptions for a couple of years."

"You sound like you know," said the ensign. "Do you have children?"

Beverly tried not to wince at the blunt question. Her longtime shipmates knew Wesley, or knew about him. They also knew when and how to talk about him. So many of these new crew members didn't even know she had a son, because she never brought him up; evidence of his existence was not to be found in her workplace. Crusher realized that she had been acting as if Wes was dead, when he was only being wildly independent as young men will do. She resolved to put up a couple of portraits of him around sickbay and to talk about him more.

"Yes, I do have a son," she said simply. "But he's grown. Gone off."

"Ah, that must be tough," said the young ensign, hopping off the examination table. "I still don't think my mom's recovered from me being here."

Crusher nodded politely, but she could feel her eyes misting up. She hadn't realized how emotional she had been lately. Their tragic and abrupt departure from Rashanar had made her feel like the end of an era was at hand. Deanna and Will had each other, many of the crew would see family on Earth, but she was alone. What Beverly wouldn't give to be going home to spend several months with *her* baby.

She finally hauled herself out of her gloom. "You and baby are doing fine," she told Winslow. "I think the date we have is spot-on. You can pick a pediatrician and hospital when you get home. Keep taking your supplements and do your stretching exercises."

"Yes, Dr. Crusher," said the woman with a salute.

"And let us know what happens, Ellen," added a third voice as Alyssa Ogawa poked her head around the curtain. "If you don't, we'll hunt you down, won't we, Doctor?"

"We will," promised Beverly, mustering a smile.

Ogawa turned to Crusher and said, "Yerbi Fandau is on the com for you."

"Oh, thanks," said Beverly with surprise. She glanced down at the screen beside the examination table. "I'll take it here."

"Isn't he the head of Starfleet Medical?" asked Ensign Winslow.

"Yes," said Beverly. "You take care of that little one, Ensign." She nodded to Ogawa, who ushered the patient toward the door.

Crusher punched up the com frequency and saw the balding, bearded visage of Dr. Yerbi Fandau on her screen. The Argelian's amber eyes widened when he saw his old friend. "Beverly, my dear, how are you?"

"I'm fine, Yerbi," she lied. "And how are you?"

"Training doctors for space is lots of fun," he answered with a cheery smile. "I just tell them they're going on a cruise and will never have to do anything. But I've got to be a bit concerned about your crew. You had a close call."

"We've had plenty of close calls over the years," she said wearily. "We'll survive this one."

The Argelian frowned deeply. "Listen, Beverly, it didn't seem like much at the time, but now people are asking about it. Can you tell me anything else about the injury Captain Picard suffered when his yacht, the *Ca-lypso,* was stolen from him?"

Her eyes narrowed, and she answered hesitantly, "It was in my log. He inhaled an unknown Androssi muscle toxin which temporarily paralyzed him. This toxin wasn't intended to kill, just to disable. It did the job quite well. He was recovering by the time he got to sickbay, and I examined him and ordered him to get some rest."

"That was after he had been back on the *Enterprise* for seven hours, right?" asked Dr. Fandau.

"Something like that," she answered. "What are you driving at?"

"Just filling in a few blanks," he replied. "Can you get me the pathology on that Androssi toxin? We want to analyze it."

"Sure," answered Beverly, wondering how she could graciously exit from this conversation. "If there's nothing else, my sickbay is full of patients."

"Give Captain Picard my regards," answered Yerbi. "What's the captain's frame of mind now?"

She tried to act nonchalant, but her doctor sense was pinging. He was digging for information. "He's a little on edge, which is understandable. We all are. What's *your* frame of mind?"

Dr. Fandau laughed uneasily. "You know, Beverly, I'm going to retire soon, and I'm holding this job open for you. You didn't really give it a chance last time."

"Head up Starfleet Medical," she mused. "I've thought about it, but not now. Not when *he* needs me most."

Fandau gave a nervous chuckle. "What do you mean? Who needs you?"

"I mean the tone of this conversation," she answered coldly. "We wouldn't be talking about this unless Jean-Luc was in for a miserable time. I know Starfleet, and their bureaucracies can make a Cardassian torture chamber look like kindergarten. What do you have planned for him? You aren't thinking of relieving him of command?"

The Argelian frowned at her and said, "He's going to be temporarily relieved of command and placed under psychological observation. That is confidential information which you cannot divulge."

"Yerbi, you know he doesn't deserve that. Even if he did, we've got one of the best counselors in Starfleet on this ship. Deanna Troi can do your evaluation."

"Counselor Troi is not objective, and you know it," said the head of Starfleet Medical. "I was hoping you could give me an honest assessment, but I realize you're not objective either."

"I hope you're as open-minded as you are objective," grumbled Crusher. She almost broke off contact with him, but she kept the frequency open just to see what he would say next.

"When is the *Enterprise* getting home?" asked Fandau, desperately changing the subject.

"Twenty-four hours. It can't be soon enough. Are you really ordering me not to tell Jean-Luc that he'll be placed in a hospital for evaluation?"

"Yes," answered Dr. Fandau gravely. "If he finds out in advance, I'll hold you responsible. Beverly, we're talking as chief medical officers here. If the *Enterprise* were blown up in peacetime by the actions of another Starfleet captain, I hope your ghost wouldn't mind an investigation!"

Beverly braced herself against the bulkhead. "All right, Doctor, you've made your point." She looked up and caught sight of an unfamiliar orderly who had perhaps overheard their conversation. He turned away and pushed an antigrav gurney into the next ward. She never got a good look at his face, but he seemed familiar.

"Beverly!" snapped Fandau, apparently trying to get her attention. "Can I count on you to keep this to yourself? And to bring me a sample of that toxin?"

"Yes, yes," she assured him. "I'll bring it directly to your office as soon as I disembark. Good-bye, Yerbi."

Five minutes later, Beverly Crusher stood at the door to Picard's quarters and rang the chime. After finding out that he was off duty, she had decided to see him in person. The door slid open, and his friendly voice said, "Come!"

Tying his robe around his slim torso and looking sleepy, Jean-Luc approached her. "Beverly, to what do I owe this pleasure? I didn't miss an appointment or a date, did I?"

"No, Jean-Luc," she said, twisting her hands nervously. The door shut behind her, and she paced to his desk, where she happened to see the photos of the three of them, she, Jack, and Jean-Luc. "I've been ordered not to talk to you about something, but I have to talk to you anyway."

He sighed and held up his hand. "You're worried about what's going to happen to me when we get home. I'm prepared for anything."

"Are you prepared to lose your command and be committed to a hospital for psychological evaluation?"

"Uh, no," answered Picard, sitting in his desk chair. "I'm sure that's standard procedure under these circumstances. Admiral Nechayev has volunteered to be my counsel, and we have Data's testimony about the mimic ship. I might also find some support around the admiralty."

"I'm sure you will, Jean-Luc," said Beverly, mustering a brave front. "Just act surprised when they tell you that you're going to be evaluated. In the meantime, we have one night left before we get home. You're off duty, and so am I."

The captain jumped to his feet, took her arm, and conducted her to the couch. "Yes, and I'm being a terrible host. Make yourself comfortable, Beverly. Since we're going home early, I can stock up on wine from Chateau Picard, so we might as well drink what we have left. I have a splendid Shiraz, vintage 2370."

"Whatever you want, Jean-Luc," said the doctor with a glint in her eye. "Let's make this last night memorable."

Chapter Fourteen

THE YOUNG TRAVELER SAT QUIETLY in a corner of the conference room at Starfleet Headquarters, looking at an oblong electromagnetic container with four tentacle-like manipulator arms. Thanks to antigrav generators, the box floated several centimeters off the table, thus allowing the user a certain amount of mobility. Inside the container was a Medusan named Korgan, who held the rank of commodore in Starfleet. Although noncorporeal, the Medusan was able to manipulate simple objects with his mechanical tentacles. He entered commands on a special padd with two of these arms. The other two tentacles writhed nervously, awaiting the start of the meeting.

Wesley and the Medusan were the only two beings in the conference room at the moment. Commodore Korgan's assistant had gone to meet Admiral Nechayev in the research library, to compare documents and evidence to make sure both sides were starting with the same materials. The Traveler was a little nervous, because the highly telepathic Medusan might be able to see through his guises. Their extraordinary perceptions of space and time made them highly valued as navigators. Wes knew that looking directly at a Medusan would cause most humanoids to go insane. He wondered if a Traveler would be equally affected. Although he was curious, that was one experiment he was not going to try.

The Medusan did nothing overt, but Wes could sense his prying intelligence. Why had Commodore Korgan become a military lawyer instead of a navigator? The Traveler didn't know that, but he knew it was a stroke of genius to appoint the Medusan to be Captain Picard's prosecutor. A non-humanoid was bound to have greater rapport with the Ontailians, and so far they were the basis for the prosecution's case, along with the reports from Rashanar.

Commodore Korgan versus Admiral Nechayev was a contest the Traveler didn't want to miss. He almost hoped this meeting would fail to produce a settlement. On the other hand, he wished the best for his old friend Picard, hoping against hope that the captain could avoid a court-martial.

The door to the conference room slid open. Admiral Nechayev and Commander Jason Emery strode into the room. Nechayev acknowledged Wes's presence with a nod; however, the tall, lanky commander looked right past him. Emery stood beside the Medusan's container, closing his eyes as if in some kind of trance. Wes knew he was communicating telepathically with his superior.

"Commodore Korgan greets you warmly," said Emery with a glance at Nechayev and her bland assistant. "He wishes the circumstances of this meeting were more pleasant."

"As do I," agreed Nechayev. "The commodore should know that I haven't really had time to talk to my client yet, because the *Enterprise* doesn't return to Earth for another three hours. But I will be happy to entertain preliminary discussions."

Emery nodded sagely, then seemed to be concentrating. After a moment, he said, "The commodore wishes to know if you have reviewed all logs and reports pertaining to this case?"

"I have," answered the admiral, "but I don't feel that the reports offer prima facie evidence that Picard did anything wrong. It's just an interpretation of events from one point of view with limitations. For example, Leeden reported that Picard destroyed the *Vuxhal,* but Picard reports that the *Vuxhal* was destroyed by an unknown third party and the ship he fired upon was a duplicate of the *Vuxhal* by unknown forces. It was about to attack the *Enterprise.* None of the wreckage was recovered, so there's no physical evidence—it's his word against hers."

"*We* may not possess any wreckage from the *Vuxhal,*" said Emery with a sniff, "but the Ontailians might. We're awaiting the arrival of their delegation, with new evidence."

"Oh," replied Nechayev with surprise. "They're coming here for the inquiry?"

"We're hoping they're coming here for an apology," answered Commander Emery with a glance at the Medusan's container. "If Captain Picard will admit to provoking the Ontailians, the inquiry will be quick, with no court-martial, and we can move on."

Nechayev held up a hand. "Hold on," she said. "The Ontailians had no justification for attacking the *Juno,* nor are we going to invent any for them. Besides, it was the Androssi, Orions, and other illicit salvagers who were doing the provoking. They're the ones who kept the Rashanar Battle Site in turmoil and who contributed to the short fuses everyone had. That same day, the Androssi tried to haul away a Romulan warbird, and they attacked and crippled the *Juno.* Two Androssi ships had already been destroyed in heavy action, plus *something* destroyed the yacht *Calypso.* Rashanar is still a dangerous zone, which we can show."

Emery closed his eyes while he communicated with Commodore Korgan. "So," he finally said, "you are claiming mistaken identity? Friendly fire?"

The Traveler could see that Nechayev was making an effort to remain cordial. "No," she answered slowly, as if speaking to a child, "Captain Picard fired on that vessel to prevent an imminent attack on the *Enterprise.* That much is clear from his own logs. The Ontailians fired on the *Juno* not in self-defense, but out of revenge. That much is also clear. *They* are the ones who should be on trial."

"We will try to establish their frame of mind," replied Commander Emery, "but since they had just seen their flagship brutally destroyed without provocation, their actions seem understandable to us."

The tall aide closed his eyes to talk to his superior, and a moment later he said breathlessly, "The only basis Picard had for believing the *Enterprise* was in danger was the information supplied by Commander Data. He had no firsthand knowledge of this so-called mimic ship, so he could have been mistaken or misinformed. We'll all understand if he just apologizes and accepts responsibility for a mistake. Then the Ontailians stay in the Federation, Captain Picard returns to his ship, and we all put this behind us. Of course, we'll try to come up with better policy, more resources, for the Rashanar site."

Nechayev folded her arms and sat back in her chair, frowning. It must have been tempting, thought Wes, to take the deal and just say, "It was our mistake, so sorry," but the Traveler doubted that would happen.

"I'll relate this to my client," said the admiral, rising to her feet. "So your strategy is to discredit Data?"

Emery listened to Korgan, then replied, "Commander Data is a sentient machine, but he's still a machine. For your strategy to work, Data has to convince the tribunal—as he convinced Captain Picard—that the *Vuxhal* had been destroyed earlier by unknown forces. And the ship the *Enterprise* destroyed was an enemy ship in disguise. I haven't misrepresented your case, have I?"

"We may come back with a counterproposal," said Nechayev, looking stung by the Medusan's blunt and accurate assessment. She stepped toward the door. Wesley jumped to his feet, anxious to make a retreat with her.

"Please take the deal," said Commander Emery,

sounding as if he were speaking for himself and not his Medusan superior. "Ensign Brewster?"

With surprise, the Traveler turned around as the door whooshed open. "Yes, Commander?"

"Commodore Korgan would like to have tea with you at five o'clock," said Emery blankly.

He knows, thought Wes. "Please tell the commodore thank you, but until this case is concluded, I am occupied elsewhere. However, I'll be happy to have tea with him then. In fact, I look forward to it."

A light on the Medusan's hovering box blinked, and Commander Emery bowed politely.

Three hours later, the *Enterprise* was in orbit around Earth. Four-fifths of the ship's personnel were scheduled for shore leave or other business on the planet. Per Admiral Nechayev's instructions, Captain Picard left the ship last among those beaming down, and he was accompanied only by Data. He and Data beamed directly to a small transporter room in Starfleet Command, not to the transporter center at the Starfleet docks. Picard could understand this low-profile return to San Francisco, because there might be curious spectators waiting for him. Data was amenable to going anywhere the captain wanted to go.

Admiral Nechayev and an unassuming ensign of medium height and build met Picard and Data in the transporter room. There were only the four of them, and Nechayev had manned the transporter controls herself. "This is Ensign Brewster," she said, pointing to her bookish aide. "Thank you for meeting me here, away from prying eyes. From now on, both of you have to watch what you say about this matter, because the entire Federation is watching you. If asked anything, it's best to say that you can't comment."

"Is that really necessary?" asked Data. "I have a difficult time lying, and I am able to make comments."

Nechayev scowled. "I'm an admiral and your counsel, and I *order* you not to comment about this matter to anyone without checking with me."

"I am under orders not to comment," said Data with a nod, sounding satisfied with that compromise.

The captain mustered an appreciative smile. "I want to thank you, Admiral, for volunteering to represent us. I know we were involved in a tragic incident—actually a series of them—but I can't understand how this process will be as time-consuming as you seem to think."

"Picard," she said sternly, "you don't realize the trouble you're in. Not only does the peacetime loss of a Starfleet vessel require an inquiry, but you're accused of willfully destroying a spacecraft from a friendly member of the Federation, without provocation."

"We did not destroy the *Vuxhal,*" stated Data a nanosecond before Picard could say the same thing.

"In court, what you believe and what you can prove are two different things," said Nechayev, gazing at the android. "You, Mr. Data, are the only one who can keep your captain from losing his command, unless he wants to take the deal I was offered on his behalf."

She sighed and took a few paces. "Their offer is actually very generous, and I don't think Commodore Korgan would have made it unless the Ontailians were willing to go along. You would have to take responsibility for destroying the *Vuxhal* and the subsequent Ontailian attack on the *Juno*. Mistaken identity, friendly fire . . . whatever you want to call it. Do that, and it will stop at the inquiry. The Ontailians will stay in the Federation, and the *Enterprise* will go on its merry way."

"No," said Picard quietly. "I'll take responsibility for giving the Androssi a Starfleet yacht to use against us, and if you want to drum me out for that, fine. But we were in extreme danger—a danger we had seen before when the shuttlecraft *Hudson* was shut down, along with every system on it. Data saw two identical versions of the *Calypso* and two versions of the *Vuxhal*, and these ships are unique in class and appearance."

"Data's testimony is problematic," said Nechayev. "I hate to be blunt, but your only witnesses are an android who was malfunctioning and a blind man. Yes, something knocked out the *Hudson* and Data—and La Forge's implants—but we don't have any sensor or visual logs of it. The only good visual record we've got is of you destroying what looks like the *Vuxhal.*"

"It was chasing us," explained the exasperated captain. "We were trying unsuccessfully to lose it, and to hail them. But we got trapped in the graveyard. You can see that in the log."

Nechayev sighed a heavy sigh. "Captain, the log shows an agitated Commander Data, and you telling him to turn off his emotion chip. Among other things which don't do your case any good."

I can't believe this, thought Picard to himself. Shaking his head, he circled the small transporter room, re-

alization dawning over him. "So I have to *lie* to get out
of this? What about stopping this mimic weapon? I was
going to ask you to let us go back to Rashanar and deal
with it, but now you're just going to ignore it?"

"If the Ontailians leave the Federation," said Nechayev
evenly, "that entire battle zone reverts to them. They don't
have to let us poke through it. We'll have to negotiate our
way back in there. That is, unless you take the deal."

"Ridiculous," muttered Picard, pacing anew while he
rubbed the back of his neck. He could certainly understand the Ontailians' acceptance of this deal; they got to
absolve themselves of blame for destroying the *Juno.*
Everyone figured that Picard's record was sterling
enough to survive this smirch, especially if he helped to
whitewash it over. It was easier to put one man on trial
than an entire planet, also easier to dredge up a stock
apology than the truth.

Data frowned slightly and cocked his head. "Captain," he said, "you should not do it. We made some
mistakes during our week at Rashanar, but we were not
at fault for the destruction of the *Vuxhal* or the *Juno.* To
say we were is . . . wrong."

Picard smiled at his trusted comrade and patted him
on the shoulder. "The poet Byron once said, 'Truth is a
gem that is found at great depth; whilst on the surface
of this world, all things are weighed by the false scale
of custom.' "

"I don't blame you for holding your ground," said
Nechayev sympathetically. "And I'll fight for you. We
have to realize that we have holes in our defense, plus
we have political forces working against us. If you turn

down the settlement, we don't have any control over the outcome."

"I've charged into trouble before without knowing the outcome," said Picard. "Just do the best you can, Admiral, and thank you."

"Yes, thank you," agreed Data.

Nechayev nodded and turned to her nondescript aide. "Ensign, what are their immediate schedules?"

He read off a padd, "Captain Picard must report immediately to Medical Mental Health I have the coordinates laid in on the transporter."

"Sounds like it will be a great shore leave," said Picard with a wan smile.

"He will be assigned a private room and be evaluated," continued the ensign. "This evening, he'll be released for the memorial service for the *Juno,* assuming the captain passes his competency test. The inquiry begins at oh-nine-hundred hours on Thursday, two days from now."

"I'll be visiting you," promised Nechayev, "and we'll go together to the service." Picard nodded.

The ensign went on, "Commander Data, you are to report to the Corps of Engineers, where you will undergo standard diagnostics. I have your coordinates laid in. After that, your schedule is similar to the captain's, although you'll have to wait in the witness room until you're called for the inquiry."

"Very well." The android looked pointedly at Picard. "We shall stand by the truth."

"It's easier to remember," added Picard.

Nechayev stepped behind the transporter console and checked the readouts. "Captain, we've got your desti-

nation laid in. You're not going to be held incommuni-
cado, but they will restrict your visitors to a handful.
You might want to give them a list."

The captain nodded, realizing that this meeting was
over, and he was going to face the next step on his own.
He stepped onto the transporter platform. Ensign Brewster gave him a friendly smile that was oddly familiar.
Picard was trying to place the smile when his molecules were disassembled, condensed, and whisked
away to another part of the Starfleet complex. After
that, he could barely remember what the admiral's aide
had looked like.

"Captain Picard!" called a voice as he stepped off a
transporter platform in the corner of a hospital lobby. An
attractive, blond-haired employee in civilian clothes
stood outside a door marked ADMITTANCE. She strode toward him, offering an outstretched hand. "This is indeed
a pleasure," she said. "I'm Counselor Colleen Cabot."

He shook her hand and mustered a smile. "Nice to
meet you, Counselor Cabot."

"You know," she said winsomely, "we're going to be
seeing an awful lot of each other the next two days, so I
want you to relax. It might help if we used each other's
first names, unless you would find that awkward."

Get along to go along, Picard told himself. *This is
not the time or place to cause any trouble.*

"Certainly, Colleen," he answered. "Please call me
Jean-Luc. Do I need to go into Admittance?"

"No, we've done all your paperwork," answered
Colleen, walking slowly toward a turbolift. "Do you
know, Jean-Luc, it takes several hours to read about all

your exploits. What was it like when you were turned back into a child?"

"Very disconcerting," he answered with a frown. "I didn't like it much, although I found out how much children are ignored."

"How true." Colleen Cabot stepped up to the turbo-lift. The door shot open. With a smile, she motioned the captain to go first, and he dutifully obeyed. The turbolift door closed. She requested, "Level sixteen, holo ward."

"Holo ward?" asked Picard curiously.

"You're going to like your room, Jean-Luc," she bragged. "In fact, we have many visitors to the holo ward who don't want to leave. It's not a full-scale holodeck, because we don't want our patients doing *bat'leth* duels or orbital skydiving, but it has all the amenities of home. In fact, any home you want."

The turbolift stopped; then the door popped open. The counselor led him into a corridor that belonged more in a five-star hotel than in a mental-health facility. The carpet was thick and tightly brocaded, while the walls were covered with tasteful tapestries.

"You could choose your quarters on the *Enterprise,*" she said, "although that wouldn't be much of a vaca-tion. Or you could be in your bedroom on the winery where you grew up. A bungalow on the beach at Pa-cifica or overlooking the ski slopes of Spiez—there's a menu of selections."

All of them revealing something about me, thought Picard. "Which is your favorite?" he asked innocently as they ambled down the hall.

"I'm partial to an old-log-cabin program," she answered with a wistful smile. "I think it's supposed to be in Canada. It's very rural, there's even an outhouse out back, and the bed has down pillows and comforters. Sometimes when we have to work late and we have a vacant suite, I sneak in there for a few hours. I grew up in Hong Kong, so I'm not reliving my childhood."

Picard smiled, quite disarmed by this charming young lady. In due time, they came to a door numbered 117, and Picard began to get a bit nervous. *Just look at it as a vacation,* he told himself. *I could sleep away two days without too much problem.*

"Is there music?" he asked. "I'm in the mood for some Berlioz."

"Absolutely," answered Colleen, pressing a panel to open his door. "The music is all programmed separately from the surroundings, and you can listen to a mariachi band in Switzerland if you like. You can call us anytime, too."

And you'll be somewhere watching me, thought Picard.

They stepped into a nondescript suite: sitting room, bedroom, and a nicely appointed kitchen, although the furnishings were a bit drab and spare. The misty gray skyline of San Francisco was visible through the picture window, but he doubted it was a real window. He would probably be under observation in every room but the bath.

"Would you like to have lunch with me, Jean-Luc?" she asked cheerfully. "That will be in about two hours."

"I would indeed," he answered. "Colleen, are you the only person I'll be seeing here?"

"From the staff, probably," she answered. "I believe

a couple of people have asked to visit you—crew members and Admiral Nechayev. They'll be here this afternoon. The holosuite can also give you a few generic companions—to play chess or cards with, to talk to about the weather. You can work on that screen in the kitchen or make vocal commands to the computer. I know you like to read, so the bookcase and computer database in each style of room is stocked."

Hmmm, two days of reading, Berlioz, and lunch with Colleen, thought Picard. *It doesn't sound all that horrible.* "I may take a nap," he said with a yawn. "I didn't get that much sleep last night."

"Relaxation is the best," she replied. "I'll see you in a couple of hours, and I'll bring lunch. So don't eat too much."

As soon as she was gone, Picard walked to the kitchen and found a teakettle, cups, loose Earl Grey tea, and a tea ball. He was quite relaxed by the time he had prepared his tea and sat down at the small domestic console in the kitchen. There were about thirty suggested locales or types of quarters from which to choose, everything from Chateau Picard to a cliff dwelling on Vulcan. That one was tempting, but he searched until he found an entry marked, "Log Cabin, Georgian Bay, Canada, Earth."

With a tap of his finger, he chose the log cabin. He found himself in a homespun example of frontier living, right down to the woodsy smell and lyrical bird calls from beyond the walls. The furnishings were Early Americana with some linens and antiques of fine craftsmanship; the only things anachronistic were the unchanged computer terminal and a large picture window that showed a view of a deer standing in an alpine forest. He didn't think real log cabins had big picture windows.

What will Colleen make of me choosing her favorite room? wondered Picard. Ah, well, they were here to play games. The captain was normally a rather guarded person, and he didn't like the idea of anyone peering into his psyche, even if it was their job. He strolled over to the front door of the cabin, which corresponded to the door into the corridor. He gave the knob a twist. It didn't move, nor did the door open. He was locked in, which didn't do much for his disposition.

When the captain checked out the bookcase, he was delighted to find several Dixon Hill novels from the mid-twentieth century. Of course, he had read them all, but they were perfect light vacation reading. He grabbed one of the more obscure Hill titles, *Kiss Me Badly,* and padded across the weathered wood planks to his bed. For the moment, he would listen to bird songs instead of Berlioz.

Pushing on the plump bed, Picard found that it was exactly as described. He threw himself on top of the goose down and sank in as if it were quicksand. *Oh, that's a feeling I'd forgotten,* he thought with pleasure. He didn't even open his Dixon Hill book but instead fell asleep with it clutched to his chest.

Captain Picard awoke from his nap feeling refreshed. He made himself some more tea, sat down in a rocking chair, and began to read his book. When his door opened, he irrationally considered running out, but he knew that wouldn't do his case much good. Colleen Cabot entered, carrying a picnic basket. She looked around fondly at the quarters he had chosen.

"So you had to try my cabin, huh, Jean-Luc?" she said with amusement. "What would you have chosen if I hadn't recommended this one?"

Picard shrugged and straightened his tunic. "I don't know. The cliff dwelling on Vulcan was tempting, or I might have seen if you really duplicated my room at Chateau Picard."

"No doubt you could find some faults in the details," said Colleen. "All we had were images from an old architectural digest and a documentary, also very little time for the programming." She set the picnic basket on the rustic dining table and opened the lid.

"Do most of your visitors choose someplace familiar like that?" asked Picard. The longer he could keep the conversation away from himself, the better he liked it.

"Most civilians choose someplace familiar," answered the counselor, "but Starfleet personnel like the cliff dwellings on Vulcan and the other exotic locales. Usually."

From her picnic basket, Colleen produced silverware, glasses, and food. "I hope you like what I brought you to eat, sort of a French picnic with pâté de foie gras, stuffed red peppers, and deviled eggs. Only because every picnic should have deviled eggs. I tried like crazy to find some Picard wine, but the best I could do on short notice was this California chardonnay. It's chilled."

"That will be fine," he said reassuringly. "Let me

open it for you." She handed him the corkscrew and bottle, and he skillfully popped the cork and poured.

"I have to ask you certain things," she said sheepishly. "Please don't take these questions personally."

"Not at all," answered Picard, taking a sip of wine. He swished the delicate liquid around in his mouth and swallowed. "This brand still has that heavy oaken taste I find in most California chardonnays, but it should stand up well to all this food."

They took their seats at the table, and she prepared him a plate. "First of all, Jean-Luc, do you understand why you're here?"

"All too well," he answered. "A mission went terribly wrong, and two Federation ships were destroyed. Whenever that happens, the captain is held responsible. An inquiry is standard procedure."

"Do you think you could have avoided what went wrong?" Colleen bit into a deviled egg and chewed contemplatively while she awaited his answer.

The answer didn't come quickly, and he finally said, "I've asked myself that several times. I doubt if you've ever been to the Rashanar Battle Site, but there are fleets of determined looters and salvagers trying to get to the wrecks before we can. We only have a handful of Starfleet vessels to stop them. Plus there are anomalies and things going on at Rashanar which we can't explain."

"Tell me about them," she asked eagerly. "I'd like to hear."

Whether that was true or not, he told her about the gravity dump that shouldn't exist, the vortex of spinning rubble, the deadly energy spikes, the antimatter asteroid that had to be avoided at all costs, and the doppelgänger ship. Colleen was very attentive, listening silently while she ate. Picard actually welcomed the opportunity to tell his story in one coherent whole. He might as well get used to it, he decided, because he would be telling this story over and over again.

"Having perfect hindsight, could I have avoided the disasters of this mission?" he asked rhetorically. "Yes. But in practical terms, I don't think I could have, because *something* is at work in that battle zone. I've spent a lifetime confronting the unknown. It's always a matter of probing and prodding until you can explain it. Some mysteries are never explained, some missions are failures. That grates on me, but I have to accept the results. The thing I really regret is having retreated from Rashanar when I *know* something deadly is lurking there."

Colleen's pretty face frowned slightly, and she said, "You understand, Jean-Luc, there are different opinions as to what happened there?"

"Not among *my* crew," answered the captain.

The counselor nodded thoughtfully. "Your crew is loyal to you, but you and Captain Leeden had your differences of opinion. How do you account for that?"

"I felt sorry for a fine officer in an impossible situation," answered Picard softly. "To do her job, Leeden asked for a specialized task force and got one ship—the *Enterprise.* For the reasons I've told you, that place is very dangerous. Turnover and accident rates were high, and morale was low. Recovering bodies, fighting off the scavengers, dealing with a vast panorama of death and destruction . . . it's not easy. A week there seemed like a long time."

Picard sighed, not wanting to speak ill of the dead, but he was determined to cling to the truth. "We didn't communicate well, until something went wrong. She kept telling us the boneyard was haunted, and there were myriad ways to die in there. But I didn't realize how right she was."

"I see." The counselor picked at her food, giving Picard a few moments' respite from talking in order to eat, but he still didn't have much appetite. "In her reports," said Cabot, "Captain Leeden told Starfleet that you were having a few problems since arriving. That must have hurt."

Picard didn't rise to the bait, and he said calmly, "I've had enough experience to know when a mission isn't going well. No one needs to spell it out for me. Leeden and I agreed on the important matters—especially that major policy changes were needed—but chaos won the day at Rashanar."

"So you had a feeling of helplessness about this assignment?"

The captain tried not to smile at that question or take umbrage. "No, I didn't feel helpless. I felt frustrated, overextended, determined to make a difference despite the odds. I really hope to go back to Rashanar and correct what I can. We have to understand those anomalies, or we can't let *anyone* in there."

"Then it's still unfinished business for you?" asked Cabot.

"It's still unfinished business for everyone," answered the captain, "or we wouldn't be having this conversation."

Colleen Cabot sat back in her chair and tapped her delicate chin. "You've used terms like 'chaos' and 'haunted' to describe what you found at Rashanar. Normally those kinds of terms don't go over real well at Starfleet."

"I'm a very rational person," said Picard with a smile. "As you can see from my record, I haven't always lived in a rational universe. 'Haunted' is a word Captain Leeden used to describe Rashanar."

"Yes," replied the counselor with a slight frown. "For me to properly explore everything that's happened to you in your stellar career, I would need two years, not two days. How did you keep going? After your Borg experience, torture by the Cardassians, and regression to a primeval life-form? How is it that you still want to go back to the Rashanar Battle Site?"

The captain cocked his head and looked at the fine pine beams holding up the sloped cabin roof. He listened to the birds chirping and the rustle of pine trees in the noonday breeze, as he gave her question genuine reflection. "I used to ride horses quite a bit. There's an old tradition about getting back on after you've been thrown off." Picard cringed at an old memory and said, "Plus I almost died in a barroom brawl just after graduation. So there almost was no stellar career or Captain Picard. After that, I've always felt I was here on borrowed time, and I've tried not to think of my personal safety—just my duty and my loyalty. Does that answer your question?"

"You're going to make a very convincing witness," admitted Colleen with an encouraging smile.

"I hope so," replied Picard.

The counselor pushed her plate away and said, "Neither one of us is eating very much. But let's leave the food out, because you have some visitors coming in."

"I do?" asked Picard cheerfully as he picked up a napkin and wiped his mouth.

The counselor took a bit of food and chewed thoughtfully. Finally she asked, "You've never married, Jean-Luc. Why is that?"

He swallowed and shook his head. "Does that really have anything to do with my competency?"

"I don't know you well enough to know that." Colleen dabbed her delicate mouth with her napkin and said, "My suggestion to you is that you cheerfully answer every question. You've decided to play hard about this and not admit to any wrongdoing, so you ordered the deluxe treatment. Now why haven't you ever married?"

Picard's chewing turned into teeth gritting, and he slowly swallowed his food.

"I've come close," he admitted, "but there was always a hitch. Usually the love affair came into my life at the wrong time, although I'm not sure there have been many right times." The captain looked wistful as a flood of memories returned to him. "I once had the honor of living another man's life in a relatively short time, and I . . . I had a family then. I could have been a good husband and father—I know I could have. But the time was never there."

"You could have that time now," said Colleen, who gazed deeply at him with her pale blue eyes, as if she could find the answers she sought in the creases of his face. "Did you never marry because you saw the devastation that Jack Crusher's death had on his family?"

Picard sat ramrod straight in his chair, as if he had been stabbed. "You're very thorough," he said through clenched teeth. "Yes, that probably hardened my attitude, but it didn't change me. I've consoled grieving families a thousand times since then, and I've spoken a thousand eulogies. It never gets any easier."

Cabot shook her head glumly. "So here you are . . . burned out, lonely, at the tail end of your career with no family and nothing to show for it. Were you thinking about these things out there in Rashanar?"

"That doesn't sound like anything I would ever think," he answered. "Out there in space, I'm generally happy to have survived the day."

She looked at him with annoyance. "You haven't survived this one yet. Why put yourself through all this, Jean-Luc? You could retire with honors. The Ontailians wouldn't quite know what was happening, only that you were gone from Starfleet. They'd probably be content with that. You are compounding a mistake by going through with this inquiry, which might spin off who-knows-where. All anybody wants from you is cooperation."

"What about the truth?"

The blond woman shook her head and sighed. "The truth is what we agree it is. If you don't cooperate, you won't have much control over the truth."

The counselor had to consult a padd for her next question, then she said, "On Stardate 45494.2, you took the *Enterprise* to the Epsilon Silar system, where you destroyed a Lysian spacecraft without any provocation. That ship was far inferior to the *Enterprise,* wasn't it?"

"No, wait!" protested Picard. "We were not in our right minds. We had amnesia, and we were being used by the Satarrans."

Colleen Cabot smiled. "Then you admit that you can be duped into making a mistake?"

Picard scowled, sat back in his chair, and crossed his arms. "Is the questioning going to go on like this?"

"Yes, for some time," she answered coldly. "I also have several questions about Ontailians and your attitudes toward them. After that, there's a psychological test to fill out on the computer. Sit back, Jean-Luc, and cooperate. You really don't have any choice."

Picard nodded wearily and resolved to take whatever they threw at him with grace and calm, for as long as he could.

Chapter Fifteen

AT STARFLEET CORPS OF ENGINEERS, Geordi La Forge paced nervously in the tasteful lobby, where there were several displays of technical marvels built by the corps in the last two hundred years. He had seen the First Starbase Diorama ten times, while waiting to find out what had happened to Data. Twice he'd been told that Data would soon come down to meet him. He hoped so. The two of them had to attend the memorial service for the crew of the *Juno.*

The android and the captain had disappeared from the *Enterprise* early that morning without saying much to anyone. Geordi had thought Data would have his meeting and come back to the bridge to join the pared-down crew, because the android usually volunteered to serve while others took shore leave. But Data hadn't returned all day, and Geordi was in command of the ship. He couldn't leave the bridge to find him. Finally Riker had taken over for him, so he had tracked his friend down by calling Admiral Nechayev's office.

He stopped to look at a model of a collider the S.C.E. had built on an asteroid, and the voice behind him made him jump.

"Commander La Forge?"

It wasn't so much a question as it was a statement. He turned expecting to see someone he knew. What he perceived through his ocular implants was somewhat odd—a human who was so bland he had no distinguishing features—yet there was something about his electrochemical makeup that was oddly familiar.

"I'm Ensign Brewster," he said. "We talked earlier today. So you still haven't gotten in to see Commander Data?"

"No, I've just gotten the runaround," answered La Forge with frustration. "We've got to go to that memorial service."

"Yes, that's why I'm here," said the bookish ensign.

"Well, let's go spring him."

"There's one problem." La Forge pointed to a hulking Starfleet security officer standing by the turbolift, checking everyone's IDs. It was obvious that security had been strengthened in this building today. He sincerely hoped that wasn't because they feared Data.

Brewster ambled slowly toward the turbolift and motioned for La Forge to follow. "Don't say a word as we walk past the guard," he warned. "If he sees you're with me, he won't say a word. But if we stop to talk, he might have to make a show of stopping us. He won't find you on the list."

"Whatever you say," replied La Forge with a curious look at the unassuming ensign.

The big security guard didn't even seem to look at them as they walked past him. When the turbolift door opened, he looked surprised, but his combadge beeped, further distracting him. Before he looked their way again, the turbolift door was closing. "Level four," said Brewster.

"So, Ensign, you must come here a lot," remarked La Forge.

"I get around," answered Brewster. "In fact, I know a way to duck out of this building with Data."

"I bet you do," said La Forge, impressed. *So this is Nechayev's fixer,* he thought to himself. Brewster was certainly the kind of person no one would look at twice; however, he seemed rather old to be an ensign. Geordi knew his perceptions were different from other people's, but Brewster had a vagueness about him that was peculiar. He wondered if his new implants were working at full capacity.

They arrived on a floor of laboratories and design studios in the robotics department, which was not encouraging. Once again, there were plenty of security officers around but very few gold-uniformed engineers; three officers were gathered around a door at the end of the corridor. La Forge was dressed in his regulation duty uniform, so he looked as if he belonged.

The two of them walked right up to the door and past the security officer, who appeared momentarily confused. La Forge spotted Data inside the laboratory, stretched out on a workbench and surrounded by technicians. Every one of his input ports was hardwired. The readouts were whirring past on a screen over his head.

A stout, blue-skinned Bolian looked up at the intruders. "Excuse me, we're conducting tests here. You're not authorized."

"Hello, Geordi," said Data, swiveling his neck to see them. "Hello, Ensign Brewster."

"He can come back tomorrow for his tests," insisted La Forge. "Right now, he's got to go to a memorial service for the crew of the *Juno.*"

"This is on his approved schedule," added Brewster. Several of the technicians seemed to notice the ordinary-looking ensign for the first time. "Unwire him, please."

A brawny Antosian security officer stepped into the room and growled. "Are these two bothering you, Commander?"

"Not yet, but they might be soon," answered the Bolian. "Give us fifteen more minutes."

"I've given you an hour and fifteen minutes," insisted La Forge, crossing to the workbench and starting to undo wires himself. "I've been down in the lobby waiting that long."

"Here are orders from Admiral Nechayev," said Brewster, producing a handheld device, which he handed to the Bolian commander. Geordi glanced at the thing, which looked vaguely like a padd but didn't have any real circuitry; to him, it looked more like a hairbrush. Still the commander seemed to be reading from it as La Forge hurriedly untangled his friend.

"The orders are valid," muttered the Bolian with disappointment. "But we have our orders, too. He can go, but I want him back here at oh-seven-hundred hours."

"Is he functional?" asked Brewster. "Does he seem to be himself?"

"I am feeling fine," replied Data, swinging his legs over the side of the bench and hopping off. "Commander Moroz has examined me before, during my Academy days. It was a pleasure to see you again, Commander."

"You too, Data," said the Bolian, his arrogant façade crumbling a bit. "Good luck in the inquiry."

"Why, thank you." The android made a polite bow, and he strode out the door with his two rescuers in tow.

"Let them pass!" ordered Commander Moroz.

Once in the corridor, they made quickly for the turbolift at the far end of the hall. As they walked, La Forge studied Ensign Brewster a bit closer. "Is there something wrong, Commander?" asked Brewster, noticing his attention.

"Ensign, have we met before?" La Forge shook his head puzzledly. "You remind me of someone I know, but I can't quite remember who."

Brewster smiled. "A lot of people say that. I have a very common face."

"I guess so," said La Forge with a shrug. "Your manner too."

When they reached the turbolift, the ensign stopped and said, "I have to make sure Captain Picard gets to the service, too. Tell the turbolift you want to go to the transportation center in the basement. From there, take the moving walkway to the basement at Academy Central Union and look for the Sarek Lecture Hall. You can avoid going through both lobbies that way."

"Thank you, Ensign Brewster," said Data. "Please give my regards to Admiral Nechayev and tell her I have been reviewing the testimony I will give on Thursday."

"Remember not to talk about the case with anyone," warned the ensign. He smiled at La Forge. "Except maybe your friends."

"I am under orders not to comment," agreed Data.

The turbolift door opened. La Forge pushed his friend into the chamber. Wanting to ask about Captain Picard, he turned to look for Brewster again, but the ensign was gone. The hallway was empty. The doors slid shut before Geordi had a chance to keep looking for him.

"He has been very helpful," said Data.

"Yes, very," agreed Geordi, feeling a bit tired and woozy. "Does Ensign . . . What's his name?"

"Brewster," answered Data. "Computer, transportation center in the basement."

"Transportation center," echoed the mechanical voice.

La Forge blinked his eyes, thinking that he could hardly recall Brewster's face now. "Does the ensign remind you of someone . . . maybe someone who used to serve on the *Enterprise?*"

"Yes," answered Data. "But then many humans remind me of many other humans. Is it rude to say that?"

"No." Geordi chuckled and patted his friend on the back. "The ship has been dead with everyone gone, but we're thinking about throwing a poker game tonight."

"That sounds very enjoyable," answered the android. "It will distract our minds."

"Well, we can try," agreed the chief engineer.

Captain Picard buttoned the tunic of his dress uniform, which he was wearing for the memorial service. He had finished the questionnaire about half an hour before. He didn't think he had sent up any red flags; no one should conclude that he had a murderous personality. The captain had spent the last hour answering questions about Ontailians, and he wished he understood them better.

If I win my case and discredit them, they might leave the Federation for good, he thought glumly; but he doubted that was a major concern for them. What they worried about was the same thing he was worried about: *What are they hiding in the graveyard at Rashanar?*

There came an old-fashioned knock on his door. "Come!" he called.

Counselor Colleen Cabot entered. She was also wearing a Starfleet dress uniform, in Special Services blue, unlike the civilian clothes she had worn earlier. "Hello, Captain, I see you finished all of your work. Thank you," she said, back to acting cordial but not insipid.

"You're welcome," answered Picard. "Are you going to the service, too?"

Cabot nodded. "Where you go, I go. Until I release you for the inquiry, you're in my custody. But I'll have to share you, because you have three more women waiting for you in the lobby."

"Let me guess," said Picard with a smile. "Admiral Nechayev, Dr. Crusher, and Counselor Troi."

"I'm probably in for it, aren't I?" asked Cabot worriedly.

"Yes," Picard answered, crossing to the door, which turned into a holosuite archway at his approach. "I'll try to protect you from them."

They stepped into the tastefully appointed corridor, and it felt wonderful to get out of his cage, although he dared not say so. As they walked to the turbolift, they passed a white-suited attendant, who nodded pleasantly at the captain. His face was oddly prosaic yet familiar, and the captain glanced back at him. But the attendant was moving swiftly in the other direction.

"Who is that attendant?" he asked the counselor.

"What attendant?" she responded. They both glanced behind them, but there was no one there.

After stepping off the turbolift and entering the lobby, Captain Picard felt like a matinee idol as he was surrounded by doting women. During the introductions, Beverly Crusher and Admiral Nechayev gave Colleen Cabot dirty looks, but Troi seemed to know her fellow counselor and greeted her warmly.

"We've been waiting for you for hours," complained Beverly, giving Cabot some more evil eye.

"I had a couple of questionnaires to fill out," he answered with a glance at his jailer.

"This is highly unusual," muttered Nechayev, her intensity ratcheting up a notch. "Admiral Ross assured me that the captain would be well treated."

"I have been," Picard assured them all. "Can we please talk about something else? I can't feel sorry for myself when I consider what happened to Captain Leeden and the *Juno* crew."

That effectively ended conversation as they made the short trek to the Academy Central Union, where they met up with Data and La Forge. Commander Riker had volunteered to stay on board the *Enterprise* for the duration, a decision for which Picard was very grateful. He knew he could lose command of his ship at any stage of this procedure. He wanted to make sure Riker was aboard when it happened. He loved his first officer, but if Riker was allowed off the ship, he would soon be parasailing in Mazatlán and be impossible to reach. If he was on board, no one else would be assigned the *Enterprise.*

They reached Sarek Hall, the Academy's largest lecture hall, and found it filled with cadets, officers, and family members of the *Juno* crew. The family members were easy to spot, because they pointed Picard out to each other and glared at him. Although officers and admirals greeted each other warmly, the *Enterprise* crew members were pointedly left alone to find seats apart from the others. Captain Picard lifted his chin and nodded politely to Admiral Ross and others he knew, although no one from the admiralty approached him for personal conversation. This was as persona non grata as he ever hoped to become.

As promised, Colleen Cabot seldom left his side, although she was content to converse with Deanna Troi while eavesdropping on his conversation with Beverly. They struggled to find topics of discussion, as did Geordi and Data. It was difficult not to talk about the tribunal or reassure each other that all would end well.

But Picard was adamant: he refused to discuss his own troubles when they seemed so trivial compared with the grief of those who had lost loved ones on the *Juno*.

A clergyman from Captain Leeden's hometown came up to talk first. He introduced himself and pointed out Leeden's family in the front row, all wearing Starfleet uniforms, except for her mother and a few young children. Her two brothers were both lieutenants. The pastor talked about how much she had wanted to follow in the family tradition of service. He pointed out that Jill Leeden had always volunteered for the toughest assignments, and Rashanar was certainly that. When she had come home for several months to recover from injuries suffered in the Dominion War, she had become a humanitarian, organizing shelters for displaced refugees.

It was difficult going for Picard to listen to the eulogy. He felt for these people. The accusatory stares made him uncomfortable, but he knew the whole point of being here was not to be comfortable. It was to show respect for the crew of the *Juno*. Three family members of others slain spoke on behalf of those who couldn't speak owing to time constraints, and their brief, tearful remarks made the veteran captain misty-eyed.

Admiral Ross spoke last. He lauded the entire *Juno* crew, mentioning senior officers and department heads by name and distinctions. He expounded on the *Juno*'s distinguished record, mentioning awards for valor and scientific discoveries. Clearly Captain Leeden had never shirked from any difficult mission, and Picard felt a deeper connection with her.

By necessity, Ross's speech was long and detailed. It

gave bored audience members ample opportunity to look his way. *No, I haven't sprouted any horns,* Picard wanted to tell them. *I'm still the same Captain Picard who used to lecture here to packed houses.* He tried to concentrate on Ross's remarks. He marveled that the admiral delivered his eulogy so well. He supposed that the war had given Ross considerable practice. The admiral could probably name every Starfleet vessel lost at Rashanar.

Admiral Ross concluded by addressing the current problem: "As we face inquiries and investigations into the tragic loss of the *Juno,* it's important to remember one thing: Starfleet is all one family. We're not always a happy family—we make mistakes and face adversity—but we have respect for each other and our shared duties and goals. One of those goals is not to put fellow officers in needless, avoidable danger. I'm afraid the admiralty and the Federation Council failed on that account . . . for not recognizing how dangerous the Rashanar Battle Site is. I apologize to all of you for that."

He scratched his chin and continued, "The holy book says 'Blessed are the peacemakers' and I think we should take our solace from that. Keeping the peace is often the most dangerous mission for Starfleet, because breaking the peace is always to someone's advantage. We're restricted, wanting to set a good example and not use full force . . . even against ruthless thieves. The *Juno* was trying to keep the peace when she went down. She was retrieving the hallowed dead from our most revered battle site. As our Klingon friends would say, 'It is an honorable death.' "

245

He nodded offstage, and a classical quartet filed in and assembled. "This is the *Juno* Youth String Quartet," explained Ross. "They were here on Earth performing in a series of concerts when their parents and family perished at Rashanar. In memory of their families, they would like to play the piece they played in competition, which enabled them to travel here: Mozart's 'Hunting' Quartet in B flat for strings."

The youngsters began to play, and play beautifully they did. But it was clear that the youngest player, a blond-haired violinist, was trying to suppress sobs. Before Picard had even realized he was gone, Data popped up on the side of the stage. While the other musicians bravely tried to plow their way through the piece, Data said a few words to the grieving young lady. A moment later, he took over for the violinist, and his perfect playing rallied the others. Together they brought the piece to a rousing conclusion and much applause. A reception was announced for another room in the building, and the memorial service was finally concluded.

Data shook a few hands while keeping an eye on the contingent from the *Enterprise.* Picard and the ladies did some milling around until the aisles cleared of traffic.

"It's time to go, Jean-Luc," said Colleen Cabot, nodding toward the door.

"Do we really have to?" asked the captain. "It's so early."

The counselor smiled sweetly. "If you cooperate, I'll let you go at this time tomorrow. You can sleep in your own bed before the inquiry."

Beverly Crusher had taken notice of the conversation, and she intruded. "Counselor," she began, "I happen to know your boss pretty well, and I don't want to hear that you're denying Captain Picard visitors, including his doctor and his lawyer."

"Beverly," he said, trying to calm her down. "I don't mind. She has a short time—"

The younger woman leveled her blue eyes at the older woman and acted as if he wasn't even there. "I don't think you'll find many volunteers to take over for me," she declared. "I'm damned if I do and damned if I don't. If I find the captain non compos mentis, then I'll have to take the heat, but he won't have to face a court-martial. He could stay under my care for a couple of months until this all blows over. If I give the captain a green light to go ahead, he could face a court-martial and lose everything . . . his ship, his rank, even his freedom."

While Beverly paused in thought, the young blond woman got more in her face to whisper, "You tell me. Was he in his right mind when this happened?"

Crusher looked at Troi, and both of them came to an unspoken conclusion. It was Deanna who finally nodded and said, "Yes."

Counselor Cabot gave Picard a sidelong glance. "Then I'll only have to decide if he's in his right mind now."

When the captain was ushered back into his room at the mental-health facility, it was dark inside. He started to say something to Counselor Cabot, but she had beaten a hasty retreat down the hall. The door slid shut behind him, cutting off all light in the room.

"Is this a new test?" muttered Picard. "Sensory deprivation. Computer, lights."

At once the lights came on, and he wasn't in his rustic log cabin, of which he had grown fond; instead he was his old bedroom on the family farm in Labarre, France. He was stunned at first, then angry, because they had chosen this place for him.

"Computer, can I change this back to the log cabin in Canada?" he demanded.

"Yes," answered the computer.

"Wait a minute," said Picard. He looked around, realizing that this version of his bedroom was from his teens, when he had stopped sharing the room with his older brother. On top of his dressers and shelves were starships displayed inside clear wine bottles, models he had meticulously crafted himself, although the holodeck did not reproduce them in much detail. If this scene was accurate, his old bed would not be as soft as the one in the cabin. Out the window, he could see neat rows of grape vines stretching into the distance. It was the middle of the season, so there was watering and pruning, but not much activity. Plus a golden twilight was falling.

"Here, Jean-Luc, eat your lunch," said a feminine voice speaking French.

He whirled around to see his mother carrying a tray of food into the room; she set it on his desk and smiled at him. He glared at the wall where the picture window had been in the cabin, because he assumed they were watching him. "I know that's not my mother."

"Who are you talking to?" asked Yvette Picard with confusion. She wiped her hands on her apron. "There's nothing unfair about your lunch, except that you missed it earlier. Now eat up, Jean-Luc, because we're going to play *Milles Borne* before dinner."

Knowing he was beaten, Captain Picard slumped into his old, rickety desk chair. It creaked realistically. "Mother," he said politely, "you don't think there's anything odd about the outfit I'm wearing?"

She smiled fondly. "You're just dressed up like your space heroes again, aren't you, Jean-Luc? But please change into something else before your father sees you."

Picard glanced at the veal cutlet on his plate and picked up a croissant, which he studied. It smelled delicious, but of course they knew how to make croissants in San Francisco. "I'm not playing," he said wearily. "I don't really care what you say about me at the tribunal."

"I'm sure I don't know what you're talking about," said his mother cheerfully. "Tribunal? What tribunal? Madame Fouché said it wasn't you who was stealing the brandy from her reserve barrels. It was that Bouchard troublemaker."

"I'm not playing." Picard jumped to his feet, took a couple of hops, and sprang into his bed, a maneuver he had done a million times but not for sixty years. He lay there, marveling that his muscles had not forgotten.

"You think everybody likes you, Jean-Luc," said his mother as she tidied up. "Not everybody likes you. There are a few who say you get too many accolades, too much credit, too many plum assignments, not to mention the brightest and best crew. Who couldn't succeed with the *Enterprise?"*

Picard had been only half listening, but now he sat upright. "Who are you speaking for? And I know it's not my mother."

"Don't listen to a silly old lady," said Yvette Picard, back to using motherly tones.

"Who wants me out of here?" he demanded.

The holoperson gave him a friendly smile. "Why, nobody wants you out of here, Jean-Luc. We want you to stay in this pretty room forever, just dreaming about the future and spacecraft. Just as always."

She moved briskly to the door, escaping from the room before Picard could even jump to his feet and chase after her. As the door shut behind the apparition, he caught a glimpse of himself in the long dressing mirror behind the door, and he gasped aloud. It was Jean-Luc Picard at the age of twelve!

Of course, his rational mind said, *they have recent records of me at that age, and Cabot even asked about the time I turned into a child.* Instead it made him introspective, and he asked himself, *Who is that young man, and where has he gone? Have I been in this game too long?*

"Computer, take me back to the log cabin," he said wistfully.

Chapter Sixteen

"Don't be nervous, Picard, we'll be fine," Admiral Nechayev assured him as they sat behind the table in the Hall of Justice, Courtroom B, Starfleet Command. That was the confident tone of voice she used when sending people off on a particularly dangerous mission, recalled the captain.

The customary gallery visitors and reporters were not to be found this morning. The simple court was more somber and dark than usual. Everyone conversed in whispers, as if enemies were hiding a few centimeters away. Two technicians had finished installing a larger-than-normal visual screen, and they were running a few tests on it. Picard looked for supporters in the crowd, but he found none; his crew or anyone connected with the Rashanar incident had to wait to be called. As before at the memorial service, people either stared at him or avoided his eyes.

He finally noticed Ensign Brewster seated in the first row behind Nechayev. The aide gave Picard an encouraging smile. The captain shook his head, thinking that Brewster had to be the most unprepossessing person he had ever met. Less than a meter away, he could still look right past the ensign.

The doors at the back opened, and an antigrav container floated into the court, followed by a tall, lanky Starfleet officer. "Your prosecutor," whispered Nechayev, "Commodore Korgan, and his telepathic aide, Commander Emery."

Picard's lips thinned. "I don't think he's ever lost a case."

"I don't know about that," sniffed Nechayev, "but I know he has risen rather quickly through the ranks. Worry more about the admirals."

It was difficult not to stare at the Medusan as he maneuvered his box on top of the table, with his aide making sure he was positioned comfortably. Emery then went to talk briefly with Ensign Brewster. Picard turned around in his seat and warned himself that he was mostly going to be a spectator here. When they let him talk, he had to be very careful about what he said.

As soon as the technicians finished, the sergeant-at-arms called everyone to find seats. Moments later, he ordered them to rise in order to introduce the tribunal as they filed in: Admiral Ross, Admiral Paris, and Admiral Nakamura, with Ross taking center seat.

William Ross nodded to the participants and said,

"Five days ago, two Federation vessels, the *U.S.S. Juno* and the Ontailian heavy cruiser *Vuxhal*, were destroyed in peacetime action in the Rashanar Battle Site. This is an inquiry to establish the facts of these tragic losses and to see if further action is required by this tribunal."

He looked toward the prosecution table, and lights blinked cheerfully on the Medusan's container. "Commodore Korgan, what is the finding you wish the tribunal to reach?"

Emery spoke confidently and said, "Starfleet will prove that Captain Jean-Luc Picard did with malice and aforethought cause an unprovoked attack on the vessel of a fellow Federation member. Since all hands were killed, we wish to petition the court to pursue a charge of murder for the *Vuxhal* crew. Also dereliction of duty for failing to prevent an earlier Androssi attack on the *Juno* and for failing to aid the *Juno* when she was under attack by angry Ontailians."

Ross sighed heavily and asked, "What evidence do you wish to present to support these petitions?"

"We have a vidlog of the destruction of the *Vuxhal*, wreckage from the *Vuxhal*, the pertinent logs and reports of Captain Leeden, Captain Picard, and other senior officers. We will also present testimony from Ontailians who observed the attack from nearby ships, and of *Enterprise* crew members Dr. Crusher, Commander La Forge, and Commander Data. Our first witness is Counselor Colleen Cabot, who has evaluated Captain Picard over the last two days at Medical Mental Health."

Picard leaned back in his seat, realizing he was going

to be here a long time, and very little of it was going to be pleasant.

"In your opinion, Counselor Cabot," asked Emery, "is Captain Picard fully competent to undergo these proceedings and any further actions this tribunal may choose to pursue?"

"He is competent," answered the attractive counselor, who looked at Jean-Luc for the first time since entering the court.

"Does he understand the charges which may be leveled against him?"

Colleen pursed her lips, and Picard wondered why she was hesitant. "No, sir, he does not," she answered, "because Captain Picard believes that he did *not* destroy the *Vuxhal.* Whether he clings to delusion or fact, I don't think he'll ever accept the court's contention that he destroyed the *Vuxhal.*"

Picard relaxed a bit, because at least that much was true. Nechayev wrote notes with a stylus on her padd.

Emery plunged onward. "Was he in sound mind from May eighth to May fifteenth, when he was serving in Rashanar and these events occurred?"

"All indications are that he was," she answered.

"In your experience, how would you characterize Captain Picard's mental state now?"

Cabot lifted her delicate chin to say, "He is suffering from grief, guilt, and low-grade depression, all of which are understandable. He makes a valiant effort to maintain his good humor."

"Is he fit to serve now?" asked Emery.

"Objection," Nechayev blurted. "May we approach the bench?"

Admiral Ross waved her off. "I was just going to overrule that myself. It goes to the matter of this inquiry. If there are no objections, I'm going to dismiss the counselor for now."

Nechayev shook her head, and Emery concentrated for a moment before he said, "No objections, sir."

As Colleen Cabot walked out the door without looking at him, Nechayev leaned close to whisper, "It was interesting what she did for you just now. I'll tell you later."

"Your Honors," said Commander Emery, bowing to the admirals, "I would like to enter into evidence Captain Leeden's and Captain Picard's logs and messages to Starfleet during this time period."

Ross turned to Nechayev and said, "If there are no objections."

"Only that I would also like to include subspace messages sent directly between Captain Leeden and Captain Picard," replied Nechayev.

The dickering over the evidence seemed to go on forever. Long passages from messages were read into the official transcript. Once again, Picard had to relive the string of ignominies he had suffered in the Rashanar Battle Site. It began with the *Calypso* being hijacked right from under his nose while they were exploring the *Asgard*. It went downhill during the encounter with the antimatter asteroid, when they had reported that an Ontailian ship had been lost, only to have the Ontailians deny it. There were endless encounters with scavengers, most of which resulted in no arrests but considerable damage to shuttlecraft and escorts. Deadly blasts from energy spikes, dramatic rescues, and much spinning of wheels—it was all rehashed in messages dating from the time, which seemed so long ago but was only a few days.

The final chapters began with the ill-fated adventures of the shuttlecraft *Hudson.* The messages showed a dawning realization of the scope of the Androssi raid, interspersed with the separate rescues of La Forge and Data. When Picard allowed the Androssi who rescued Data to escape, that elicted an avalanche of frantic messages from Leeden. In her account, they had failed to chase the Androssi convoy, which allowed the scavengers to fire upon the *Juno* and disable her. The only lull in the storm was when both ships had paused to make repairs on the *Juno.* Meanwhile, the Ontailians were heavily involved in the hunt for Androssi scavengers.

Picard listened intently to messages about the disputed destruction of the *Vuxhal,* and the very real destruction of the *Juno.* He saw members of the tribunal wincing at times. He wanted to shout at them that this was a compression of events; at the time no one knew that everything was spinning out of control. Chaos was the natural condition at Rashanar. Worse yet, there was very little in the disjointed narrative of the reports that showed the mimic ship could be real. Thus far, it seemed like a dubious explanation for a lot of unexplainable phenomena.

He was beginning to realize why Admiral Nechayev was worried.

At long last, they had a meal break, but the respite was brief. When they got back from lunch, the new, larger viewscreen was activated. Picard really didn't want to watch what was probably coming up—the bridge record of them firing on the duplicate *Vuxhal*. *You're going out of sequence,* he wanted to tell them, but he knew that vidlogs carried a lot of weight in Starfleet investigations. Because they automatically recorded in key areas of the ship, they could be taken at face value and were tough to discredit. Much of his future depended upon what the tribunal saw . . . and how they perceived it.

As the log played, Picard felt as if he were watching an ancient silent movie. He tuned out all the exposition from the lawyers and even the words spoken by himself and his crew. He could remember the actions and the emotions he was feeling as if it were yesterday. He knew every unfolding of the narrative as if he had written it, rather than lived it. Every now and then, audible portions shot into his consciousness:

Data gasping out loud and saying, "Captain, there it is—the replica of the *Vuxhal*."

Everything that came next made it clear to Picard that the *Enterprise* had tried to hail the pursuing ship and tried to escape from them. But their maneuverability inside the graveyard was extremely limited. He saw Admiral Nakamura squirm a bit and Admiral Paris frown deeply in thought.

"You're sure that's the mimic ship?" asked a voice he recognized as his own. "There can't be any mistake."

"That *is* the duplicate!" On the video, Data jumped to his feet. "Captain, I advise you to destroy it. Do not let it get close to us, or the *Enterprise* will be like all these other derelicts . . . dead bodies and smashed circuits."

The captain ordered, "Data, turn off your emotion chip."

The android cocked his head, looked visibly calmer, and dropped his hand. "I have done so. Is that better?"

After that, Data had been himself, but it was a compelling moment in the log. *It's true,* thought the captain, *my entire defense hinges on the fact that I believed Data—even when he had been damaged and was emotional. The only way I have to save myself is to destroy Data, and they would let me do it.*

"Data, target a brace of quantum torpedoes," ordered his video image from the past.

"Yes, sir," the android answered, his fingers a blur on his console. "Ready, sir."

"Fire!" roared the captain.

It's clear from the log that whatever was pursuing us, I shot and hit it, Picard decided. *There's no debate about that. So what* was *that ship?*

Picard was thinking so hard that he almost missed the actual destruction of the *Vuxhal.* The tribunal watched in stunned silence as the elegant spacecraft blew apart, followed by interference and static that obscured the image on the viewscreen.

If there was any mercy in the universe, the record should have ended there, but the worst was yet to come. First Leeden screamed at him about overreacting and for firing on a friendly ship. To him, it seemed as if the Ontailians overreacted, but perhaps that was his lack of

258

knowledge about them. If they had been talking about Klingons, he could well imagine instant retaliation after seeing their flagship destroyed.

In truth, the retaliation wasn't instant, because Leeden had thought she could negotiate with the Ontailians. While the *Enterprise* crew waited on the bridge, Counselor Troi made a profound statement on the video log:

"It must have been like this during the Battle of Rashanar," said Troi. "The doppelgänger caused mistaken identity . . . deadly hostilities . . . vengeance with no thought of surrender. Ships were disabled by the force beam. Whole crews died while they were unconscious. No wonder there was no record of all this."

Is anyone listening? Picard wanted to scream at the admirals.

The attack on the *Juno* took them all by surprise, both the people on the vidlog and the ones watching it in the courtroom. Despite the entrance of the *Enterprise* into the melee, all four Ontailian ships pounded away at the hapless *Juno*. Before they could do anything to help, the *Juno* broke apart.

When the record ended, Admiral Ross wisely asked for a short recess before they continued. During the break, Picard turned to Nechayev, smiled wanly, and said, "So I should have taken the deal, right?"

"Right," muttered the admiral. "I've seen the log before. Every time I see it, I draw the same conclusion. Your defense rests on this doppelgänger being real, but the only proof you have is Data's testimony. Unfortunately, that's like having Bigfoot as your star witness."

Picard frowned. "I thought the Ontailians were supposed to present physical evidence . . . wreckage from the *Vuxhal.*"

"They claim they couldn't find any," answered Nechayev. "They say an antimatter pack from one of the graveyard ships must have come through there and destroyed the wreckage. Believe me, I intend to ask them about it, because the lack of evidence from the *Vuxhal* weakens their case."

"Then again," said the captain, "an antimatter pack could completely obliterate any debris, and we often encountered them in the graveyard."

"I was afraid you would say that." The admiral sighed and looked down at her notes. "It helps, but there isn't much we can do to refute the log. At least your *pretty* counselor friend did you a possible favor."

"What did she do?" asked Picard, thinking Cabot's testimony had been fairly accurate.

Nechayev lowered her voice to say, "She didn't give you an entirely clean bill of mental health. She made it sound as if you're a bit obsessed with this mimic ship and that you would never admit you're wrong. Ross let the inquiry continue, so he gave me a possible avenue to appeal the findings."

"You mean argue that I really *am* crazy," muttered Picard.

"Well, it's not a perfect plan B," admitted Nechayev, sitting back in her chair. "Besides, they will probably try to discredit Data."

"Why?" asked Picard angrily.

"Because he has no constituency," answered the admiral. "There's no planet of androids who might threaten to leave the Federation. No Android Council members. It's the way a trial goes—aim for the most vulnerable spot. Besides, everything about Rashanar is murky. I've seen that video log a number of times, and you lived through it—and I still can't figure out exactly what happened. The tribunal has a rough job and only complicated, bad options from which to choose. The tribunal is going to start looking for an easy solution."

Nechayev tapped her chin thoughtfully and said, "I intend to portray the Androssi as the main bad guys here. They were the spark that set off the forest fire, and they aren't here to defend themselves."

"They didn't destroy the *Juno* or the *Vuxhal*," said Picard, "although it wasn't for lack of trying. We should investigate the three ships of theirs that were destroyed in this action."

"Every new detail makes the situation murkier," Nechayev pointed out.

"For our first witness, we'd like to call Dr. Beverly Crusher," announced Commander Emery.

Although Beverly glanced at Picard on her way to the witness stand, she was careful not to smile or act overly friendly toward him. With her most professional demeanor, she answered questions about the paralysis Picard had suffered when he was gassed by the Androssi who stole the *Calypso*. There was no sugarcoating the fact that he had been physically incapacitated by the muscle toxin, and he might have died if not for the quick arrival of La Forge and Data, followed by a shuttlecraft that had already been dispatched from the *Enterprise.*

"You did not personally see Captain Picard in this condition, did you?" asked Emery.

"No," admitted Crusher. "He came to me afterward."

Emery asked sharply, "How many hours had elapsed after this incident before Captain Picard came to you to be examined?"

"Approximately eight hours," she answered truthfully.

Emery paused to get prompting from the Medusan in the container beside him, then asked, "Isn't that highly unusual, not to see a patient for eight hours after he was paralyzed and nearly died? You castigated the captain for taking so long to see you, didn't you?"

"Yes," she answered, "but he had gone to see Captain Leeden and done other—"

Emery cut her off. "So, Dr. Crusher, is it accurate to say that you were unable to observe any of the actual short-term effects of the Androssi muscle toxin on Captain Picard, because he reported to you so long after the incident?"

"That's accurate," she answered, casting her eyes downward.

Lights on the Medusan's box blinked, and Emery asked, "Upon returning to Earth, did you deliver pathology on the Androssi muscle toxin to Dr. Yerbi Fandau of Starfleet Medical?"

"Yes," replied Crusher, sounding relieved to change the subject from Picard's dubious behavior.

Emery lifted a padd and said, "With the tribunal's

permission, I would like to read into the record the conclusion reached by Dr. Fandau of Starfleet Medical."

"Permission granted," replied Admiral Ross.

The commander read aloud, "The Androssi neuro-muscular toxin, dimafluerine-narcosomatic, is a powerful and dangerous substance that induces in a human being a total body paralysis for a duration of ten minutes to permanent. It is not unlike the toxin of a puffer fish, which has been known to cause a condition that resembles death. If the lungs and heart were paralyzed, it would cause death in some individuals. Although the short-term effects of this toxin are easily observable, the long-term effects cannot be established without considerable testing on volunteer subjects."

Emery sighed after his reading and asked, "Is there anything in Dr. Fandau's conclusion you wish to dispute?"

"No," muttered Beverly.

The tall commander smiled. "Then quite frankly, Doctor, you were unable to study either the short-term effects or long-term effects of this toxin on Captain Picard. You have no idea what it did to him, do you?"

"Objection," said Admiral Nechayev.

"I withdraw the question," said Emery, having made his point. "Your witness, Admiral." Looking smug and satisfied, the prosecutor took a seat beside his superior, Commodore Korgan.

Admiral Nechayev rose to her feet and asked, "Dr. Crusher, how long have you known Jean-Luc Picard?"

That brought a smile to the beleaguered doctor's

face. "Twenty-eight years," she answered proudly, "serving with him for twelve years."

"And you have no doubt observed him under many circumstances and conditions," said Nechayev. "You have treated him for illness and injury numerous times."

"Oh, yes," she answered.

"Have you ever classified Captain Picard as unfit for duty?"

"Yes, a few times."

"In your opinion, was Captain Picard incapacitated or unfit for duty when you examined him after the *Calypso* was stolen?"

"No," answered Crusher forcefully.

Nechayev nodded gratefully. "Thank you, Doctor. No more questions."

"Next we would like to call to the stand Commander Geordi La Forge," intoned Commander Emery.

La Forge was on the stand a long time. The first part of his testimony centered on their exploration of the derelict starship *Asgard* and the subsequent hijacking of the yacht *Calypso*. This account brought nothing new for anyone to chew on, thought Picard, as the *Calypso* incident had been rehashed ad nauseam. Commander Emery asked forthright questions without much bias. The story came out fairly accurately, the captain decided.

The latter part of La Forge's testimony focused on the misadventures of the shuttlecraft *Hudson*. He related how he and Data had spent hours searching for the Androssi ship that supposedly fired on the *Juno,* chasing her around the dangerous center of the graveyard. They had played cat-and-mouse with each other, alternating among acting dead, hiding among the wrecks, and sudden bursts of frantic chase. La Forge drove home how unreliable sensor readings were in the middle of the boneyard, but he stressed that they could pick up impulse engines firing, at least enough to keep the chase going.

The *Hudson* crew hadn't been entirely sure the vessel they were chasing was the stolen *Calypso*. They feared they had lost it until they stumbled upon not one *Calypso* but *two*. Once again, Emery and his Medusan master did a good job of eliciting the facts. The engineer told about the added photon torpedoes on the *Calypso*, the new paint, and new name, *Tempo*, and how they were astounded to see that the ships were identical down to these small details. Finally Geordi related how the shuttlecraft and everything in it, including Data, went dead before they could form any conclusions.

"There was a high-pitched whine," said Geordi, wincing at the memory, "and it caused me to black out. But I managed to put on my environmental suit before I did. That protected me from the cold, and there was air in the shuttle."

Emery nodded sympathetically and said with concern, "How 'dead' was Commander Data?"

Geordi swallowed uncomfortably and answered, "He was frozen in his last position. There was no internal activity—at least to my normal observation. Since the other systems on the shuttle were dead, too, I reached that conclusion quickly."

Emery nodded. "You have deactivated Commander

Data a number of times for maintenance and repair, have you not?"

"Yes," answered La Forge, and Picard could tell he hated talking about his friend as if he were a machine. Admiral Nakamura leaned forward to listen, and his face was an inscrutable blank.

"So Commander Data was as broken as he could be without being disassembled?"

"Yeah, I guess so," muttered Geordi. "But unlike a human being, Data can be reborn as good as new."

Emery smiled and closed his eyes to communicate with Commodore Korgan. Then he said, "Your own optical implants malfunctioned at the same time, did they not? That made you effectively blind."

La Forge heaved a sigh and answered, "Yes."

Emery circled around the table and asked, "You were rescued a few minutes later still inside the shuttlecraft *Hudson,* but Data was not with you. Is that right?"

"That's right."

"So you were unconscious, the shuttlecraft was dead, and Commander Data was inert. Do you know how Data got out of the shuttlecraft?"

"No clue. Neither had anyone else," answered the engineer.

Emery turned to the tribunal. "The details of Commander La Forge's rescue are to be found in First Officer Riker's log, exhibit eighteen. Commander Riker is currently acting captain of the *Enterprise.* We didn't wish to call him away from his duties. To summarize, the *Hudson* was found with all video and sensor logs erased, also it was in the vicinity of wreckage from the *Calypso.* The yacht was destroyed by unknown forces. Do you concur with that summation, Commander La Forge?"

"Yes."

"Did Riker find the wreckage of one yacht or two yachts?" asked Emery.

"One," admitted La Forge reluctantly.

Emery nodded sagely and seemed to be listening to a distant voice. "In your report you ventured the theory that one of the identical yachts you saw could have been a holographic illusion? Or some other mechanical illusion?"

"Objection," said Admiral Nechayev. "Conclusion of the witness."

"The commander is the most experienced engineer in Starfleet," answered Ross. "I'll let him answer that."

"It could have been," agreed La Forge.

"And the Androssi have been known to fool us before, have they not?"

"Yes," murmured La Forge.

Emery concluded, "So we have no proof there were two yachts and no idea how the *Calypso* was destroyed. We also don't know how Commander Data came to be where he was later discovered, but we do know that he was malfunctioning. Is that a fair assessment, Commander La Forge?"

"Yes, it is." The engineer bowed his head sadly.

"We wish to call Commander Data to the stand," announced Commander Emery.

The android was ushered in to take the hot seat. He was the only one in the courtroom who wasn't nervous about it. Even the Medusan, Korgan, seemed hesitant. He took longer to converse telepathically with Emery. The tribunal members—Ross, Paris, Nakamura—were cordial toward the android, but Picard realized that none of them actually knew Data very well.

Under questioning, Data corroborated Geordi's accounts of the actions on the *Asgard* when the *Calypso* had been hijacked. Obviously, he couldn't add much information about the encounter with the twin *Calypso*s and his subsequent deactivation. He didn't know how he had ended up floating in space. Emery wouldn't allow the android to express his theory that the mimic ship had taken him from the shuttlecraft, examined him, and found him to be uninteresting. Since this contention couldn't be proven, it wasn't a terrible oversight, thought Picard.

Unfortunately, there was very little in Data's testimony that could be proven. He was the only one who had seen the mimic ship paralyze and replicate the Ontailian heavy cruiser *Vuxhal*. He was the only one who had seen the *Vuxhal* spontaneously destruct after the mimic ship had turned into a reasonable copy of it. By his own admission, he continued to black out periodically while he floated in space, and he had memory loss akin to amnesia.

"You were malfunctioning, weren't you?" asked Emery.

"Yes," admitted Data. "I also relived memories from my past as my positronic brain attempted to do a memory update of my neural network."

"Would you normally trust your observations during a time when you are malfunctioning?" asked Emery.

"No," answered Data, "but I eventually recovered all of my short-term memory loss and was functioning as normal."

Emery shook his head with disbelief. "After what you'd been through, how would you know if you were functioning normally?"

Data turned to the panel. "I performed my self-diagnostics."

"Didn't you do something else too, Commander?" asked the prosecutor. "Didn't you activate your emotion chip?"

"Yes."

"Why?"

"Activating my emotion chip puts me in touch with those areas of reasoning beyond mere logic, such as intuition," answered Data. "I was confounded by a situation I could not solve logically. I was spiraling toward the gravity dump and the vortex of debris."

The prosecutor paused to listen to the Medusan in the box, and he nodded. "Would you activate your emotion chip for the tribunal?"

Nechayev sprang to her feet and barked, "I object!"

"Overruled," replied Ross thoughtfully. "The entire rationale for the *Enterprise* firing on the *Vuxhal* is fear over this mimic ship. The validity of that hinges on Data's competence during the time he formed his theory. Activate the chip, Commander."

Data cocked his head slightly and said, "Emotions are activated."

Emery closed his eyes, getting his instructions. He finally said, "Isn't it true, Commander Data, that you stole the emotion chip from your brother Lore after you killed him?"

"I object," said Nechayev vociferously. "No one is on trial here, least of all Commander Data."

"I am asking for the origin of the emotion chip," insisted Emery. "Commander, you took the emotion chip out of your duplicate, Lore, before you dismembered him, correct?"

Nobody breathed in the courtroom, and Data seemed to be struggling with the answer. "We had to dismantle him—he was defective."

Emery strutted before the tribunal, pointing to Data. "Lore had the emotion chip, but he was defective. However, when *you* use the emotion chip—even while you're in a damaged state—you're perfectly fine! Is this what you want the tribunal to believe?"

Data hesitated. "I . . . I believe I am fine."

"Why don't you use the emotion chip all the time?" asked Emery. Captain Picard cringed, because there was no good answer to that question.

"There are times I wish to be more efficient," answered the android.

"Hmmmm," said Emery. "So the emotion chip makes you inefficient and possibly psychotic, like your duplicate, Lore?"

"He is not my duplicate," insisted Data as Admiral Nechayev leaped out of her seat to object.

Emery waved her off and said, "We'll get back to the case. Commander Data, you have stated that the *Vuxhal* was actually destroyed by an unexplained anomaly near the middle of the Rashanar Battle Site. Is that correct?"

"Yes, it is," answered the android.

"Can you give us the coordinates where you say the *Vuxhal* was destroyed, and can we find it there?"

"Not precisely," answered the android. "By now, that wreckage has been pulled into the vortex."

"So there is no actual proof you can give the tribunal to refute what the Ontailians are about to testify?"

"No," answered Data glumly.

Emery nodded confidently. "No more questions for Commander Data. He may turn off his emotion chip now, if he wishes to be more efficient."

Admiral Nechayev questioned Data and got a good account of the transformation of the mimic ship into the *Vuxhal*. Dispassionately, Data told of the destruction of the *Vuxhal* and his daring rescue from the derelict in which he had taken refuge. Data admitted that he had asked his superiors not to fire at the Androssi salvage vessel that had saved him, but explaining that one minor infraction didn't negate all the larger ones.

Data's story still hung together for Picard, but he couldn't tell how many others in the room had been swayed. They respected Data, but he wasn't their shipmate, an officer they trusted with their lives every single day of the week. This fateful event had just been one of countless occasions when Picard had based his actions on Data's word. He would do it again tomorrow.

The Ontailians followed Data to the stand and presented their own logs and visuals of the *Enterprise* firing upon the heavy cruiser. Under Emery's gentle questioning, they insisted they thought they were under attack when they turned on the *Juno*. After all, they had been battling scavengers all day, and some of those looters had been disguised as Starfleet vessels. The destruction of the *Vuxhal* right before their eyes left them no choice.

When Admiral Nechayev rose to cross-examine her first Ontailian witness, she asked, "Where is the physical evidence? If the *Vuxhal* was destroyed near buoy twenty-five, why weren't you able to recover any wreckage?"

"First, we were involved in an action with the *Enterprise,*" answered the mechanical voice of the universal translator. "Then the aberrant antimatter pack swept through the area and dissolved all traces of the wreckage. At least that is our theory. We were unable to enter the area for several hours."

"That's awfully convenient, isn't it," remarked Nechayev snidely.

"May it please the court," interrupted Emery, "no one has produced any wreckage of the *Vuxhal*—from either the middle or the outer part of Rashanar. We can name dozens of vessels which vanished there without a trace."

"That says something about Rashanar, doesn't it?" she added. "No further questions."

The hearing room had been reduced to a somber hush, and whispers sounded like shouts. It was the third day of the inquiry, but for Picard it was beginning to seem like one night's long nightmare.

Appearing last, Captain Picard took the stand and answered all of Admiral Nechayev's questions as truthfully as he could. The prosecution refused to ask the captain any questions at all. *Why should they risk show-*

ing me disrespect, thought Picard, *when they have their case sewed up?*

He could do little but say, "Yes, I believed Data, and I did everything I could to help the *Juno.*" As Counselor Cabot had predicted, he wouldn't be shaken from his belief in the mimic ship.

As she had also predicted, the result was a foregone conclusion. Admirals Ross, Nakamura, and Paris went into seclusion for about an hour and emerged looking grim-faced. They sat at the dais, and the sergeant-at-arms called for the room to come to order.

The court fell into a hush, as Admiral Ross folded his hands in front of him. Somberly he intoned, "The tribunal has reached a preliminary finding on this matter. After hearing and reading the testimony presented, we find that Captain Picard acted negligently in not doing more to prevent this tragedy. That is our only finding at this time, but there may be further action in the future. Until our final determination, Captain Picard will be remanded to the custody of Starfleet Medical Mental Health. This hearing is dismissed."

There were a few gasps from the gallery, but neither Picard nor Nechayev was surprised. Captain Picard felt a pat on his back. He turned around to see unassuming Ensign Brewster, who looked crestfallen. "It isn't over yet," whispered the aide.

"What does this mean?" the captain asked a thoughtful Admiral Nechayev.

"It means you were found negligent," she answered.

The admiral bolted from her chair, a look of determination on her pinched face. "Give me a little time to see what I can do, and I'll visit you tonight after dinner. I'll make sure you won't spend much time in the holding cell, Jean-Luc, but go along for now."

"Thank you," replied Picard, although he wasn't in a very thankful mood. He felt a tug on his arm, and he knew it was time to go with those whom he had grown to think of as his jailers. If they thought he had felt helpless in Rashanar, they were wrong, because now he really felt helpless.

Chapter Seventeen

GEORDI LA FORGE WAS ALREADY STUNNED from hearing the outcome of the inquiry when he got even more bad news. Data was back with the S.C.E. They wanted advice on how to take him apart. La Forge moved at light speed to get down to the Starfleet compound and into the labs of Commander Moroz.

Once again, he walked in and found Data stretched out complacently on a workbench, with the Bolian and his assistants gathered around, ready to take apart his best friend.

"Hello, Geordi," said Data pleasantly.

"What's going on?" demanded La Forge. "Why is Data back in here?"

The Bolian frowned and answered, "By order of Admiral Nakamura, Data's emotion chip must be removed and handed over to the S.C.E."

"You can't do that!" exclaimed Geordi. "It's a very delicate operation—it's not supposed to be removed!"

"Then could you do please do it for us?" asked Moroz sheepishly. "I don't want to hurt your friend, and I'm sure you could remove it better than I could."

"Yes," agreed Data, "La Forge has clocked many hours with his hands inside my head."

"Thanks, Data," said the engineer, rolling his eyes. "It's not that I can't do it—it's the principle of the thing! I don't agree that his emotion chip is dangerous to him or anyone else. He hasn't been convicted of any wrong-doing. You don't have the right to take his emotion chip!"

Data turned his head and replied, "Yes, they do, Geordi. Because I did not have the emotion chip when I was admitted to Starfleet, it can be considered add-on equipment. Regulation ninety-four, section three, paragraph twelve clearly states that Starfleet gets to determine the equipment and clothing I am to bear on my person while on duty. Admiral Nakamura has decided that my emotion chip is not standard equipment and should be removed."

The android frowned slightly. "I will miss my chip, but perhaps someday it can be restored. In the meantime, I have the memories of my feelings."

La Forge took a deep breath, and his voice was hoarse when he replied, "This is one time I wish I could turn off my emotions, but I can't. This isn't fair, Data—you haven't done anything wrong!"

"We're talking about orders from an admiral, not

right and wrong," said the Bolian. "Commander, will you help us or not?"

"Step aside," grumbled La Forge, grabbing a spanner out of Moroz's hand. "Starfleet's done enough damage to us already. I'll take it out, but this is a dark day. For two bolts, I'd give you my commander's bars to go along with Data's emotion chip. You can give them to Admiral Nakamura, too."

"Do not be angry," cautioned Data. "Perhaps I aspired too much to be human."

Geordi sniffed back a tear and put an arm around his friend's shoulder.

Picard sat in a spartan but comfortable cell in the bowels of Starfleet Command. He tried to read one of the Dixon Hill books they had brought him. On a small table built into the wall sat his dinner, hardly touched. *The condemned man did* not *eat a hearty meal,* he thought disgruntledly.

As he sat alone, in silence, Picard began to realize that he couldn't blame Starfleet for his woes. He had made genuine mistakes in Rashanar, including that he had failed to comprehend how much danger they were in. He had ignored the warnings of Captain Leeden, also he had failed to protect her. *Something* in that ships' graveyard was alive and deadly. It was fulfilling its own twisted agenda without any regard for the living or the dead. It had to be responsible for the wholesale destruction that accompanied the Battle of Rashanar. Eventually it might tire of its devastated fish bowl and go elsewhere.

That entity landed me in this cell, he told himself.

I've got to find out what is haunting Rashanar—what has destroyed my life.

A security officer walked past his doorway and looked in through the shimmer of the forcefield. "Captain, Admiral Nechayev is on her way to see you. She should be here any minute."

"Thank you, Lieutenant," said Picard, closing his book and setting it on the table beside his uneaten dinner. He took a drink of the tea he had ordered, but it had gone cold.

At my age, I don't have that much longer. Do I really want to spend the rest of it as a prisoner?

"Picard," said a familiar voice, snapping him out of his reverie. It was Admiral Nechayev, looking winded, as if she'd been running. She looked expectantly at the guard and grumbled, "Open the door, Lieutenant."

"But visitors usually talk through the forcefield," said the security officer.

"Now," she ordered softly. Sensing the danger he was in, the guard quickly killed the forcefield, allowing her to step inside Picard's cell. Nechayev seldom exchanged pleasantries, and she wasn't going to start now. "I've been to see Commodore Korgan," she began, "and we may have hammered something out."

Picard rose and pointed to his lone chair. "Won't you sit down, Admiral?"

"Don't mind if I do," she answered, slumping into the proffered seat. "I don't imagine you mind standing."

"No," he murmured.

She slapped her hands on her thighs. "Well, Picard, we need a way out of this that will save face for everyone. To put it bluntly, we need you to take one for the team. It's an old phrase; it means—"

"I know what it means," he answered with a scowl. "A little blood to appease the masses."

"No, just the Ontailians," she muttered. "They've withdrawn their threat to leave the Federation."

"I see," he said, wondering what that meant for him.

The admiral bristled at his look of disapproval. "I need you not to fight this, Jean-Luc," the admiral said. "I need you to give up any thoughts of appealing the decision before your evaluations are completed. When you pass them"—and Picard noted gratefully that the admiral did not seem to harbor any doubts about the outcome of the tests—"you'll be found to have done nothing less than any other Starfleet captain would have done in those bizarre circumstances. That will give us some breathing room and some time to get back into Rashanar. Once we're there, we hope to find proof that will exonerate you completely. The Ontailians say they'll still be looking for debris from the *Vuxhal,* and let them. Given time, I think we can find enough to back up Data's story."

She mustered a smile. "Worst-case scenario, in a couple of months all of this will have blown over, and the Ontailians will have lost track of you. This case will never be reopened. Cabot is on board with this—the only one who still needs to sign off is you."

"I realize this gets all the paperwork signed and sealed," said Picard, "but what will actually happen to me?"

"You'll be in the custody of Counselor Cabot at Medical Mental Health."

The captain stopped pacing, and his lips thinned. "When do I get a chance to prove my innocence?"

Nechayev winced slightly and rose to her feet. "We've still got to negotiate to get Starfleet back into Rashanar, and then we can correct all the problems."

Picard chuckled. " 'Correct the problems.' You sound like *me* when I first went to Rashanar. Admiral, you had better go to the boneyard ready to hunt some *targ,* because a big *targ* lives in there."

"So do you agree to this deal?" asked Nechayev impatiently. "If Admiral Ross could come in here and beg you, he would. He begged *me* to convince you. Say the word, and you're out of here tonight."

"For a nicer cell," Picard muttered. "I can't believe I'm agreeing to this. What if *everyone* loses track of me in the system?"

"You get three or four weeks' vacation," answered Nechayev. "Buy us some time, Picard. Help us hold the Federation together at a critical juncture."

He finally nodded, telling himself that it was only temporary. Admiral Nechayev nodded in return and bellowed, "Lieutenant! Let us out of here!"

"This is nice," said Will Riker, making a show of admiring Captain Picard's log cabin inside Medical Mental Health, which he now called home. "Is there a trout stream out back?"

"I wish," answered Picard, working his rocking chair harder. He was dressed in a flannel shirt and khakis in order to look more at home in his fancy cage. It seemed absurd to sit around in his uniform as if he were about to take charge of the bridge. At least entertaining visitors now was no problem; also he no longer had to take psychology tests. He was already certified "impaired" and "guilty," which meant that his trials were over, along with his career.

"What is out back?" asked Riker, growing uneasy with the captain's silence.

Picard shrugged and kept rocking. "I don't know. The doors don't actually function, at least not for me. How is the crew holding up?"

The commander shook his head. "Not well. It's like we've all got a dark cloud hanging over us. Beverly, Geordi, several of the crew, are talking about resigning from Starfleet."

"No, don't let them do that," said Picard with alarm. "I made this deal to buy us some time."

"After we get under way on a new mission, maybe they'll have the old spirit," muttered Riker, although he didn't sound convinced.

The captain rose to his feet and gave his old first officer a chipper pat on the back. "Hang in there, Number One. You've got to hold that crew together until you get another ship—the *Enterprise* needs you."

"I know." The acting captain squared his big shoulders and tried to shake off the gloom. "We've had a few repairs. Then we've got a test flight scheduled later today. So I'd better get back. You hang in there, too, Captain. They say you won't be here long."

After two days, his stay already seemed an eternity, but the captain didn't say so. He kept hoping that his eventual release was not a figment of his friends' imaginations. They kept saying he would be out soon, but nobody ever said when.

"Thank you for visiting, Will," declared the captain, mustering a smile. "I'm sure they'll assign you to a great ship."

They shook hands, and Riker tapped his combadge and called for an orderly. When the door opened, orderlies stood guard outside. The captain sighed and slumped back into his rocking chair.

As he rocked, he thought about the mimic ship inside Rashanar—the thing that had taken away his life. Had he blown it up? Somehow he didn't think so.

Morose and thinking about resigning her post in Starfleet, Beverly Crusher wandered through the lush gardens of Starfleet Academy. It was spring and the first sunny day after a rainy week; the blossoms were bursting with life and color. The air smelled like a perfume store. But none of this brought her much solace, not when Jean-Luc had been imprisoned indefinitely.

Walking through this garden, Beverly couldn't help but think of the many happy times when she, Jack, and Wesley had frolicked here. Jean-Luc had been their best friend in those early days. The world had been their oyster back then, and they had no inkling of the tragedies and turmoil that awaited them.

Beverly hadn't spent so much time at the Academy since the year she took off from the *Enterprise* to run Starfleet Medical. They wanted her back for that job, but her confidence in Starfleet was severely shaken.

She had almost thrown up when she had to write an explanation of how she ignored Jean-Luc's "condition" to let him serve in an "impaired" state. It had been very difficult not to pen a resignation letter at the same time, but she bit her tongue for his sake. She knew Geordi was equally upset over the treatment Data had gotten. He was considering resignation. They had trusted Admiral Nechayev to look out for Jean-Luc's best interests, but now she realized he had been sold out for the sake of political expediency.

As Crusher wandered between rows of daffodils and pansies, more Academy memories came flooding back to her, especially those involving Wesley. The Academy had been the scene of her son's greatest shame, although that was difficult to say for sure anymore, because he might have done something truly hideous since leaving with the Traveler. Still it would be hard to top having lied about the details of a fatal crash in his flight squad.

So much has happened to me in this place, she mused. *Is this where I will chuck it all? If only I knew why I keep going . . . when there's no hope of seeing him again.*

"Mom," said a gentle voice that seemed to float on the breeze.

"My imagination," grumbled Beverly, thinking she was going crazy. Then a tall shadow darkened her path, followed by a face that had aged and lost its baby fat but was still youthful and handsome.

She gasped and staggered backward, and he had to reach out to catch her. "Mom," he said with a smile, "it's really me."

"Wes!" She collapsed into his arms, weeping with joy. "Wes! Wes!" She ran her hands all over his face and into his hair, which looked as if it had been cut by bald humanoids. He was wearing a civilian suit of clothes and looked very handsome. "Is it really you? You're not a dream or a hallucination?"

"No, Mom, you know I'm real." A few pedestrians strolled by, smiling at their joyful reunion.

Beverly staggered on her feet and said, "I think I have to sit down."

"There's a bench right over here." His strong grip guided her down the sidewalk to the oaken bench, and she marveled that her son was a man. Actually he was much more than that—how much more she didn't know.

As they sat on the bench, she stammered, "How . . . how did you get here? Are you still with the Traveler?"

"I *am* a Traveler," he replied, "at least for now. I've wanted so badly to come home, but I had to finish my training. I sneaked a peek at you a few times while you were sleeping, just to make sure you were okay. I wish I could have let you see me, but my training was very strict. I've witnessed things you wouldn't believe, Mom, but nothing as unfair as what happened to Captain Picard. I tried to ignore it and turn my back, but I can't any longer."

"So you know what happened!" she said with relief. Then her face drooped, and she gripped his hands in hers. "You're too late to help him, but he would love to see you. Why have you come back now, Wesley?"

The young man answered, "To save the *Enterprise.*"

ABOUT THE AUTHOR

John Vornholt is the acclaimed author of numerous *Star Trek®* novels, including *Genesis Force, The Genesis Wave* Books One through Three, *Gemworld Books* One and Two, *Sanctuary, Mind Meld, Masks, Contamination, Antimatter, Rogue Saucer,* and *The Dominion War* Books One and Three. He lives in Arizona with his wife and two sons.

The saga continues in March 2004 with

STAR TREK®

A TIME TO DIE

by
John Vornholt

**Turn the page for an electrifying
preview of *A Time to Die*. . . .**

Jean-Luc Picard sat on bare red stone, gazing out the archway carved in the side of a sheer, deeply striated cliff. His dwelling was about a hundred meters from the top of the bluff. Beneath him floated sulfurous mists which hid a murky river that ran with potable water only a few weeks a year. Above him was a hot, desolate plain. The heat of the day would reach him when the sun struck his level. This humble abode, hollowed from the red rock itself, was no more than a hovel; he had a few clay bowls and utensils and a pile of linen on which to lie. In the corner sat a large clay pitcher shaped like a *brujgar* horn in which to catch water from the spring just above him. Vulcan tribes had inhabited such cliff dwellings for millennia, dating back to a time when they had been violent savages. The warrens in the cliff were easy to defend and stayed relatively cool for a village in the Vulcan high desert.

The captain's only nod to modernity was a stack of dog-eared Dixon Hill novels in the corner. He had pens and a journal in which he had yet to write a word. There was nothing in his present circumstances he wished to record for posterity; he wished only to wake up from this horrible nightmare and get on with his life.

As befitting his hermitic lifestyle, Picard had let his beard grow. He wore Starfleet exercise garments, which were more comfortable than the thick Vulcan robes everyone around him wore. Humans tended to sweat much more than Vulcans, and a shower was not available to him, unless he switched to a different holodeck program.

Jean-Luc heard footsteps on the stone walkway just beyond his open door. He wondered if it was a visitor come to see him. A moment later, he was disappointed to see it was just another holodeck character—a wise-looking Vulcan who often stopped to dispense pedestrian platitudes and try to engage him in conversation.

The old Vulcan cleared his throat and said, "Only Nixon could go to China."

"I've heard that already," muttered Picard. "Go on your way."

The Vulcan stood for several seconds, as if the hermit might change his mind and talk, and Picard considered yelling at him to go. No, doing so would look very bad on his next evaluation, and that one was crucial, whenever it would be. Now it was time to take the kettle off the fire and let the boiling water come to a rest. *And I'm the kettle,* thought Jean-Luc.

"Conditions are favorable for rain this afternoon," remarked the old Vulcan, studying the golden sky.

In response, Picard rolled onto his blankets and stared at the rugged wall at the back of his cavern. He presumed that Counselor Colleen Cabot and her assistants were watching him through the fake wall, if they even bothered to pay attention to him anymore. He supposed that some of this neglect was his own fault, because he had let it be known that he didn't want to see many of his shipmates under these circumstances. They were respecting his wishes . . . thus turning him into a recluse.

He had avoided further proceedings on the Rashanar matter, but now he was beginning to miss the day-to-day interaction with others. The incident was over, as far as everyone else was concerned; for him, it had only prolonged the embarrassment and started an open-ended incarceration.

I have to find some way to cope, he decided, *or I really will go mad.*

"Good morning, Jean-Luc," said a friendly voice from the doorway. He turned to see that the Vulcan had departed and was replaced by a fair-skinned woman who looked rather youthful, her blond hair blowing gently in the warm breezes of the cliff. As usual, Counselor Cabot wore flattering civilian clothes. He had seen her in a Starfleet uniform only twice, during his inquiry and at the memorial service for the *Juno*'s crew. She made a few notes on her padd, and he felt like a zoo animal being visited by the zookeeper. According to Nechayev, Colleen Cabot had done him a considerable favor by allowing more psychological evaluation, but it didn't feel that way to him.

The counselor motioned toward his dingy, austere surroundings. "You know, Jean-Luc, I always figured you would pick the Vulcan room, if left to your own devices long enough."

"It's the most like a cell," he remarked.

"If you say so." She gave him a bemused smile, then ducked her head to step inside his hovel. "People keep making requests to visit you, but you have a very short list of those you approve. You really don't have to be alone, as long as the *Enterprise* is at home port."

Picard sat up cross-legged and looked at his "jailer." "They have repairs and test flights to make, followed by a new mission. Let them get used to Captain Riker without being overly concerned about me."

"That's very selfless of you," said Cabot, sitting down across from him.

"The welfare of the *Enterprise* and her crew is my first concern," he answered. "Always had been."

The counselor nodded. "That's right. If you hadn't been sure the ship was in danger, you wouldn't have fired on the Ontailians."

"They weren't Ontailians," said the captain, his jaw clenched tightly. With considerable self-control, he managed to relax and muster a smile for his keeper. "But you haven't come here to rehash the inquiry, have you? I hope not, because I hate to keep fighting battles I've already lost."

"Isn't that what Rashanar is all about?" she asked. "Fighting that never stops."

"Yes, that's one theory. This doppelgänger ship—or more than one—could explain why the Dominion and Federation vessels fought to the death at Rashanar. They didn't know *who* or *what* they were really fighting. They died at their posts, with surrender never an option."

Colleen Cabot frowned, then asked, "But isn't that how Jem'Hadar and Dominion ships always fought—to the death?"

"No," answered Picard. "If a Jem'Hadar ship becomes too crippled to be effective, they look to board an enemy ship as soon as possible. The Cardassians were never ones to die needlessly—if there was a way to escape to fight another day, they would take it. But not if the whole crew is blacked out with the ship paralyzed. Think about it, Counselor: How can you have a battle with no survivors? You're a psychologist—you know the will to survive is one of the strongest instincts."

Cabot sat forward. "Yes, Jean-Luc, and you went to Rashanar *wanting* to solve this mystery, didn't you? And you *solved* it—you were successful."

Picard narrowed his eyes warily at his keeper. He could see where this line of questioning was going. He had to hand it to Colleen Cabot—she was always working one angle or another.

"I didn't make up the replicant ship just to fit the facts," he said firmly. "Data and La Forge didn't expect to see what they saw—two identical ships—but they did."

"You take me the wrong way, Jean-Luc," said Cabot with disappointment. "This replicated ship is not only at the basis of your defense, it's the basis of your mental state and confidence. As long as you are unshakable in your belief in the mimic ship, your case makes sense to me and everyone else."

He snorted a laugh. "You mean, I'm either right or delusional, therefore it doesn't really matter to you."

"It matters to me a lot," said Cabot somberly. "And it should matter to you, too, if you want to get out of here."

"But how do you prove me right or delusional," asked the captain, "except to go to Rashanar and see for yourself? To me and my crew, Data's word is proof enough. But it wasn't enough for the tribunal, and I can't offer you anything else."

The young blond woman shrugged and rose slowly to her feet, brushing the fake red dust off her pants. "If Data were a humanoid, we could use hypnosis, a mind-meld, or some other process to verify his story. But he's not, and no one else saw the transformation. You're convinced, but you didn't see it firsthand either. I guess you're right, Jean-Luc . . . . Starfleet has to go back to Rashanar."

Picard noted darkly, "If we don't stop this threat, more ships will be destroyed."

Don't miss

STAR TREK
A TIME TO DIE

**Available March 2004 wherever paperback
books are sold!**